TEQUILA HIGHWAY: LAST EXIT

TEQUILA HIGHWAY:
LAST EXIT
SECOND EDITION
by
R. J. MATTHEWS

TEQUILA HIGHWAY: LAST EXIT

ISBN: 978-0-9980965-7-5

Cover design: CjBell Photomation

TEQUILA HIGHWAY: LAST EXIT

Prologue

One day.

That's all it took to change everything I had ever known or worked for up to this point in my life. All my dreams, goals, and desires disappeared on that one fateful day. Could I ever get them back? Could I ever retrieve the life I worked so hard for and have it be like nothing had changed? Will I ever be the same person that I was from the day before that dreadful day? The answer is all too obvious: absolutely hell no.

One day.

Rachel and I, Jim Seagram, lived our happy life in Nashville, Tennessee. We were both from the Northeastern area of the United States, me from western New York and she from southern Vermont. We both went on to university: for me, it was the University of Notre Dame—go Irish—and for her, it was the traditional New Hampshire State University. I actually had forestalled my entry to scholastic studies by enlisting in the army for an exciting four years. I got to see the world, meet interesting people, and shoot guns.

We actually met in New Orleans, Louisiana, while both of us were traveling with friends, and it was just one of those nights on Bourbon Street. As I think back, it was after the second Hand Grenade drink from the Tropical Isle bar when I saw her partying in the one of many music venues up and down the street. The next morning, we saw each other again in Jackson Square while we were recovering, and I convinced her to join me for a beignet, the tasty French pastry. This woman sitting across from me must have thought I was the right man for her. Whoever could love a sugary French pastry and share it with her was the man she would marry someday.

Our courtship blossomed as we conversed on the phone for weeks before meeting again, this time in New York City, around the time we both graduated with our bachelor's degrees. She already had job offers in New York City, Kansas City, and Nashville. Though I was no fan of country music, Nashville did have great appeal in terms of culture, weather, some sports, and geographic location. The choice of where to move was decided that day, sitting with a woman whom I barely knew in a town I was visiting over an authentic Italian meal in Midtown Manhattan. That was a good day.

Fast-forward a few years.

Rachel and I went to work throughout the week. Each day, we commuted and came home, cooked dinner, and relaxed in the evening. This was repeated day in and day out year after year. We went out to dinner with friends sometimes on the weekends or traveled around the area during our time off. We lived a happy life and counted our blessings each and every day that we shared it with each other. There was nothing about our life that could even remotely be considered in the realm of the bizarre or unusual.

So it was quite a shock to the system to find one day that Rachel was gone. I mean completely gone, without-a-trace gone. Her car was still in the garage, and her purse was on the kitchen counter where she always put it every day. Strangely, no clothes were taken other than the ones she had worn that day. When the police later questioned her financial office coworkers, they described nothing unusual about Rachel that day or any other day. There were no strange or unknown phone calls except for one that turned out to be an annoying telemarketer. There were no mysterious letters or unusual emails, no questionable texts either. She literally vanished without a trace as though she had never existed.

In the days that followed, I took a turn for the worse that I never fully recovered from. I mean, come on—who really gets over the disappearance of their one true love and wife? Who just says, "Oh well, I tried to find her, and I failed. I have to get on with my life, don't I?" You don't, and you never do.

Sadly, I had not one clue to go on. Surprisingly, the police had nothing either. All they could do was interview everyone, file a missing person's report, and assure me they would call if they heard anything. Not exactly words of comfort, but there was honestly nothing they could do. There was no ransom demand or suspicion of foul play. The police interviewed me over and over. They searched the house tirelessly and found nothing. The local news channels aired my pleas for help, any clue to lead the police and I to my wife's whereabouts.

Eventually, the news channels grew tired and switched to another hot news story. Over time, people stopped asking me about her, and the hope of ever seeing my wife grew fainter with each passing month. Everything and every means to find her were exhausted. Everyone had given up and moved on. What could I possibly do at this point other than move on also? There had to be something I could do as a last resort because attempting anything was better than failing at doing nothing.

Everything changed on that one day. I took a new direction, emotionally, beginning on the day after.

I heard from some people who knew a guy that helps people with problems. Kinda like the A-Team, and for an additional price, you could probably get the guy to drive a black van, too. My whole life had changed, and my wife was gone; I had tried to do everything legally, which hadn't accomplished anything, and I decided to verge on the border of illegal to find her. What kind of man would I be if I did not honor the vows that held me so dear to her?

It was time to take action. I left my job, citing depression and needing time off. They understood without showing too much judgment in their eyes or coldness in their mannerisms. I could hear them say, "That sad man. He was so promising with the firm, so much potential and a future ahead of him." It was written all over the faces of those judgmental bastards. I never really liked working there anyways. Hell, I didn't really like working, period. At least now I had an adventure ahead of me. I had to find Rachel again if it were the last thing I accomplished in this world.

I had a neighbor watch the place while I contemplated my next course of action. All I had to go on was the name of a guy who could help me, but he had last been located in Mexico. In order to see him, I had to prove myself to one of his associates. Easy enough, as I have handled tougher challenges back in my army days. You see, I have one special skill that is the most valuable skill. It isn't being a good shot (comes in handy, though) or the quickest draw (also handy). I'm not an expert knife thrower or bomb maker. Rather, I have the ability to survive any situation. Call it pure luck or pure crazy. I can assess the situation, analyze it, and still get out of it alive no matter how bad the odds look. Call me a survivalist, and obviously, I'm great at it, aren't I? After all, I'm still alive.

So this associate decided to test me one night in downtown Nashville. I had just finished watching the local ice hockey team, the Predators, with the game decided in overtime. Thank goodness it didn't go to a shootout. Anyways, I left the game happy and in good spirits. I decided to take a stroll and enjoy

4

the moment of euphoria, something I had not felt in a long time. I stumbled in and out of nearly every bar along the Strip after the game and had a celebratory drink with newfound friends in every place.

It was getting late, and I was getting hungry and needing food to help absorb the vast amount of alcohol I had recently ingested. I made my way toward an eatery known for their greasy burgers and even greasier cheese tater tots. Halfway there, I sensed I was being followed. It was a feeling, and I'm usually right when I get those feelings. The guy caught up to me before I planned to turn a corner and cross the street. He silently pressed the point of a knife in my lower back and demanded I turn the other way toward an empty street.

I slightly "tripped" just enough to turn around and face the perpetrator. He started shouting at me and showing the knife, demanding payment so he could pass word about meeting with the guy in Mexico that I was requesting an audience with. The guy held the knife at an angle in front of me, which was not a very smart move on his part. If one is going to flash a weapon at someone whose capabilities they don't know, then they should be better prepared to use it. This guy wasn't, but I was. With my best predator-like reflexes I could muster while inebriated, I quickly grabbed his wrist, twisted his arm, and plunged the knife into his right thigh.

The man, wailing in pain and gushing blood, was too much in shock to make demands anymore, so I decided to make a couple of demands upon him. I requested that he pass the message of me requesting an audience up the chain and took his wallet and phone as collateral. I told him amid the continual screams of pain that he could call his phone when he received word in regard to the meeting I had requested. I let him go, and he stumbled off with a limp to the right. I heard some choice words directed toward my family and I, but overall, I felt I had passed the first test.

I turned around and jumped in the first taxi I could flag down. I looked in the wallet and discovered a rather large amount of cash, which I quickly pocketed before the wandering eyes of the taxi driver spied it. I thought a nice dinner was in order and asked to be driven to a fancy Japanese restaurant near the expressway. When we arrived moments later, I graciously tipped the driver courtesy of the guy who ironically had tried to rob me earlier. As I took the first bite of the Godzilla sushi roll, I contemplated where this new path would take me.

Chapter 1

I make my decision to pack it up and head south to Mexico for that possible lead to solve the disappearance of my wife. After I "proved" myself in Nashville, I now have to do a small task this side of the border to authenticate my meeting with this Hector fellow.

The weather had turned cold in Nashville, and so had the world. I begin pondering as I look out the window at my old yet reliable Subaru hatchback ready to begin the journey. It is time to move on and complete this delivery job and maybe start fresh somewhere else where they don't know me or my storied past. Yes, I am willing to look for my wife, but I am also looking for a new life, a life after the tragic events of the last few months. Maybe I will make it to Mexico to have a chat with this Hector or maybe not. Maybe he will help me on my journey. In the end, it's either I find Rachel again or I don't. But I must push on to see where this road will take me. A well-planned exit is not needed for this descending chapter in my living epic.

There is one other thing that I have to sort out. It is my precious baby, an heirloom Triumph. Willed to me from my dad, it now sits patiently in a prepaid storage unit outside Salt Lake City, Utah. God only knows if it is still there, though the three carbon-steel locks and the secret trap on the garage door give me some security and peace of mind. The other baby, my trusty Subaru, may have seen better days, but it still runs after a hundred and fifty thousand miles, and I just put new tires on it and had it serviced. Hopefully, it looks like an ordinary car on the road and won't attract the attention of the law patrolling the nation's highways.

The journey out of Nashville begins with a stoplight one mile from my house. I wish it is more climatic, but the light turns green and off I go. I drive in a southwesterly direction for hundreds of miles and stop only when I run out of gas, food, or smokes. Oftentimes, it is a quick stop before I am back on the road.

As I get closer to my destination, fate has a different hand for me that has to be played first. South of Waco, Texas, in a no-name town, my instructions were to find a cinder-block dive bar with no windows that serves cheap draft beer in a dirty glass. This is not a big town, and there is a bar that matches that description to a T, so I stop and decide to check it out, believing this must be the place. The instructions told me to go on a Wednesday afternoon and speak to the bartender, who might go by the name Mo, and gave the impression that he might or might not at one point have worked for the mob and that he looked like he was an ex-marine. It is confirmed by the talk I hear as I walk in about the glory days when he was back in the corps. In the envelope I received a few days ago, the instructions inside stated I was to be at this bar on Wednesday afternoon and talk to the bartender. I assume the meeting with Mo was to be discreet and something different.

Mo the barkeep does not look up when I walk in on a Wednesday afternoon. Two other patrons are yakking away with him. However, I know he is watching me intently with those eyes in the back of the abnormally large bald head. One of the patrons start to raise his voice toward Mo and possibly reach for a weapon of choice. (Side note: this is not a place where one checks their weapons at the door.) The volume of Mo's voice matches the rambling patron's, and he very discreetly starts to reach under the bar. A baseball bat or a shotgun is my first guess as to what he is reaching for. Instead, he already has my beer in a bottle top opened and raises it over the bar countertop. He then slides it in front of me the very moment I sit down at the bar. This guy either has practiced this way too many times or thinks it is cool enough to help fill the tip jar that looks rather scant.

After about an hour, I consume just enough beer to stay within the legal limit. I flag over Mo, who is watching some sports talk show on the TV, to cash out. The highly vocal patrons had left to do what they do every day, which is probably nothing. Mo simply looks at me for a moment and says a twenty should cover the bar tab. I am impressed that he keeps a running tab in his head, or maybe he is just too lazy to write it out. Either way, he probably overcharges everyone, figuring they are not going to argue with him.

I sheepishly hand over a twenty and tell him to keep the change, knowing I wasn't going to get change from this shifty bartender anyways. He half-heartedly smiles, showing his teeth that are badly in need of a dental plan, and tells me to wait a second. He turns and goes into the back office. At that moment, I have thoughts of fleeing, with the adrenaline rush telling me that I can do it and run out the door without looking back. I also sit there calculating if I can scam a free bottle of beer for the road. It is too late to run for it, as the jarhead bartender comes back with a manila envelope in his hand, throws it at me, and goes back behind the bar. I guess it is his way of saying good luck. I glance at him one last time before turning and walking out the door with an unopened bottle of beer hidden in my right-side coat pocket.

This is not the time to stumble to the car or do anything to raise suspicions that I might have been drinking, especially

9

exiting from a bar at 2:00 p.m. I look to the left and right nonchalantly and do not spot any vehicles that look like police cars. It is a lucky break for me. I fish for the keys to my reliable Subaru. I start the engine, waiting for the moment of a *click-click* and the car erupting in a huge fireball explosion because I did not check for a mob-style plastic C4 strapped to the starter. I did not turn into a huge fireball; however, the radio did explode into Van Halen's "Eruption" once the engine turns over, so I guess fate is being a comedian today.

It is a matter of minutes before I am heading onto the highway and back in a southwesterly direction. The sun is declining from its apex but is not quite in my field of vision, though eventually during this long drive it would start to blind me. In the end, it is fatigue that gets me to stop driving. I must have blacked out from the exhaustion and fall into a deep sleep.

It was a typical day in our lives. The sky was clear, the sun's rays were shining brightly, and in the distance was the sound of birds singing joyfully. Rachel and I were looking for seeking something unusual to happen but were more concerned tonight with an evening without too many hiccups. We would settle for a simple yet relaxing evening. By chance, we received a call from our friend, Selena, who was normally sharing our same zeal for life but not at the current moment. She was being as lazy as we were and asked us to meet up for food. Pizza was often the premier choice for us. Who doesn't like pizza?

I would love to tell you that it was on that night when the events were about to transpire that would forever change all of lives. But it wasn't. In fact, we all met up at the local pizza joint, but as usual, Selena was fashionably late. Rachel and I, exercising our patience for others, met her with stern yet warm smiles for her fifteen-minute tardiness.

With our first round of Cokes nearly depleted, we got our second round as Selena was still trying to get settled in and close out her Facebook and texting functions on her phone. She was dressed in very revealing attire. She had on a small halter top and wore very teasing Daisy Duke shorts.

"Have you all been waiting long?" The sarcastic looks on our faces probably told her the truth of her question versus the standard answer of "We have been waiting all our lives for you to show up."

After the meal, we decided to go for a walk around town but started walking down a street that opened up to a grassy field with lots of radio antennas. Up the street from the antennas, the road led onward around a building. Why were we drawn to this building? In the end, only by walking toward it would we find the answer.

As we got closer to the building, a cold shiver overcame me. Something was not right; something felt cold and empty, like death. My prediction was correct as there was a funeral being attended by many people. Well, the marquee told me so.

We walked closer to the building and going inside, and Rachel had a sudden urge to take a sneak peek from behind the wall. However, she was not sneaky enough, as an unusual man wearing a fitted black suit called her out. Soon others were welcoming us to join them in the service as they sat in a semicircle around the open casket.

I watched Rachel from behind in the vestibule area. She shout out to me. "What are you doing? There is a funeral Mass going on. Why are we interrupting?"

11

She proceeded to walk around the corner and address the mourners calling to her. Finally, an older-looking lady stared at Rachel and invited her to sit among the semicircle of mourners as a way to pay respect.

I assumed this was the widow who was staring at Rachel, and she guided Rachel to sit next to her as people shifted one seat down. For some odd reason, the old lady reached in her handbag and fetched a book. She gave the book to Rachel, and with a confused look, Rachel graciously accepted it. Looking at me for a rope to hang on to, I only shrugged my shoulders in joint confusion.

Rachel stood up and walked over to me. She showed me the book: it was On the Road by Jack Kerouac. It looked pretty worn, and the grayish cover showed signs of being well read. I thumbed the book, and don't know why but I was looking for a mystery piece of paper tucked away inside for some cosmic message from beyond. A piece of paper fell to my feet when I flipped the pages.

I picked up the piece of paper and opened it. On it was written, "Dead man." I then flipped to the inside of the book cover and found something even more unusual. There were four signatures obviously naming the previous owners of the book. The last signature, I assumed, was of the man the funeral was being held for. His name was Julio.

I turned to look at Rachel's face when I revealed the inside cover to her. I would never forget her face as I showed her that the first signature on the inside cover was mine.

By then, we were standing in front of the memorial in the park near the lockers. I opened one of the lockers and noticed a bottle of whiskey and two glasses. We sat there holding our *glasses of a two-finger pour of Jack Daniel's, reminiscing of a time long ago. It felt as though we were in a commercial.*

That was one crazy dream. But who believes in messages from dreams. I don't but maybe I should start paying attention to them from know on. Or not.

Chapter 2

I awake to find myself in what appears to be a parking lot. As my eyes begin to focus, I look around and decide it is a truck stop. I see several 18-wheelers parked around me when I look in the rearview mirror. Off to the right, some people are sitting on a picnic table smoking and sharing a laugh. Are they laughing at me?

As my coherence and the wheels turning in my head notch into full gear and I become fully attuned to my surroundings, I suddenly realize I have several days' stubble on my face. Next to me appears to be the last meal I ate. It is in the form of dried-up vomit in the carrier bag sitting on the passenger-side floor. A quick check of the wallet, keys, phone, and the 9mm underneath the seat gives my racing mind a temporary pit stop of peace.

I don't remember stopping for a rest, but my bloodshot eyes and the aches and pains of every joint in my body tell me it was probably a good decision. I guess drinking at Mo's until 2:00 p.m. yesterday and then driving all the way here probably wasn't a smart decision. Except for the remnants of my last meal, I feel semi—ha, ha, get it: semi, truck stop—OK. I check my phone for obvious reasons and discover various missed calls from friends in Nashville. I also have strange texts from some truck-stop groupies that I might have shared experiences and whiskey with last night. I really hope I don't find a tattoo of one of the groupies' names on my arm, but at some point, I will have to check. Maybe later. Perhaps I should lay off the booze until I get across the border.

Since I am at a rest stop, I might as well utilize the facilities, maybe partially clean myself up, and dispose of the dinner bag. I get out of the car, lock the door, and start to turn toward the bathrooms. It is only then I notice the sign informing me that I am less than thirty miles from the Mexican border.

It is a funny thing about our Mexican neighbors to the south. As an American, crossing into Mexico is relatively easy. The border guards all look nonchalant and bored. I could be carrying a kilo of cocaine, and they could probably care less. They would just wish me good luck trying to get back into the United States.

I arrive at a nondescript motel about a mile away from the border crossing. I book a room for a week and pay cash in advance. The clerk gives me a once-over and decides I don't seem like I am going to steal the TV or the nasty towels. I take the room key—how twentieth century—and go out of the office and down the row of doors to my room. I turn my head around to glance out past the highway. The sun that is high in the sky and beaming down upon me feels like it is out of an Ansel Adams photo—well, except for the nasty smell of the town and my rundown motel. I can only imagine the view from the second floor is even less appealing.

I'm not supposed to meet up with Hector until around 10:00 p.m., and it is only three in the afternoon. I can see the sights of Mexico or stay in my what-is-that-stench-emanating-from-the-back-room suite. Why does dust stir up every time I walk across the seventies-style carpet? When was the last time it was vacuumed, or, even better, has it ever been vacuumed? Should I even bother to use the shower? My stomach starts to retch at the thought of pulling back the shower curtain. I guess next time I should look into staying at the Marriott. And I could have earned hotel points, too.

I leave my Subaru in the motel parking lot. I really feel bad subjecting it to sitting there for a few days in the blistering

Texas heat, but I can't drive it into Mexico. Well, I *can* drive it into Mexico without insurance coverage, but I adamantly refuse to do so. Unless I just want to hand it over to some stranger pointing a gun at my head on the first right turn from the main street in the border town. Instead, I call for a taxi courtesy of the motel clerk, who has probably called more taxis for Americans that any other concierge duty. Besides, it would be a shame if he didn't get a kickback from the taxi company.

The taxi driver has to be some retired army veteran of a bygone war or conflict, and I am willing to bet he has a Mexican wife or maybe an ex-wife taking half of his retirement pay. This guy is a real hoot; I never thought someone could talk so much during a two-mile drive. Apparently, he thinks it is really funny that I am going across the border so early when all the entertainment commences when it gets dark. To plead innocence will only make him laugh louder. Honestly, I am going for a nice meal and a couple of cervezas and maybe do some shopping.

I tell him, "I want to buy a big sombrero."

"Yeah, right, buddy! And the Panthers are gonna win the Super Bowl this year!"

He is probably reflecting back on the last time he went over the border, and it wasn't to go to a Mexican hat store. The taxi driver, aka Mr. Laughs, keeps advising me on where to go for the best food, cheapest drinks, prettiest girls, etcetera. Does this guy work for TripAdvisor on the side? I bet he can tell me what I could get for twenty bucks at three different seedy places. Please, I'll pay you an extra ten bucks if you drive faster so I can get the hell outta here. Twenty bucks if you will just shut the hell up.

16

He drops me off right in front the Mexican customs building, and from there, I manage to catch a glimmer of the unusual hue of the mighty Rio Grande. I tip him generously and tell him to buy a round for himself. He tips his hat and peels out of the parking lot, squealing tires and drawing unwarranted attention to myself. I bet he is going to drive to the motel and break into my Subaru to steal the change in the car.

I walk into the building and immediately move to the first line I see. I try not to look too happy, like I am only going to Mexico to get laid, or too relaxed, like I going to attempt to smuggle some drugs back in. As I would have guessed, the guards look me up and down, wondering how much they can extort from me and if my belt will fit them. The one on the right is really eyeing my shoes. Note to self: next time, wear a cheap pair of shoes and a fake leather belt. However, I do look pretty benign and pathetic, so they let me through without any incident or extorting a "border-crossing fee."

I cross on the pedestrian side with the gorgeous view of the river. The smell, and it hits you immediately, is starting to get to me, and I walk a little faster to get across the border quicker. I proceed to walk right into town after leaving the customs gate, forgetting to take the touristy photo of one foot in each country. If I am still alive on the way back, I will try to remember that cheesy photo opportunity.

It starts right away. Here is a mid-thirties American white male all by himself standing just outside the Mexican border gate. I must look like a meal ticket, someone's payday, and a real easy target all rolled into one. Everyone is taking notice of me, but who is going to snare this cash cow? Everyone calls out to me or grabs my arm to buy their wares, eat at their delicious restaurant, and drink a Corona or a margarita—the best in town, the coldest, blah, blah, blah. However, little did they know that I have been here before several times on weekend passes when I had to get away from the military base. Those were the days, but I'd rather forget some of those weekends I spent in a Mexican jail.

I did remember to put my wallet in my front pocket and plant a fake wallet in my back pocket. I was going to tuck in a message like, *"Sorry, maybe next time,"* but then the thief would just hunt me down eventually. Instead, I planted some business cards, a US five-dollar bill, and a photo of a motherly type older woman that says, *"Mom, 1991,"* on the back. The thief will make a small score, and maybe they will feel guilty after seeing the photo. Sucker.

I already have a destination in mind and head in that direction. I just have to get through all the tourist traps and annoying vendors in the beginning. It starts to thin out the farther I go down the street. I continue to walk down the main street, keeping an eye to the left and the right for potential gang members who might be thinking about their chances of robbing me. It seems pretty safe to walk around, even for midafternoon, but one never knows. I need to pick up a weapon for my stay here to better my chances of survival.

Ironically, I turn around, and I happen to be standing in front of a vendor selling such legal and illegal weaponry. In a matter of minutes, I easily buy a cheap knife and a beautiful, handmade blackjack. I really admire the craftsmanship of the blackjack and would hate to whack someone over the head with it. I need to remember to tell them first to look at the fine stitching before knocking them out. It would be funny if they replied, "Oh, you must have bought that from Julio in town. He always makes the best blackjacks. Thank you for knocking me out with the best you can afford and supporting local merchants. Ouch, that really hurts my head. Can you aim better toward the back of the head next time?"

I don't trust the knife too much, but it always acts as a good deterrent in a standoff, should the opportunity present itself. More like a last resort before I get my ass kicked and left for dead. Here is twenty bucks, Mr. Julio the Weapon Vendor. These two items may very well keep me alive in your beautiful town. Gracias.

I head farther down the street and into the heart of this Mexican border town. There are a lot less tourist vendors and more normal businesses. Wait a minute; I swear I just saw a goat running down a side street. Not something you see every day, but hey, I am in Mexico. I will try not to order a goat taco off the dinner menu tonight, but if I do, at least I will know it is quite fresh. What exactly is the difference in taste between goat and beef anyways? I hope not to find out later at a restaurant, but I assume they will serve the cheaper of the two meats to unsuspecting gringos. I would hear something like, "It is the chef's secret sauce. That's why the 'beef' tastes so much different than you are used to. Would you like another Corona to wash it down?"

As I continue to walk down the street, I look over on the left-hand side and see a place called La Tequila. You can't get a more Mexican-sounding name than that! The food in there must be the most authentic Mexican food it can be in this town.

I walk into La Tequila restaurant on a typical mid-afternoon day. The kitchen appears to be switching from the completion of the lunch rush and preparing for the dinner crowd. There are only a few people milling about inside. I think this is a good time to go while they were not too busy from the lunch crowd and maybe less hostile. But not this place and certainly not the feeling I feel as I walk through the front doors. I scan the place from left to right, noticing a group of three people sitting at a table off to the left side of the restaurant and the empty bar on the opposite side toward the back of the dining room. I am not really hungry, but a cool, refreshing drink to quench my thirst sounds appealing. I walk over to the bar, sit down, and stare straight ahead at the few bottles of liquor on the shelf.

I know I am being watched by everyone in this place, even those I can't see yet but know are there behind the elaborate CCTV system all over the ceiling. The bartender is not present behind the bar and there is no self-service sign, so I decide to let what happens happen, figuring someone will come talk to me eventually. It does not take very long, as the silence from the table on the opposite side becomes more prominent and the other telltale sign is now obvious: there is a long, cold, metal cylinder now pushed against the back of my neck.

Click.

Chapter 3

With the firing pin cocked and ready to shoot, this will certainly end my day in a hurry. Though it will make a mess all over the bar and floor, it probably won't make much of a difference, judging how dirty the floor was when I last looked down on it. I proceed to glance up with only my eyes to look at the angled mirror positioned behind the bar to see the man behind me.

"Gringo, I think you are in the wrong place."

Normally, I would have laughed at this futile attempt at the English language. Further, I was half expecting him to say something cool and slick. Now is not the time to relive old western movies with my life one click away from ending.

With a gasp of breath, I muster, "Hector is looking for me. I...I have an appointment with him." It is difficult to respond with the barrel of a gun protruding into one's neck. I close my eyes, waiting for my untimely demise.

And there it is. The silence of the calm before the storm. The man freezes in his tracks, as he contemplates whether my response is correct or a lucky guess. Maybe he hesitates to decide if I really am meeting with Hector or if he should just rob me in order to pay for his enormous bar tab. I can feel the barrel of the gun relax a little and withdraw slightly from the back of my tense neck.

"There is no Hector here." Pause. "What...what do you want from him?"

Well, which one is it? Either he doesn't know Hector and is pretending to play along, or he is the front man for Hector and is trying to screen me. I really should play poker with this guy; he is terrible at reading people. Maybe he is better at shooting people. Maybe I shouldn't play poker with him after all.

Now comes the moment of truth. I present the item I have for Hector that he requested: a 1993 US Silver Eagle coin. Not in mint condition, but they don't know that. I tell the man I have an item in my left shirt pocket and am reaching to retrieve it. I try not to make any sudden, jerky movements, lest Trigger Guy might decide it is a hostile move. I slam the silver coin on the bar so that everyone in the place, in view and hidden, hears it hit the surface. I take a deep breath and whisper, "Hector will be very interested in this coin. Perhaps he should come out and take it. Good ahead. Look at it, hombre."

I hope for the continual sound of silence. Trigger Guy peers over my left shoulder, sees the coin, and snatches it up all in one fluid motion. The gun never leaves the close proximity of my neck. This man is really good at his job. He lowers the gun and tells me to turn around and face him. He looks at me once more, says to wait here, and marches off.

A beautiful woman with long brown hair suddenly appears to right side of Trigger Guy. I never saw where she came from. Trigger Guy hands the coin over to her and then proceeds to walk back to the table with the other two guys and nurse his now much warmer Corona. The three of them all share a laugh in the background.

Meanwhile, the woman stares deadpan at me before cracking a smile, then looks at the coin once more before returning my gaze.

He must be the one that Hector is waiting on, Selma thinks. *Clearly, this is Jim, the one who would have the coin, as Hector said.*

The woman says, "You look thirsty. Why don't I get you a shot of tequila and a cold beer? You could probably use both about now."

"That would be much appreciated." I am more relaxed now, especially since I do not have a gun in the back of my neck. "The name is Jim, by the way."

She motions me to a table and tells me she will fetch me something to eat. I go and sit down, away from the other table, and breathe a sigh of relief. I continue to watch the woman head toward the kitchen. I wonder if this is a bad time to ask for her phone number. In retrospect, this was the very day that altered the course of my life. This was the day I met Selma.

The woman returns with a bottle of icy-cold Corona and some tortilla chips. I am still in a state of high alert, so the cold beer, even if it is Corona, helps ease away the pain. She also brings some salsa that is too spicy for my taste, but the beer washes it down quite nicely.

She stares back at me with those sultry green eyes of hers that look familiar in one sense and yet so distant in another. Have I met her before in another time, another land, another bar? She seems comfortable and relaxed with me, and yet she hardly knows me. She probably assumes I am Hector's American lackey and will be outta here sooner rather than later. Should I make small talk with her? She seems so...I can't think of the right word. Sophisticated, or high society? Educated? She just seems out of place. She is not dressed as a waitress, yet seems bent on serving my needs. Right now, food is a need that must be satisfied.

The woman brings over carne asada tacos and reposado tequila already poured in a big glass. I start to thank her for the food and drink, but she pushes the glass at me and tells me to

23

drink, while everyone is watching me. I give her a look of derision but decide to do the manly thing, like what tough hombres do, and drink the glass of tequila straight up. I may play the naive card but go along; it's not like I haven't ever drank tequila before. In fact, it is one of the permanent bottles in my liquor cabinet.

"Salud, mujer bonita." I down the drink and slam the glass on the table. She starts to blush. The guys at the other table look over to see what's going on, but she waves them off.

I wolf the tacos down and tip the beer bottle to her as she clears my plate. I finish the bottle of beer and am ready to ask her for another. Is that pushing my luck? She comes back and sits right next to me and puts her hand on my thigh. Hmm. I start to say something, but then I begin to feel funny.

She leans closer to me and whispers in my ear, "You're probably feeling the effects right now. It helps to have food in your stomach so the drug doesn't cause worse side effects."

Dizziness. Nausea…stomach pain. Headache…

"Drug…stomach…wat dig ya put in the glasssss…"

"Oh, you're going to sleep for a while. You should be all right when you wake up in a few hours. Remember, my name is Selma. Don't forget it."

I slump head first on the freshly cleaned table, jarring an empty beer bottle that almost falls over. At the last instant, Selma whispers softly in my ear and slips a piece of paper in my shirt pocket—coincidently, the same shirt pocket that housed the silver coin.

I wake up some time later in a place unfamiliar to me. Out the window, the sun is setting. That tells me the time of day, but which day is a different question. I quickly survey my surroundings: single room with a window and a great view of the town and sunsets. There are no bars on the window, but I suspect the door is locked from the outside. There is a twin bed that I slumbered on for an indefinite period of time and a bottle of water on the bedside table. I guess they don't drink the tap water in this place either. As far as I can tell, I have almost all my possessions: my wallet, though there is a fifty-dollar bill missing; keys to the Subaru; and the finely crafted blackjack in the jacket pocket. The knife is sadly missing, but it was a cheaply made knife, so no big loss.

I have a flashback of the waitress named Selma looking over me after she drugged me and saying something I could not make out. The last thing I remembered was her touching my chest on the right side. I start to feel aroused until I remember the shirt pocket. Oh yes, there is a note in it. I retrieve the note and open it, but it only reads, *"Muerto hombre."* Dead man.

A wave of depression overcomes me. Is this a sick joke? Is it a warning? Is she just messing with me? If I am a dead man, then why am I still alive? I flip the piece of paper over, and it is nearly blank. Out of desperation, I hold it to the light and see if I can make out something. It looks like an address—something plaza and 42 next to it.

I start to think about the cryptic message and the address, but then I hear footsteps with voices in the distance. It appears the welcoming committee is coming to have a chat with me. I quickly stash the note in my wallet and sit down on the bed in time for the door to unlock as two men walk in. I take a gulp from the water bottle and then scream out, "Howdy!"

The first henchman walks in, followed by the other. Both are wearing hit-man-style suits along with snakeskin boots. They probably killed the snakes to make the boots. One of them has an open jacket to make sure I see his .44 glistening in the holster on his right hip. The other guy flicks a knife, opening it and closing it. It suspiciously looks like my knife that was "borrowed" from me earlier today.

"We are here to take you to see Hector now," the first henchman says to me.

He did not say, "Please," so I quip, "Do I have time to put on a suit?"

The first guy quickly pulls the gun out of the holster and slams the barrel underneath my chin. Wow, that was fast. I would congratulate him on his skill, but I can't really talk at the moment. He looks at me with such an intense stare that I really think for a moment he has never heard a smartass response in his life. He blinks and exhales as I brace to hear the final pull of the trigger, but the second guy grabs his shoulder to ease off.

I must think twice before making any more witty commentary to these fellas. Note to self: make better decisions and shut the hell up, especially when outnumbered and outgunned.

The second guy grabs me, and we walk out of the room and down the hall. The first guy is behind me shutting the door.

"Hey, don't forget to lock up!" I shout to the first gunman as I scurry to catch up to the second one. He does not seem as violent as the other guy, who seems hell-bent on shooting me before the end of the night.

We drive to a quintessential Mexican border-town bar and nightclub. The smell of stale beer and other foul odors permeate for at least a one-hundred-yard radius. This bar has everything: lukewarm Coronas for one US dollar, friendly prostitutes, and really greasy street tacos. Or is it one-dollar tacos and greasy…never mind. I start to wonder what the deciding factor is going to be on whether I will walk out of here tonight or be carried out in a body bag. I bet they would charge for the use of the bag. Probably that guy who stole the fifty-dollar bill earlier would try to collect on that debt from me, even though I would be dead. I should probably start coming up with a plan to survive.

I am forced to walk "the correct path" through the patrons and female workers of this fine establishment by the two hired goons. As I stroll in the direction of a gentleman in an expensive tailored mobster-style suit and the three females desperately trying to attend to his every need, I can't help but look off to the right toward the stage. There I see, and it is difficult not to look away, Selma gyrating to a typical stripper-bar song. I might have heard this song before, in another strip club, in another time. Selma, waitress by day, is looking even hotter and sexier when removing the essential clothing that warrants dollar bills and peso notes to be precariously placed in her waistband for safekeeping. She recognizes me instantly and actually looks a bit distraught upon seeing me. Hopefully, it's for not tipping her when I walked by. I wish I can stop and watch the rest of the show, maybe donate some dollar bills to the cause, but present company urges me toward a different meeting that I was not expecting.

"You son of a bitch," Hector says upon seeing me walking toward him.

I recognize him right away, though I didn't know him then as Hector. "Happy to see you," is my only reply.

It has been a long time since our paths crossed. Hector walks right up to me and stares me down. His eyes never blink and are transfixed on every word I utter.

"I can't believe you're still alive." Even after that bizarre night in Detroit years ago. I want to say that I can't believe it is really him. Of course, I knew Hector by another name in another time, but that is a different story. However, I am willing to go along and see how this plays out.

Hector knows immediately that I remember his former identity and points a gun to my head as if daring me to spill the truth. Instead, I ask how the wife and kids are.

He is silent for a moment. He smirks at me and proceeds to withdraw the gun from my head. I have had way too many guns pointed at my head today. Not the best day for me.

I can only add, "Amigo, to what do I owe this honor?"

Apparently, I have chosen wisely in my response, as he motions me to sit down and snaps his fingers twice at the hired help. The first time is to whisk away the hired goons and the second is to have one of friendly female attendants place a glass of tequila in front of me. I hesitate to drink from this glass after the last one resulted in me being drugged. However, the unemotional attendant sits next to me with her arm placed around my waist. She says not a word. I guess I should feel more secure with this silent girl watching over me. Besides, how many times can one get drugged in a day? I must commend Hector on the prompt service in this bar. I should make a point to type up a good recommendation on TripAdvisor for this establishment.

Ah, Hector. The same old Hector, or whatever name he is going by these days. I might have known him by Phil or Enrique or a host of other aliases, but he is still the same guy whose ass I saved from being buried in a six-foot-deep permanent residence along the Lake Erie shore years ago. Of course, he may have saved my ass on one or more occasions, so

I guess that makes us even. At least he has done well for himself, so who am I to spoil it. Besides, it is keeping me alive, and I am sure as hell not paying for any of these drinks or "extras" tonight. He owes me that, at least.

I turn my attention to the stage and start to be entranced by the show. The girl next to me is not bothered; I assume she sees me as an easy assignment to sit next to all night. I stare again at Selma onstage. I give the woman next to me more credit than what's due, even if she is forced to sit here and entertain me. At least she is paying more attention to Hector than I am and signals me (via a swift elbow to the ribs) to listen when Hector is speaking to me (like right now). My mind is clearly more on Selma and her entertaining routine at the moment. Thank you, girl, I will remember to tip you well tonight. Too bad for me though, as the song changes and Selma removes her hot-red lace top and tosses it over to the side of the stage.

I quickly catch up when Hector says, "I need you to help me out, amigo." Hector looks at me square in the eyes. "Jim, I know I can trust you to finish a job all the way to the end. And right now, you are the only one I know in this room that won't fail me."

Translation: "You do this job for me and I won't kill you right away."

I hope he does not need me to bury another body. "No problem, Hector. No worries. You can trust me, can't you? What do you need me to do?"

Translation: "Hector, don't shoot me now. I've never told anyone about the various incidents in our past, though I know whatever job I do for you, I'll probably die in the process."

I continue to sip on my third or fourth round of rather expensive tequila. At least Hector has good taste in fine liquors.

Hector ponders my last sentence but is still wearing a poker face. He continues. "If I remember, my friend, you know New York City like the back of your hand. I need you to make a delivery to an address in Lower Manhattan. Easy enough, compadre."

Translation: "I want you to smuggle thousands of dollars' worth of cocaine or something else illegal across the Mexican-US border and drive all the way to New York City. Oh yes, and try not to get shot, caught, or killed."

"Sounds like an easy job. What do you need me for? Surely you have dozens of men to do this at your disposal."

Translation: "Hector, I know I'm going to die, so why are you sending me to do this? You must have other mules to do this for you."

I motion to the girl next to me that my glass is empty. She looks at me empathically, looks at Hector for acknowledgement, then goes and gets another drink for me. I casually watch her walk off before I look back at Hector. It is just he and I at the table, minus his bodyguards hovering around the next one. "You are about to find out momentarily."

He leans over the table and starts to laugh. Hector looks over my shoulder and watches Selma confidently step down off the stage and put a shirt on to be a little less exposed. She obviously had a great dance session, as evidenced by the numerous dollar bills circling her waistline and the loud round of applause. I wish I could have added to the collection of dollar bills, but other matters are more pressing, like whether I live or die tonight. Hector starts talking while I am still glancing at Selma, who is heading toward our table. This is my vision, my fantasy that is now becoming a reality as she sits down next to me.

Hector shouts over the blaring music, "Ah! My dear Selma, this kind gentleman is going to drive you up to New York City tomorrow." I turn bright red as I raise my head to look at her eyes, which are examining me intently.

He then points toward me. "Don't forget what we discussed and our deal, are we clear?"

My assigned girl returns with my drink, and I take the glass and chug the fine tequila in one gulp. I am starting to feel its effects and probably will readily agree to anything. I look at Selma and then at Hector, but he can only laugh in retort. Selma studies me as if waiting for a reply. I can only show my poker face.

Hector proposes he will pay handsomely for completing this job and, as a bonus, will contact a few people to assist and hopefully lead me in the right direction about Rachel. He assures me that when I arrive in NYC I will be much closer to knowing what happened to her. There is nothing else I can do, as the police have closed the case and listed Rachel as missing and presumed dead.

I put all my faith in Hector and what he can find out in a week's time. I trust him somewhat, and though I have known him for quite some time, I still have that gut feeling that I should watch my back very closely. However, Hector's team has a lot more power, men, and guns against my team of one. I am screwed if he reneges on the deal; I guess it doesn't matter, as I will probably be dead anyways. That's how I see it on the scoreboard: Jim lost, Hector Juan (or, uh, won).

Hector gets up and leaves the table. Now is time for the awkwardness to begin. I look at Selma, thinking about the show I missed, but my attendant girl elbows me once again, asking if I want anything else. Clearly, my attentions are on another female, but it doesn't seem to bother her for the moment. Perhaps my lack of lustful desire is a relief to her, even if my lack of bathing today is something she has had to put up with for the last hour. I am really hungry, and food would be nice, even if it might cause complications later tomorrow.

"Hey babe, can you get me something to eat when you're refilling my drink?" I ask, pointing to my empty glass. "And take your time." It was a nice way of saying, "Take a break, and I won't tell your boss." Besides, I need time to talk to Selma since I am going on a road trip across the country with her.

So now it is just Selma and I. Off in the distance, another woman is doing her thing onstage while the DJ plays another clichéd song. This time, I am not interested in that woman, but rather in the one directly in front of me. Here is this strange woman who, in the last twenty-four hours, fed me, drugged me, and now preformed for me. What is her role in the grand scheme of things? She continues to glare at me as if waiting for a reply. She seems to be studying me like a scientist does a test subject; maybe I should be more intellectually stimulating.

"Well, I hope you like road trips," is the only thing I can muster. I clearly failed on that one.

"You really don't get it, do ya?"

"I'm not following you, sweetie." I have had way too many drinks already.

"Ha, ha, he hasn't told you, has he?" Wow, she has such a beautiful smile when she laughs. Oh yeah, focus, man, focus.

Now I am confused. "Uh...told me what?" I am not playing the mental genius card tonight.

Hector and his entourage come back to the table, and so does my female attendant. And yes, she managed to bring back food—whether it is edible might be a different question—along

32

with a refilled drink in hand. I really should thank her, or do I need to tip her? If I tip her, is she expected to do an extra service for me? I think I have had too much to drink and just found out my new assignment is to drive more than twenty-five hundred miles cross-country. Regardless, the food is needed, and my attendant is a rock star and doesn't even have to sleep with me tonight. Evidently, I am infatuated with another woman this evening.

Hector comments on how well Selma and me hit it off. He looks over my shoulder again to see the next girl dancing away onstage. He glances back at me for only a second to give me words of wisdom.

"Don't fuck this up, and keep her alive. You have one week to get her to New York City. You will be well funded for this trip. Adios, amigo."

I really hope that in doing this job, Hector will be able to give me some lead on tracking down my wife. How can this possibly go wrong? All I have to do is drive this woman to New York City. Selma is still looking at me, as if waiting for the right time to pounce.

At least my green chile pollo tacos taste good, and I drink my tequila as though it is my last meal. Probably not far from the truth. I might as well enjoy myself tonight and pull my female attendant closer with Selma sitting on the other side and watch the next girl dance away onstage.

Chapter 4

Near the center of the Mexican border town is the plaza square, not far away from Hector's nightclub. It is the time-honored tradition in most villages where the town well is located near the city center, but this town happens to have a nice open-air park. Vendors usually take it over during the day to sell their wares, but at night, it is a peaceful place to sit and relax and gaze upon the stars. It is also an advantageous point in town, given all the inbound roads lead to this particular park. In addition, at night you can sit there and see all the people coming and going up and down the various streets. You can also see people in their apartments above the businesses that occupy the plaza.

By chance on this evening, there is a window open in the apartment above one of the buildings, covered only with a translucent curtain. The form of the person in the window is undeniably female. The address number on the building below the window is 42.

After a couple of hours, I am just a little bit past drunk, and it is late into the night. One of Hector's junior associates comes up to me and kindly asks me to join him outside. Is he gonna kick the shit out of me, or does this mean my taxi has arrived? I follow him hoping for the taxi, but where is it going to take me tonight? Probably the locked room, though a real hotel room would be nice right now, maybe with extra-firm pillows, too.

I look around and realize everyone else has already left the fine establishment. I am one of the last ones left as they turn the lights on in the club. Patrons and dancers start to look really scary once the alcohol wears off and the lights are on. That is a sobering thought, and it is definitely closing time. I don't remember saying goodbye to anyone, especially to Selma, and my female attendant has already disappeared. I never got a chance to thank her or generously tip her. I should tell Hector she was great as an attendant and nothing more. I wonder if Selma lives far from here, or is she staying at the Hector Hotel? Am I really going to spend the next week driving across the country with her? Does Selma even like me, or do I repulse her? More importantly, why doesn't she just fly to NYC, and what exactly is her relationship with Hector?

Outside, barely able to stand, Taxi Man is yelling at me and directs me to the right side of some flashy black Mercedes-Benz C-Class vehicle. I realize that I did not pay for anything tonight: nothing for the food, nothing for the dozen or so drinks. I start to tell Taxi Man that I need to go back inside and pay what I owe. It is only right. He looks at me for a second in seriousness but then lets out a hardy chuckle.

"You got to be kidding, amigo." He now encourages me to get into the back seat, courtesy of a right-arm twist and a slight nudge forward. If I were sober and left-handed, I could flip him and have my left boot against his left cheek in less time than it takes to say it. Instead, I play out the drunkard role and go along; at least I am getting away with paying nothing tonight, including the chauffeur service to a bed/hotel room.

"No, I'm serious. I drank and ate way too much to leave without paying some bar tab." I turn around, stumble, and escape his grip. My newfound strength could possibly be due to the five or six Jack and Cokes, or was it the four liberal tequila pours? I don't know or can't remember. I start to walk back toward the door haphazardly, bracing the wall for stability.

Taxi Man runs toward me as if he is my personal bodyguard tonight and grabs me by the shirt collar, this time in a tighter grip.

"Hector owns the place. You don't owe anything, gringo."

"What about the girl. I owe something to...her?" I blurt out. Clearly, the alcohol is taking over.

"She went home, and so should you. Gringo, you don't want to mess around with her. Take my advice, amigo. Don't do it."

"But I...I want to..." I rethink what I am about to say, but I am fighting the alcohol speech. "I am supposed to drive cross-country with her."

"Then you need to get some sleep. Right now. I will take you to your room that has been arranged for you." He forcefully motions me toward the passenger seat of the Mercedes, blocking my escape this time.

I get in the vehicle, admiring the comfy seat, and settle in. Ah, I could sleep right here. I start to doze off until he slams the door shut.

Taxi Man gets in the driver's seat and starts the engine. It purrs like a kitten, and we are off. He starts to yak away about something in Spanish but realizes that I already look half-asleep. Though I am somewhat coherent, I only pray I don't throw up right now, especially in this fine vehicle. It would be a crying shame to leave my mark this way on the soft leather seats.

Taxi Man rolls down the window a quarter way and reaches over for his smokes. He fires one up and breathes out the smoke, with most of it exiting the car. I barely smell the remaining cigarette smoke, but I am not bothered by it. I stare out the window watching the buildings go by on this humid Mexican evening.

The vehicle's occupants do not notice the open window above the address of Number 42 with a silhouette of a person looking out the window on this cloudless evening. The vehicle drives on by and continues up the street. The person in the window watches the vehicle the entire time. Once it turns the corner, she shuts the curtains and disappears from sight.

We turn the corner and continue on our way back to the apartments above La Tequila Restaurant, which Hector clearly also owns in this town. Will they give me my old room? Has the cleaning staff had time to clean it and make the bed? I hope Hector is not expecting me to pay for this room either.

Meanwhile, Hector and Selma sit in a private room back at the club. She asks, "He really doesn't know anything, does he? Do you really trust him, Hector? Just how long have you two known each other?"

Hector reaches over and tops up the glasses with the finest Jack Daniel's around. He lights up another cigarette and exhales the smoke to his left, away from her.

"No, I don't trust him, but he's the perfect mark. He'll think he's protecting you, and he won't hesitate to shoot anyone for your safety. Besides, I know his type; he wants to find his missing wife and thinks I've got all the answers to find her. Oh, I'll have the information and will give it to him after this is all done with, but he won't like it." Hector smirks as he takes another pull from the whiskey glass.

"Does he really believe you'll help him? Gosh, I feel so sorry for him!" Selma lights a cigarette as well but blows the smoke in front of her toward Hector. She is supposed to have been smoke-free for two years but has one every once in a while.

"Now, Selma." Hector raises his voice more than raising his whiskey glass and looks directly at her. "You can't tell him anything. All he'll know is he has to pick up and drop off various items en route to New York City. He just assumes it's drugs. I'll tell him he has to collect various packages from these people. He shouldn't suspect anything." He pauses. "Selma, my dear, he doesn't know anything about you. You can lead him on or do whatever you want, but I swear, you cannot tell him anything else. You hear me? It will jeopardize everything, and she will be *really* pissed at you and me. Now remind me, can you assemble it once you have all the pieces?"

"Honestly, do you think I'm a dumbass or something? I'm not one of your girls shaking their stuff onstage because they're too stupid to do anything else. Though it was a lot of fun being up there. Ah, it was empowering. Check this task off my bucket list! But I didn't graduate with a PhD from Caltech so I can dance on a Mexican stage. However, the amount of money I made tonight is tempting me, given how good I am at it."

She laughs so hard that she starts coughing, a bit of a testament to the effects of the cigarette she is trying to smoke. She catches her breath and continues. "Are you sure the parts will be there when we arrive at the destinations?"

"Yes, my dear, they will be ready for pick up. The question is, can you do this and get him to play along? By the way, you looked amazing onstage. I have a job for you here if you ever change your mind." Hector checks her out one more time.

"Of course I can, and I'm glad you liked the show." Selma turns five shades of red in the face. "So when do we hit the road?"

"Sooner than you think. And keep him alive until Rachel wants him dead. Can you do that, sweetie?"

Normally, it would sound like some bad B-rated movie: waking up in a cheap motel south of the border with tequila on my breath, the memories of some unknown female's sweaty perfume lingering in the air, and discovering I am robbed of my wallet and clothes. Fortunately, that is not how I awake the next day, apart from the tequila breath. I wake up wondering if today is going to be the strangest day of my life, and yet I feel a sense of calm about it. I have a paying job to do for Hector, and it may lead me to finding out whatever happened to my wife. I feel a sense of failing Rachel as the weeks go by and I continue to have no clue as to what happened to her or how to find her. Somehow, I even feel guilty for embarking on this road trip across the country with a beautiful woman whom I just met hours ago.

First, I have to cross back into the United States. Easy enough: I am supposed to play the American schmuck who has the "drank too much tequila/ and cheap beer, spent all his money, and bought a Mexican blanket to prove he was in Mexico" travel experience. All I have to do is go buy a blanket in the market, not shower, and just look sad and pathetic.

I try to tidy up the room, but there is no point. I gather my wallet (still contains most of my money) and car keys, and shut the door on the way out. I walk down the stairs and find the desk clerk who I think was the bartender from the other day. I throw the room key down on the counter, and he picks it up and goes about doing something else.

"What do I owe, amigo?"

"Huh? Oh, nothing, señor. Courtesy of Señor Hector. Buenos días."

"Gracias."

He clearly is not bothered by me, or anything else, for that matter. I simply shrug my shoulders, turn around, and walk out.

I stroll down the street and head toward the border. I pass a few shops before stopping to peruse some blankets at one particular vendor. She is an older lady, and I feel sorry for her. It doesn't take me long to find a Mexican blanket that I like and doesn't feel cheaply made.

"How much for the blanket, señora?"

"Four hundred pesos or thirty US dollars."

"Fifteen dollars would be more reasonable. I saw a similar blanket for less at a vendor one block over."

"I need to feed my family. Couldn't you afford twenty US dollars?"

How can I argue with that? Five bucks extra is not gonna break the bank.

Having negotiated a reasonable, though probably overpaid, monetary offer, I open my wallet and pull out a crisp twenty-dollar bill. At this point, various vendors start circling me and fighting over who gets to sell me their favorite Mexican-crafted tourist items. I really look like someone's meal ticket this morning, so at least I got to pick the old lady who I thought would benefit most from my generosity. Too bad that she probably ripped me off the most.

As I continue making my way down the main drag and trying to avoid any more pushy vendors, my mind begins to wonder about Selma again. Not in the dirty, lustful way, although her stage show certainty left a memorable impression that will long linger in my visual mind for a while. I also wonder whether taking her to New York City is a good idea or if this will be my last trip. Perhaps I should just ride it out to NYC and not worry about anything. Was Selma sent to take me out and bury me? Take me out to dinner, maybe, but I doubt that girl can shoot anyone. Maybe I am underestimating her, but I don't get a bad vibe from her. Even so, I also don't like the idea of transporting thousands of dollars in drugs in my car either, but that, for some odd reason, isn't bothering me as much.

In the near distance, I can see the border crossing up ahead. I also see the duty-free store right before it. Now is the time to buy one more souvenir at discount prices. I open the door to the store and beeline straight to the tequila section. It takes me less than two minutes before I spy what I am looking for: one bottle of La Cava de Don Agustín tequila. Only the best and only found in Mexico. I also pick up a bottle of Sauza Conmemorativo Añejo as well. Hey, it's on sale.

Now I really look like a touristy American on a weekend pass to the wilds of Mexico. I am armed with passport, blanket, and duty-free-emblazoned bag full of tequila. I am ready to stare down the dreaded US passport control.

Thank goodness they have two lines: Americans and everyone else. I jump in the American line just behind some obnoxious couple from Boston. They one-upped me and bought a sombrero; they must be drug runners. The couple looks at me and steps forward away from me. I guess the lack of showering might indicate that I need to get back across the border more than they do. I smell fear in them as they smell cheap cologne and day-old sweat on me.

When my turn comes, I step up to the US customs officer, who just starts to laugh at me. Obviously, he must see this a million times a year.

"Citizenship and purpose of your trip to Mexico." The officer strains not to burst out laughing at the sight of me.

I plead the schmuck look, and he asks if I have anything to declare. Though I want to say, "Don't go to Mexico," the better part of me decides if I just go the normal route and not be the funny guy, it should go all right.

"United States. Went down south of the border for some rest and relaxation. I tried working on my tan as well."

I show off my duty-free bag and Mexican blanket, and it doesn't interest the customs officer one bit. He stamps the passport and just bellows, "Next!"

I quickly move down the corridor and walk out the building onto American soil. Yay. The message of "Welcome to the United States" on the big billboard is overshadowed by the taxi stand. I jump into a taxi and have the horrified feeling that maybe it will be the same taxi driver I had on the way over. Luckily, it is some guy from Dallas, and he is not a talker, double bonus. I tell him the motel I am staying at, and with dust screaming from the back tires, so ends my foray into Mexico.

Apparently, a petite brunette with faded blue shorts has an even easier time crossing the border. Selma uses her passport that has her photo from her grad school days at Caltech and is not questioned about anything, like the fact that she has been staying in Mexico for a week and is toting a really small piece of luggage behind her. Maybe it is because the US customs officer is more interested in her smooth tanned legs than what she is bringing with her to really care. He stamps her passport, and off she goes back to the USA.

Selma has one stop to make before she meets Jim at the run-of-the-mill motel. Her transportation is waiting for her as she exits the customs building.

"Hello, Selma. Did you have fun in Mexico?" He opens the passenger door for her.

"Seriously, Bob, did you think it was all fun?" She adjusts in the seat, and Bob pauses before shutting the door. He takes Selma's bag and puts it in the trunk.

"You love it, and you know it." Bob slams on the gas pedal and blends into traffic. In no time, they are on their way.

"I really wonder sometimes why Hector keeps you on the payroll. Maybe it's for your incredible driving skills?"

"Because I'm good at what I do, and Hector knows it. You know it, everyone knows it. Oh, and here's an update for you: your boyfriend is already back at his motel."

"He's not my boyfriend, Bob." Selma quickly changes the topic. "Is everything ready as we discussed two days ago?"

"Sure thing, ma'am, just as you requested."

"Then let's go so we can rendezvous in time to meet Jim and get his car ready for this trip."

"Anything for you, sweet thing."

They drive to Bubba's Pawn and Gun on the west side of town where there is a package waiting for her. All she has to do is ask the clerk who his favorite Cowboys quarterback was. The clerk looks at her and says he has something special for Cowboys fans and goes to the back of the store for a minute. Another man working there eyes her suspiciously as the clerk comes back with an old dark-blue Trivial Pursuit box.

43

"Here's the item you've been looking for, ma'am. I'm sure all the pieces are in there. No need to open it. Since your uncle came in last week and paid for it, all you need to do is sign this receipt."

Selma signs some fake bill of lading with a fake signature.

"Pleasure doing business with *your family*. Good day, ma'am"

Selma leaves the pawnshop feeling satisfied that she has the proper protection. She means to shoot Jim when told to do so. Her newly acquired 30mm Glock is a little heavier than expected, but she takes it out of the Trivial Pursuit box and puts it in her shoulder bag.

Bob is playing on his phone when he looks up in the rearview mirror to see if she is ready to go.

"All set, dear? Did you stash it properly? Did you check the permit to make sure it will pass if you get stopped?" he asks her.

"I almost forgot about the permit. Where is it?"

"It should be in the box as well."

She retrieves the permit and puts it in a zipped part of her shoulder bag.

"Don't worry about the box; I'll take care of that. Just remember to tip generously at the end of the fare." He lets out a hardy laugh at his own joke.

"Do you know which motel Jim is staying at?"

"Heading there right now, unless you want to grab a quick bite to eat."

"That's fine. Anything is fine except for Taco Cabana or Taco Bell."

"Don't forget to text Jim that you'll meet him in an hour."

"Good thinking. There's a Five Guys up ahead on the right. Let's go there first. I'll text him afterward."

I am sitting on the bed at the no-tell motel. What is taking her so long? She is supposed to be here by now. I wonder if something happened at the border. Hector would have told me. Surely, he would have called. He told me not to call him except from a pay phone. I just hope she is all right. Maybe she doesn't like me or doesn't want to…

My phone lights up, and a chime rings out. I have a text: *Sorry I am running late. Border was busy. See you soon. S*

Ah, what a relief! At least she is coming. I am really nervous about this whole thing anyways. What happens if we find each other annoying or have nothing to talk about? Maybe she doesn't trust me and decides to run off with some other guy the first chance she gets. What if?

I check the route and go over the instructions that Hector gave me one more time.

Drive normally. You need to act like you and Selma are together, so just play along. Don't attract attention by arguing or fighting. Go the fastest route. You have a few stops to make, with the first in Wichita, Kansas, and the second in Niles, Michigan, to pick up a couple of small packages. Don't worry; they'll know you two are coming. Selma is taking care of the details for the pickups.

You better keep her safe on the way to New York City. If she doesn't show up there by Saturday next week, well, you don't want to know. Call the special number I gave you only if the police stop you. I don't want to hear from you until the job is done and Selma is at a specific address on Saturday in Lower

Manhattan. In return, I'll have something for you about your wife, and it'll be waiting for you when you arrive.

I push back the curtains and take a look out in time to see a brunette in shorts get out of a taxi in the middle of the parking lot as the driver retrieves her luggage out of the trunk. She thanks him and turns toward my door as the taxi drives off.

Selma has arrived. It is now just me and her.

Chapter 5

Selma is dressed typically for a hot Texan day. She is wearing a sleeveless light-pink T-shirt with incredibly short faded denim shorts. Her legs look as tan as they can be, and one can only assume they are as smooth as silk. She stands there for a moment, only switching her sunglasses down to glance up at me as I open the door to my crappy domicile in this horrible motel. I feel embarrassed yet thrilled that this young beautiful goddess is going to ride along with me. She is so secretive, yet I feel the desire to talk with her, to protect her, to get to know her. Well, last night I got to know and see a lot more of her. Let's see if she can walk the talk.

Jim opens the door as I walk toward the room. He is staring at me as though my guilt is showing right through. He saw me on that stage last night and knows that I am untrustworthy. I feel it. I know it. How will I convince him I'm interested in him? He's potentially the port in the storm that has been like a hurricane the last year since I got involved with Hector and Rachel. I know that they have a plan for what lies ahead, but I feel it could be written better. I know in my mind that I shouldn't get close to Jim, yet my heart is sensing something different. What's going to happen on this trip? What will the future bring after we arrive in New York City? I only wish that I could tell Jim what I really know, but another time.

"Hello, Selma." I check her out again, up and down. Twice for good measure.

"Hi, Jim, are you ready to actually do this?" *I can't believe we're doing this. This is crazy.*

"Would you like to come in? At least get out of this crazy Texan heat for a moment." Is that the best line I can give her? I guess it is better than telling her I want her right now.

She quickly replies, "Only if you have something cool to drink inside." She walks past me in a slow and methodical manner as if to suggest that her intentions are more than what was said.

"I have some bottled water in the fridge." Probably not the best pickup line ever uttered, but at least I should get points for practicality. The water bottles are really cold too, which helps in this heat.

She winks at me in affirmation as she grabs one of the bottles and guzzles it. I only sweat even more.

"By the way, Jim, did Hector tell you that we're taking a different car on this journey? Don't worry. Somebody will drive your Subaru to wherever you want."

Perish the thought of someone else driving my vehicle, my love, my baby. On the other hand, surely Hector will give us a nice ride and not some piece of shit.

"So what are we to drive then?"

"A Ford Escape. Fully loaded."

"That shouldn't attract too much attention." I am glad it wasn't some gangster car that tells the world, "Look at me. I'm a gangsta."

"As long as it has AC. It'll be a long, hot drive."

Looking out the window of the motel room, I can only nod my head in affirmation of the miserable heat.

Selma makes a phone call, and fifteen minutes later, a man that goes by the name of Lenny comes by in the Ford Escape complete with AC and what I assume to be drugs stashed away in the side panels. He flips the keys to me and smiles a "good luck" smile that only a man can understand. I am sure he is thinking, "Good luck, sucka, and don't get caught by the po-po," but who am I to speak gangster speak.

I only joke, "At least it has leather seats." Only to realize that leather seats are awful on really hot sunny days.

I get a half-hearted smile from Selma. Wow, if she smiled at that, then she must really like me. I can only wish.

We load our luggage into the back of the Ford Escape. I toss the keys of my beloved Subaru to Lenny.

"Take good care of her. She fishtails on wet pavement." Am I describing my car or my child?

"Where am I driving her to?" Lenny asks.

"Salt Lake City. The address is 147 Broadway. It's downtown." I add, "You'll be careful with her, won't ya?" I'm acting as if I'm parting with my first-born child. I think Selma is laughing inside.

"No worries, amigo. I'll even wash her at the end of the trip."

He really is going to hotdog it for the next thousand miles. Sorry, Subaru. I really am.

I turn to Selma and say, "I guess I'm driving first?"

She only nods in agreement.

Learning to drive takes time and skills that are developed over many years of practice and patience. Learning to ride with someone you hardly know and embark on a journey of thousands of miles and not knowing if you are going to live or die at the end is purely ludicrous. I really should open a bottle of duty-free tequila and smash it against the back of the Escape for good luck. Then again, I should just drink it for better luck. I hardly know Selma apart from a pleasant memory of her dancing on a stage while I was drinking tequila and her parting with her outer clothes. That is a fine memory, and I am sure it is a good basis for a newfound friendship or driving companion. Yeah, it is time to hit road.

I am riding cross-country with a man I hardly know yet have the impulse to trust implicitly. Why, I can't fathom. Only fate knows the answer. I'm willing to bet on Jim and play it out over the next seven days. What a strange road trip this will be.

I adjust the mirrors and the seat. I start to play with the radio when Selma asks when we are going to get the show on the road. Patience, my dear, as I make the final adjustment to the outer mirrors. All right: ready, set, one more look at my passenger, one more look at those thighs that seem ever so smooth from the end of the shorts downward. OK, look back, and now I am ready to embark on this sojourn.

I drive approximately a thousand feet and get stopped by a stoplight. That was really exciting. I guess the journey of a thousand miles really does start with one step. Somehow, I missed the part about the stoplight though. The light turns green, and we progress forward.

I turn on the radio only to hear The Proclaimers singing, "But I would walk five hundred miles/And I would walk five hundred more." I quickly shut the radio off. She laughs, catching the joke, too. I really am starting to like this woman sitting next to me. I only pray she is the perfect one—you know, the perfect driving companion. Please don't put your bare feet on the dashboard. I do have limits I must follow.

The AC provides the coolness for our comfort in the South Texas heat. We head in an easterly direction, as it is the only way to catch I-35 out of San Antonio. Texas is a big state, so unless you have never driven it, you never fully appreciate the pure size of it until you are on some Texas road for hours upon hours. I glance over to Selma just to check her out. Not in the man check-out sort of way, but just to make sure she is alive and not bored shitless yet. She is staring off into the Texan countryside but then turns toward me with a slight, half-hearted smile. At least she is tolerating me thus far. We shall see what she thinks of me after five hundred miles. I hear the end of "If You Leave" by OMD and switch radio stations until I find another non-country station. In this state, that might be trickier than I thought.

Hector picks up the phone after the third ring. "Hola?"

"Hector, you know who this is." *I only have been calling you practically every night.*

"What do you want, dear?" *What is it now? I'm busy.*

"How is our happy couple?"

"I'm tracking them as we speak. They're on their way to the first point. Hey, they really make a great couple, don't you think?" That should piss her off.

"I should know. I was married to him, and, no, they don't," Rachel snarls.

"You gutless bitch, he really loves you. I didn't tell your little secret, and Selma promised not to tell him either. I hope you're happy. We're all covering for you."

"Yeah, well, too bad for him. I hope your girl shoots his ass dead. Is she really gonna do it after all this?"

"I trust my girl to do the job. Business is business."

"You better be right on this one. We can't afford any mistakes or loose ends."

"Love you too, dear."

Hector hears the phone on the other end hang up. He turns to his computer, punches in the unique vehicle code, and waits for Jim and Selma's vehicle's location to show up on the map. *They have a long drive ahead of them. I hope they don't kill each other out of pure boredom.*

Hector turns off the computer and calls one of his girls into the office. Make it the Hornitos tequila, he tells her, and she signals an affirmation. *These days, it seems it's the same night after night, but at least I'm drinking the good stuff.*

The girl enters the office, smiles at Hector, and walks toward him with a glass of tequila in hand.

Chapter 6

The first hour of the road trip is uneventful. I think I saw a different tree on the side of the road. Maybe there were two together. I can't remember. A couple of cars passed us approximately five minutes ago. One might have had out-of-state license plates, possibly from the Midwest. I don't know. This is a boring drive. Blah.

Selma awakes from her slumber. Was she asleep or just really quiet? Maybe she was thinking about something important, maybe someone important (like me, for instance), or just thinking about when she was going to stop and get something to eat. I am getting kinda hungry myself but haven't seen anything in the last twenty miles. I should probably stop when we get closer to San Antonio.

In the silence, Selma blurts out, "How are you doing?"

"You know, just driving along. Not much to look at. We're going to have a lot of that on this drive." There's nothing like building up the fun and excitement in the vehicle. It's practically a party mobile in here.

"You can turn on the radio, Jim. Not sure what we're going to pick up out here. Maybe some country or western. Here, I'll get it."

She reaches over to turn on the radio as I am about to reach for the On button, almost brushing her hand in a creepy sort of fashion. Luckily, I pull away before contact is made and smile in her winning the race to turn on the radio. That was the most exciting thing to happen in the last hour. I am waiting for Willie Nelson's "On the Road Again" to start blaring out of the speakers, but as luck would have it, it's an advertisement for the local Ford truck dealership. God is smiling down on me today.

"We can stop for a bite to eat and fill up the gas tank once we get closer to San Antonio. And if you want to drive, we can switch. Though I must say, it isn't any more exciting behind the wheel."

She snorts out a laugh. "Yeah, that's fine. I'm not really hungry though. It's your decision wherever you want to stop and eat."

Hmm, maybe she is testing me. Is she thinking: does he go for the healthy choice, or does he go for Mickey Dee's? Surely, it's a trap! All women do this to men; they don't want to appear to like McDonald's, but everyone loves McDonald's. However, logic dictates that I have to go for the safe choice of finding highly visible restaurant parking where I can see the vehicle at all times. I really hate eating in any vehicle. But I can't call Hector and tell him we misplaced the SUV while eating at an Applebee's. Sorry, Hector, it's the darnest thing. Whoops. Suddenly, I kind of lose my appetite after thinking about how that phone call would turn out.

We make it to San Antonio in the early afternoon. I would love to park and take a stroll with Selma along the River Walk and maybe check out The Alamo. But we are not on a date or a sightseeing tour and have to reach Wichita by tomorrow evening. Still, it would have been nice to think how things would be with my traveling partner under different circumstances.

I don't think about Rachel as much as I should be, though it has been over a year since her disappearance. I never had a lot of time to mourn for her being gone, as there was never any closure. When someone disappears, one hopes that they are eventually found, as you don't want to write them off as dead. There's always gotta be hope that stays with you. But that hope does eventually fade a bit, and after a while, you start believing that they are not coming back, and you must move on. You must survive.

I am not even sure what I will do if I ever see Rachel again. How do I react? What do I say? Do we just go back to being a couple again like nothing happened? Will she be the same person as I once knew? The one I loved?

Maybe I am just too distracted by this assignment and the prospect of a long drive across the country with a complete stranger who happens to be quite attractive. I thought it would be a good thing, peace of mind and not a care in the world. I was wrong about that. I am toting around drugs in the vehicle, and I have a woman whom I hardly know that I am supposed to keep alive and deliver in a week. I really should be...

"Hey, Jim, your turn to the interstate is coming up. You'll need to get on I-35 in two exits."

"OK, thanks. Got it." I was drifting off in deep thought there. I am glad I didn't drive off the road and into the ditch or something.

"You all right, Jim? You look tired or distracted."

"Yeah, I was thinking about driving to New Braunfels just to get past all this San Antonio traffic. Besides, if memory serves me, I think that's where they make Shiner Bock beer, and I always wanted to stop and do the tour and tasting."

"Ah, a cold beer would taste good right now. Thanks, Jim!" Selma replies sarcastically.

I can only agree with that. Maybe we will drive back through here one day and get that beer. Well, at least I will. I really can't speak for Selma right now.

I glance over to her. "Are you ready to take over?"

I see the next exit coming up and decide it is a good time to stop and take a break. I take the exit and turn right, drive down the road, and turn into a Subway, a safe choice. Well, at least healthier than any burger place. Selma seems to perk up as we enter the eatery and decides she wants to order a six-inch sub. I go for a foot-long sub only because I am starving. I did ask for it on wheat bread, so I should get some healthy points in Selma's mind. I pay for the meal courtesy of the Hector bankroll, and we sit down near a window so I can see the Escape.

"OK, Selma," I say as we both unwrap our respective sandwiches.

She looks at me strangely.

I quickly reply after swallowing the first bite, "This is our first meal together." I smile back at her.

She pauses to take it in and smiles back before chomping down on her sub.

I really am starting to dig this woman. I take another bite but lose some vegetables in the process that end up on my shirt. She laughs at me but in a friendly sort of way.

We leave Subway, and I climb in the passenger side. I really hope Selma is not one of those woman drivers. I feel I will be wide awake for the first fifty miles of her driving. After about ten miles, I am less tense and start to relax. This is the easy part for the navigator. Stay on I-35 until, well, forever. Oh, you will get a chance to decide if you want to go 35 East or 35 West, but I will be driving by then. That's it though. My job is done at least until we are north of Waco, when we will probably switch.

After the ten-mile marker, Selma turns on the radio and begins her search for a decent radio station to pass the time.

Meanwhile, I decide that playing with my phone, reading the map, and just plain staring out the window is starting to get boring. She hasn't found any station that has played at least two songs in a row that I like. Should I invoke some light-hearted conversation to help quash the silence and ease the tension between us? It is time to find out the ever-important answer to the perplexing question that has been bothering me since we began this sojourn: is Selma a silent person or a chatterbox? I am about to find out.

There's this thing about long road trips. Sure, they have been glamorized by Hollywood in *Route 66* and Jack Kerouac's classic *On the Road*. Throw in a little "California Dreamin'" by The Mamas & The Papas in the background, and you have this incredible journey of one's self in search of adventure while traveling the highways of America. The reality of driving long distance is a different picture: the seat gets uncomfortable, and the scenery switches between two visualizations. The first is the corporate America big-box stores, the same sit-down restaurants and fast-food chains galore at every major exit. The second is the flat verdant pastures of farm after farm, miles of cornfield after cornfield. Sometimes it is mile after mile of wheat fields just to mix it up a bit. If you are lucky, you may get a bit of empty, undeveloped land or the endless woods and forests where one can never seem to see past the three rows of trees.

I think this is the reason that God decided to release satellite radio technology on the populace: to add some soul to the drive. In by-gone eras, it used to be the cassette tape and CD, which were the saviors of their day. It was always better than trying to scan for a new local radio station every time a station you liked went out of range. Yes, we could have flown, ridden the train, or taken the bus, except for the issue of transporting illegal drugs on public transit. But what fun would that have been?

Ah, back to the open road, the limitless views of the countryside as we explore the endless highway to reach our inevitable destination. This is the way to pass the time: in a moving four-by-four metal can versus suffocating in a six-foot-by-six-foot cubicle in Cubicle Land. And it even comes with rockin' music versus the annoying hum of the HVAC blowing down on the cubicles. Even the outdoor air is cleaner than the recycled air in the office building. I should be so lucky to be driving two-thousand-plus miles. Why would I want to live my life any other way? Ode to the open road. I can't wait to see the endless corn and wheat fields in Kansas. In fact, I am dreaming of the cornfields right now.

"Are you going to start talking soon to keep me awake?" Selma asks as I snap back to the reality of the passenger seat. We are just past downtown Austin, heading north across the great state of Texas.

"Hey, I've been here before. Austin is an awesome town. Sixth Street rocks. You so gotta go there some time. Bars, live music, drinks, you get the idea! I used to live not far from here, way back when."

"When was this?"

"Years ago. I was stationed at Fort Hood when I was in the army. HUA and all that army stuff!"

She looks at me quizzically.

"What, I don't look like I was in the army? Should I get a buzz cut? Do some push-ups next time we take a break?"

Looking embarrassed, she says, "No, no. It's not that. It's just that I really don't know anything about you, and here we are, driving across the country together for the next seven days."

Wow, she didn't really sound thrilled to be traveling with me. Maybe I should play the cool hand now. Time to play the ace I have up my sleeve.

"What do you want to know? I can talk about myself for hours. There's so much to tell. I have a lot of war stories." I literally can and have bored to death a great many people in the past.

"We have the time. Tell me where you're from, who you are, why you were down in Mexico, and how you know Hector."

I quickly reply with a wide smile, "Are you sure we aren't on a date?" Emphasizing the word *date*. My ace of spades has been played, and now it is time to reel her in.

Selma looks flustered and gives an unconvincing, "No," but her body language suggests something else. She starts to swerve but straightens the vehicle out. She quickly recovers her composure and switches back to a more serious tone. "Have you ever smoked? I don't mean weed or crack, but just cigarettes?"

Neutral topic. I will play along. "I used to smoke for about ten years. As I said earlier, I was in the army, and everyone in the army smokes, especially when we went out to the field for two weeks. Rough times," I say with a macho smile.

"And how long ago did you quit? You quit just like that? What did you smoke? How many times a day? Don't you miss it?" She is getting excited, as the speed of the vehicle is increasing.

"Ah, too many questions!" I gather my thoughts for a moment. "I decided to just give it up. Besides, my wife never liked me smoking anyways. She always complained of secondhand smoke. She—"

Selma shrieks, "*You* are married?"

59

OK, Jim, I hope you believe me and buy my fake reaction. You don't know that I'm related to your wife through marriage and distant cousins. Hector told me about Rachel and why she disappeared, but I have to make sure you believe that I don't know about Rachel and that you're married to her. She's a bitch, by the way.

Her tone and accusatory demeanor suggest she is more upset to hear that I have a wife than that I used to smoke. I will try to be honest with her, as it is not my intent to hit on Selma, though, if the situation were different...nah...she would never go for a guy like me.

"I am, well, technically, still married, but it's complicated. My wife disappeared over a while ago. I was asking Hector for a favor to help me track her down or at least help me find out what happened to her. I just gotta know what happened. He said he could help me if I do a favor for him. Voilà, here I am with you, traveling to New York City."

The vehicle slows down, and Selma steps on the brakes as we drive off to the shoulder of the interstate just outside of Waco. She throws the vehicle into park and turns on the hazards. She pauses for a moment and then slowly turns to me. Her face has no expression. She coughs and then starts to speak in a soft tone. It is almost like she knows something but is selecting her words carefully.

"Jim, look, I am so sorry. I didn't mean to bring up anything in the past that's painful for you." She pauses, then continues. "I didn't mean to upset you. I hope Hector can help you find your wife. I know it must be painful for you."

I can only muster an obligatory "thank-you," as I am locked on her eyes, searching for the truth in her voice. I firmly believe she already knew anyways. What else does she know? What has Hector told her, and, more importantly, should I trust her?

She flips the car into drive and gets back on the interstate. We don't say a word for quite a while. She is playing the eighties channel on the satellite radio, having given up hope of finding anything remotely related to classic rock on the regular radio stations. This is Central Texas: the choices are either country music or country music. I look over at her, and her head is positioned forward, though her eyes briefly dart to me for second and then forward again.

I decide to break the silence. "We should probably take a break and switch driving when we come up to Waco."

"Good idea. I could use a break. The heat is starting to get to me."

She is not the only one who could use some fresh air.

Chapter 7

We stop off at a rest area just north of Waco. I was getting tired of driving, and it seemed like a good time for Jim to take over. He has had a long enough break, and now it's my turn to relax in the passenger seat once again. It's midafternoon. The sun is shining brightly overhead, and Jim is probably waiting patiently outside wondering why I'm taking so long in the bathroom. I have to call Hector to let him know how we are doing and to ensure him everything is going to plan.

The phone rings. Hector answers on the third ring. *"Bueno, chiquita."*

"Hola, Hector. Everything is going fine. We are north of Waco. We should be able to make it to Wichita and be ready for the first pickup in time."

"Excelente. I know you can do it, dear." *I just hope you can do what we hired and are paying you a lot of money for.*

"Hector." Selma sounds worried.

"What? What is it, Selma?"

"He...Jim's on to me. He started to tell me about Rachel, and I played it way too much. Now he doesn't trust me. I can feel it. I don't know. He seems too suspicious. I think I fucked up it. You know I'm not good at this stuff. What do I do now?"

"First thing, stop talking about fuckin' Rachel. He doesn't need to be thinking about her any more than he has to. Talk about sports or the news. I don't know. Talk about something about him."

"OK, I can do that."

"And second, he needs to believe you like him. He'll be all right. Where is he right now?"

"He's probably at the vehicle wondering if I did a runner."

"Just act like everything's fine. He'll trust you eventually. I've known Jim for many years; he always is more trusting toward females. Just smile at him. It works every time. Call me when you stop tonight if you can. I need to have the vehicle at the location I instructed you the other day. Adios."

Hector hangs up.

I am standing near a park bench that is close to the where the vehicle is parked. Where is she? Surely a woman can't take that long? I better start checking all the 18-wheelers to make sure she didn't ditch me. Why is she is on this trip anyways? I am starting to wonder about what the relationship is between Hector and her and how this ties into Rachel.

OK. I see her exiting the rest area door and heading toward our vehicle. I stand up and turn toward her so she can see me. She is moving with this unique swagger, and I am not the only man to appreciate it. Hey, buddy, in your family minivan with two kids in the back—this woman is with me, so stop gazing!

She finally sees me and half-heartedly waves. As she approaches, she comes up in front of me and stops. She begins to apologize and goes on about "women's issues," but I put my hand up to stop her dead. She seems relieved to not have to explain the issue in any more graphic detail.

"Hey, do you need a bottled water from the vending machines?" I point to the separate building off to the right.

Selma stays quiet, as if she is hesitating in deciding what to do. Has a guy never bought her a drink before? I mean, come on, it's freakin' bottled water. I was hoping to buy her an alcoholic drink at some point, but on this trip, bottled water is gold.

I try to sweeten the deal. "I got the money if you want some potato chips to munch on as well." I am trying really hard and hoping she doesn't bring up Rachel again. Though I must question at some point if and how she knows Rachel. I feel this is not the best topic to discuss on this trip, as I need to stay focused and build a friendship or working partnership with Selma over the next seven days.

She seems more enthusiastic once I mention snacks. "Let's see what they got!" she yells back at me and starts to run toward the building.

I am glad she is in a happy mood. I hurry to catch up to her, focusing on the building and not her for my target to sprint to. Today is starting to turn out to be a good day after all. Our first bit of tension was about my wife, but we are all good now. We are still driving through Central Texas and have been all afternoon. It is a hot day, but the satellite radio is rocking out more eighties alternative songs, and the AC is keeping us cool.

I guess it is no surprise to see the median on I-35 is on fire. The recent dry temperatures have literally caused the grass to burn in a fiery blaze. I assume this is a normal occurrence because none of the other drivers seem to be bothered at all. Selma neither swerves nor makes witty commentary about the fires; am I the only one who sees them? I hope this is not some vision of my final resting place, though I am starting to feel the urge to get some proper Texan barbecue. Perhaps this is all a marketing ploy to sell more of it.

"Hey, you see the fires, don't you?" I have to ask.

"Oh sure, it happens all the time," she says nonchalantly. "It's a real scorcher today."

Without missing a beat, she quickly reaches for the AC, this time adjusting it to the Arctic blast setting. I found the previous setting already too cold to begin with, but the alternative is the hot air outside that is too much for me to even breathe. I'd rather sit here and freeze to death. It is funny that she is still hot despite wearing shorts and a small top. She must be a lot more acclimated to the temperature variances than I am. So much for growing up in the North. I have lost my ability to adjust to the cold.

"So, Jim, we should be able to drive through Dallas after rush hour, given we are making good time. Where were you thinking of stopping for the night?"

"I think we should grab a hotel by the airport. It would be our best choice, you know, with high visibility and low risk. Besides, airport hotels always have a bunch of eateries nearby, which means there will be better choices for dinner. If stop near DFW airport, it would only put us about six hours away from Wichita."

"Hector didn't tell us what we should do about the vehicle and its contents. Do you think it will be safe in a hotel parking lot?"

"Good point." I think back to earlier about what would happen if I had to tell Hector...my shoulders shudder at the thought. And not because it is starting to get really cold in here either. I adjust the AC to a less-than-freezing setting when Selma isn't looking.

She suggest after googling hotels on her phone earlier in the day, "We can stay at the Hilton by the airport; they have a valet service that uses the secured parking lot adjacent to the hotel. Besides, Hector is flipping the bill. He gave me a bunch of prepaid Visa cards and lots of cash."

I relax a bit and smile at hearing that Hector is covering all the expenses via these prepaid cards. Maybe I should upgrade my future choices. Next diner, it will be the filet mignon over the chopped steak now. Gracias, Hector, though that cheap bastard only gave me a grand in spending cash. I can plainly see I am not Hector's favorite between the two of us.

Now the uncomfortable, yet necessary, question of the day. "I assume we're getting separate rooms," I have to ask.

She must have been thinking the same thing because her response is almost immediate. "You mean we aren't sharing the king bed? I was hoping you didn't snore loud or hog the sheets."

She still is looking at me with a straight face. Then there is a pause before she laughs out loud.

"We can get a suite with two doubles, silly man. That will be all right. Just don't try any funny stuff. I sleep with a gun and know how to use it. You know, we have to keep up appearances as a couple traveling, don't we? Hector gave us fake IDs, too. And for your information, I do snore loud. It probably will keep you up all night!"

Well, that covers any issues or questions in regard to this matter. I am not so sure if I will rest easy tonight, or any night on this trip, for that matter.

We start to approach the outer-southern-ring road of Dallas, where Interstate 20 crosses 35 East. We have made it to Dallas and get to have our first night together, in a matter of speaking.

We arrive at the Hilton by the airport, and though we have no reservation, Selma's charm, with her sweet accent and a little flirting with the naive desk clerk, score us an awesome suite. As a bonus, we even get it at a reduced rate. We happily sign in as the exhausted Mr. and Mrs. Phil and Susan Banks who drove clear across Texas. I must commend Hector's printing

66

department, as my fake ID is spot-on. Sadly, Selma's photo— well, it must have been a bad day, 'cause she looks older. But you didn't hear that from me.

The debit card has been working all day, so it's not an issue when she uses it to pay for the hotel room. It might be too much to order a movie on the room charge, but Hector can be pissed off at us later on. I must tell him he is missing out on Hilton points; maybe I should sign Phil up for a Hilton Honor Points card. I feel better that the valet parking is secure enough, providing they don't patrol the fenced lot with drug-sniffing dogs. We should make it easy and just order pizza tonight rather than go to a sit-down restaurant. I want something quick and easy. Pizza is always a safe bet. Who doesn't like pizza in the hotel room with some beers, chilling out after a long drive? After all, we do have a kick-ass suite. Might as well enjoy it.

Surprisingly, Selma OKs the dinner menu consisting of a large pizza and six-pack of beer but negotiates to add some breadsticks with dipping sauce. I thought she would have frowned upon the pizza idea, but the drive we accomplished today took more out of us than we realized. It's too bad this hotel doesn't have a spa or a masseuse; we would have added that to the hotel bill in a heartbeat.

I am not sure what is happening between us. Are we starting to become comfortable in each other's presence and happy to drive around the country? Or will this trip just kill the both of us? Am I thinking about her way too much? Apparently, it seems I am.

Have I really moved on from Rachel, knowing that what is past is past and she is never coming back? Should I just start looking out for me and find what makes me happy in life? I really should not think of Selma in that way, but I am finding myself starting to become haunted by thoughts of her. Perhaps I need to open one of my tequila bottles tonight, as tequila consumed in mass quantities is always an icebreaker. The truth is always told better with a drunken tongue versus a sober one. Or so a drunken person told me once.

Why is Jim always watching me and staring at me intently? He doesn't trust me, and I'm sure he can see right through me. Maybe Hector hired him to befriend me and then take me out, literally, once I finish assembling the device. Yet I feel so relaxed with him. He seems like a decent guy, but there is the rift between us that I cannot close. Or haven't figured out how yet. I think I'll call it the Rachel Rift; gosh, she really did a number on him. He doesn't even know the full story, and I don't want to be the one to tell him. I feel like I'm lying to him every moment, yet he has no idea how much he can fix the predicament that I'm in. Oh yeah, pizza for dinner, what woman wouldn't want that...I hope we can chill out tonight and enjoy each other's company, as tomorrow it will be a different game. I don't even want to think about what's going to happen tomorrow with the first meeting and after that. I really should live for the moment and enjoy these happy memories that we are creating. At least I'll remember these good times, as they are the only few that I have at the moment. I am so sorry, Jim. I wish there was another way, but you'll find out soon enough.

After opening the hotel room door, I immediately go over to the thermostat to set it before she even thinks about chilling the room to near-freezing levels. Selma heads toward the large window and opens the curtains to gaze upon the horizontal view of DFW Airport in the distance. I start to check out the amenities of this awesome suite despite there only being one king-size bed. Not bad. I haven't had a decent room like this in a long time, maybe since my honeymoon. The suite even smells like it has been properly cleaned, not masked with obnoxious sprays to make it appear to have been sanitized.

We turn to each other and are locked in a momentary stare down as she realizes the sweet suite has only one bed and a sofa. It is also the result of not all the issues being resolved and thus this awkward stalemate ensues. Hear ye, hear ye: the negotiations will now commence.

The issue: we ended up getting a king bed and a sleeper sofa. Who is going to take what is paramount, as all matters are put aside until this one is agreed upon. We can go no further, and this appears to be a slam dunk for Selma. I assume I am probably getting the sleeper sofa, but I should bargain for something in exchange. Hell, I will probably be crashing out on the sofa before the night is out, as I am too lazy to pull out the sleeper and make the bed. Who has the time to do all that when lying down and throwing a blanket over yourself is much faster? Those mattresses are always crap anyways. I have slept on many a sofa in my past; this one doesn't look lumpy or too badly butt-imprinted.

She must have seen me eyeing the sofa with a bit of disappointment and proposes to sleep on it; after all, she is the smaller of the two of us. I counter-propose she take the bed, but I get first pick of the pillows, and I add the caveat that we get to play a fun game tonight. She ponders the meaning of *fun game* for a moment and requests that it is nothing sexual or dirty or freaky. My eyebrows rise for second when she says, "Freaky," but I nod my head in affirmation. Negotiations have gone well, and the peace accord is signed for the evening.

Selma is exhausted after the sleeping discussions. "I really could use a long hot bath after that drive today. You should take a shower first because I'll be in there for quite some time. I'm assuming you're not a bath kind of guy?" She follows this up with a wink toward me.

"That's fine; I can go secure us some beer at the gas station next door after I shower."

"Well, get in there then!" she barks at me. "Time is wasting, and we both smell awful."

I am already heading toward the shower with some clean clothes and my toiletries bag. While I am showering, I can hear the room door shut. She must have headed out. I hope she is filling up on ice with the ice bucket.

Chapter 8

Selma grabs the ice bucket, along with a room key and her phone, and walks toward the end of the floor. She opens the door to the stairway and walks down one flight and opens the door. She dials a phone number and waits until he picks up on the other end.

"Well, hello, sweetie. I haven't heard from you in a while."

"Hola, Hector. What's going on?"

Selma speaks in a monotone voice, as though she isn't thrilled to be talking to Hector. *Hmm*, he thinks to himself, *that's not her normal bubbly voice.* "I assume Jim is not standing next to you?"

"No, he's not," Selma says in a very harsh tone.

"Good. Good. Are you in Dallas? Have you stopped for the evening?"

"Yes, we're at the Hilton by DFW where you instructed me to stop. We were lucky that your man was working the desk when we arrived. I made sure we parked the vehicle with the valet. Will the valet have the vehicle back by the time we leave in the morning? Jim will freak out if your guys don't have the car back by the morning."

"Don't worry about that. Everything is taken care of. Jim will never know the vehicle was taken out and returned much lighter." *She's starting to worry about what Jim would think. That's not a good sign.*

"We're on schedule to be in Wichita tomorrow for the first pickup."

"Good. I'll contact you if there's a change in plans, but I don't expect any delays. Are you handling Jim OK? You know

71

what you need to do very soon, so I don't want you too...distracted."

"Yes, Hector. You don't need to keep reminding me. I'll do what needs to be done." Selma closes her eyes and lets out a big sigh.

"Excellent, my dear." Hector hangs up.

Selma is still holding the phone when she hears the terminated-call tone. She must go fill up the ice bucket and take the elevator back up one floor to cover her disappearance.

Meanwhile, another phone call is placed, this time by Hector.

"What is it, Hector? What do you want?" Rachel answers.

"Nice to talk to you too, my dear."

Rachel cuts to the chase. "How are they doing? Did they arrive in Dallas yet?"

"Yes, yes. They're at the hotel I always use near the airport. My guys are taking all the drugs out and installing the tracker on the vehicle. It'll be a lot easier in two days for Roberto to keep tabs on them after Wichita."

"Does Jim suspect anything? He's very intuitive, so don't underestimate him. What has Selma told you? That he's easy to manipulate? Because I could have told you that. Sometimes it's an act, and we don't want her falling for him." Rachel lets out a big cough.

Hector is relived that Rachel is finished babbling away. "Selma said everything is fine and going to plan. I told her she's supposed to do it after Wichita, which is why we will have Roberto heading there to take over and complete the task."

"I am warning you, don't underestimate my former husband. You should have tapped his phone. He's probably calling for backup."

"You know, you'll have to explain you and him to me someday when this is all over."

"Certainly, my dear. Perhaps over dinner tomorrow night?"

This time it is Hector who hears the terminated-call tone.

Selma returns to the room as I come out of the bathroom. My hair is still wet, but at least I am dressed nicely and smelling a heck of a lot better.

"I went to get ice," she quickly throws at me.

"Ha, I didn't realize you were gone. I figured you were on Facebook or taking a nap."

I notice that she looks awfully nervous. Selma quickly recovers. "We can't have warm drinks, can we? All right, mister, it's time for me to bathe and look better. If you're going to get beer at the gas station, can you buy some munchies too? Potato chips are fine; you should remember for future reference these are my favorites. Thanks, hon!" she says while removing her shoes and gathering her toiletries.

"Do you have any preference in beer?" I check to make sure I've got a room key and my wallet.

"I trust your decisions." She closes the bathroom door, and I hear the sound of the locking mechanism being engaged.

"See you in a bit."

I walk out of the room, close the door, and check that it is secure. I take the elevator down to the lobby and go sit in one of the comfy chairs that overlooks the pool. I see people splashing around having fun. I punch in the phone number on my cell phone from memory. The phone rings twice, and then someone picks up.

"Well, look who decided to call me," the male on the other end answers.

73

This guy never could just say hello. "Hello, old buddy. What's up?"

"Nothing on my end, but I assume something's going down with you. After all, it's the only reason you ever call me."

"OK, OK. You got me. I took a job with our old buddy Hector or whatever name he's currently using. You know, the one you told me never to do business with because you never trusted that bastard back in the day?"

Upon hearing that, Aaron pauses and laughs. "I warned you, didn't I?"

I can tell he really wanted to say, "I told you so." "We're heading your way in a few days."

Translation: "I really, really need your help, old friend. I suspect something's going to go down."

"Sure, what can your old buddy Aaron do to help?"

"I think it's an ambush, and Hector's going to take me out. Not sure what the girl's role in all this is, but Hector wants me to escort her to New York City."

"Hold on, did you say, 'Girl'? What girl?"

At least Aaron is more interested now. "Her name is Selma. I met her at Hector's club the other night. Brunette. Nice body. Really smart, so she's not your type."

"I'm in. I have a soft spot for brunettes. Too bad about her being smart and all that. What do you need me to do?"

"Can't say much now. But I need to you to start heading this way. Where are you now?"

"Chicago."

"Great. I have a pickup tomorrow in Wichita. Then I'm supposed to head to western Michigan next. Can you meet me in Columbia, Missouri, on Friday morning? If I'm still alive?"

"Sure thing, bro. Anytime. See you Friday, Jim."

"Thanks, Aaron."

Click.

I sit there for a moment reflecting on my phone call with Aaron. Sure, he and I have called on each other from time to time, often one of us bailing the other out. But this time seems different. It was like Aaron was waiting from me to call and spring into action. It is a good thing, I guess, because I need someone to watch my back.

I think Hector is plotting something against me. I just don't know the what and the why. I need to figure out what Selma's part is in all of this. I get up and decide to think more in the present. I walk over to the gas station to grab the provisions and return to the hotel room with beer, chips, and some chocolate just in case. What woman doesn't like chocolate brought to them?

I slide the room key in and wait for the green light. I cautiously open the room door. "Selma, is it OK to enter?"

"Yeah, you're fine," I hear her say from the other end of the room. I get a nervous feeling. I don't know why, but it feels like I am walking into a trap. I check the bathroom in my peripheral vision and stay on guard. I walk past the bathroom carrying our supplies for the evening when I spy Selma sitting next the AC unit playing with her phone. She is wearing this skimpy summer dress and sandals, sitting on the sofa, aka my bed, with her feet up on the table. Her thigh shines toward me. As soon as she realizes what I am staring at, she stands up to greet me. I still check around the room, waiting to be whacked over the head, but the fear subsides once she walks toward me. I open the bags for her inspection. She approves of the beer choice and potato chip flavor. Her eyes only get bigger when she sees the Reese's Sticks. Bonus points for me.

"Shall we call for a pizza now? It's near dinnertime."

"I thought I saw the menu over by the TV."

Thirty-five minutes later, we feast on a mighty nice pepperoni pizza and cheese breadsticks washed down with a few beers from some local brewery. We clean up and decide to go sit near the window to stare at the Texas evening sky.

"Would you like to play a game?" I say after finishing my second beer.

"OK, what do you have in mind?" She signals to me that she is done with her beer and requests a third.

"How about Truth or Dare?" I am throwing all the cards on the table tonight and waiting to see her call my bluff.

"Sounds like fun. Who goes first?" She is already pushing the table aside so we can sit on the carpet near the sofa.

"I'll flip ya for it."

"You're on. I call heads."

Tails come up. I go first. "Truth or dare."

"Ah, *truth*," she blurts out. She is playing with her hair while starting to knock back the third beer. I made the right call in suggesting the game. This might be a very interesting night after all. "OK, let me see. I got it. How long have you been stripping?" Oh yeah, this should be good. I lie back on my elbows waiting for this juicy response.

Selma blushes for a bit. She takes another swig and exclaims, "So, you're not gonna believe this, but that was the first time I ever got onstage!"

"What? I don't believe that. You mean this is all a coincidence?" I scream.

"No, no, it's true. Hector wanted me to excite you. You know, to sweeten the deal. I was a little drunk that night, and I thought it would be fun to do just one time. Who was gonna see me? What do you mean—didn't you like the show?"

She is staring at me dead in the eye right now. I am still replaying her dance from that night over and over in my head. My face turns beet red.

"Yes, yes, of course I loved it. Every man who saw it loved it. It's just that, you know—you looked like you performed it *professionally*." Oops. Maybe I had too many beers.

"I'm not sure to take that as a compliment or not." She has the glassy-eyed look, maybe buzzed from the beer but laughs and leans over to kiss me on the cheek.

"OK, my turn. Truth or dare?"

"What the hell. Dare!" I shout out.

I don't think she was expecting that. She thinks for a moment. "OK, OK. I dare you to beat me in drinking." She looks around, stands up quickly, and runs over to the hotel fridge with her extremely short dress flapping in the breeze to catch up. She goes on, "I dare you, Jim, to beat me in shooting these Bacardi Rum mini bottles." She produces two mini bottles in her hand.

"You're on."

I barely win, but my tolerance is a little higher than hers. We sit back down. I see the alcohol is starting to hit her, but she still has that happy face, so I press on.

"Truth or dare." This time, I am really hoping she says, "Dare."

This time is takes her longer to decide. "Truth."

Damn it. I am going for the coup de grace. "How do you know Hector, and what do you owe him?" There. I said what has been bothering me since we started this trip.

Her mouth is hanging open, and it appears I hit a nerve. Perhaps I was a little too harsh and should have asked what color is her underwear or something. Either way, I think we are done for the evening.

Selma responds, "Aw Jim, I'm not feeling so well. Maybe the rum was too much. I think I'm just going to go to sleep. I'm so sorry."

"OK. Probably a good idea. We got a busy day tomorrow."

She crawls into bed. I take a pillow and pull the sheet over her shoulders, covering her. I stare down at her and whisper good night. I go over to the thermostat and make a quick adjustment before crashing out on the sofa. I start to snore exactly seven minutes after my head hits the pillow.

I wake in the morning and look over to the bed, but Selma is not there. She apparently got up in the middle of the night and threw a blanket over me as I slept soundly. She is not in the suite, as the bathroom is empty when I quickly run to it to make a call of nature. I exit the bathroom in time to hear someone trying the door handle. I mentally prepare myself for whoever may enter but find myself excited when I see her come walking through the doorway.

"Good morning, Jim. I didn't want to wake you up. I went down to grab a quick bite to eat. I brought you some coffee and a muffin."

I appreciate the gesture of peace. "Sorry, I don't drink coffee, but I'll take claim on that blueberry muffin. Thanks."

"You don't know what you're missing, buddy. The coffee is actually pretty good, as far as hotel coffee goes."

I am eating the muffin and can't reply without spitting food all over her. That would not be cool. I only shrug my shoulders. She turns to start packing up.

"Thanks again for breakfast," I say. I grab a water bottle from the fridge. I decide not to pursue anything further about the events that transpired last night, and her silence suggests to me that this is a good course of action to follow. We finish packing up and go downstairs to check out. Though it is silent between us this morning, we both feel a little more comfortable with each other.

I take the first shift in driving, and off we go in a northerly direction.

Welcome to the grand city of Wichita, Kansas.

Selma and I have been driving a good portion of the day and keeping the conversation to innocent and general topics. I finally ask what the instructions are when we arrive in Wichita. She insists that we have to pick up the first package at 8:00 p.m. local time at, of all places, the back of a Walmart parking lot. If this all goes down tonight, I really don't want the papers to read the next day that a man and woman were found dead in the back of a Walmart parking lot and there is a sale on towels today only at the store. I guess getting shot at Taco Bell or McDonald's does not sound any more dignified. I'd rather not get shot at all and have the newspaper find another source for a headline.

Selma looks at me as we get off the expressway exit in accordance with the GPS. I glance back at her for a second and see something in those pretty eyes. I better get my own eyes back on the road when she tells me to turn left at the light. I rapidly return to my driving duties and turn left, seeing the Walmart sign way down road on the left-hand side. We eventually turn into the parking lot and park on the left side toward the back. Having arrived a little early, I really hope she doesn't want to pop into the store to do some shopping. It has been a long yet interesting forty-eight hours with her, and we have become partners, like Bonnie and Clyde, in this crazy journey conjured in the head of Hector. I bet ten bucks he is probably torturing some other poor soul right now while drinking his tequila. Private-stock tequila, not the house stuff.

So here we are sitting in the Escape. We gaze at each other, uncertain what is supposed to happen next, as we have no script to follow. I offer to turn on the radio, but The Police are playing on one channel. I quickly switch to another and hear "Jailhouse Rock." Not wanting to tempt fate a third time, I switch it off.

She looks at me quizzically. "What did you do that for? I love Elvis."

"Never mind."

As I say that, I glance over her right shoulder and see a Wichita Police cruiser slowing down and then turning into McDonald's in the parking lot adjacent to where we are sitting. The tension starts to build. The cop may have been responding to a report about a suspicious vehicle and was looking at us, or was he just naturally looking to the right as he turned right? Do we look suspicious sitting in the car at 8:00 p.m. doing nothing in the back row of the Walmart parking lot? The cop is probably calling in for backup right about now. Why are two people sitting in their car this late in the evening and so far from the door? He is thinking it must be a drug trade about to go down. Or am I getting pinged for trafficking the woman next to me? Oh yeah, I also have a shitload of cocaine in my car. Sorry, Mr. Officer, I know this looks bad, but I have a really good explanation for all of this. I should have put a "Support the FOP" sticker on the bumper before I started this road trip.

I look over her shoulder, and this time, the police officer is in the drive-through lane, and I see he has instead responded to the call of the evening Big Mac meal. I don't see him exit on the other side of McDonald's, but I pray that greasy burgers are a more pressing matter than busting drug traffickers. Oh, and throw in prostitution and loitering, just for good measure.

As I ponder how many years I will be sentenced by the judge, I am startled by the buzz from Selma's phone telling us the deliveryman is about to arrive.

She says to me, "Are you ready for this?"

A skylark-blue Oldsmobile Cutlass shows up and parks next to us. Honestly, can we attract any more attention? If this does not scream, "Drug exchange about to happen!" then there is a real issue with the training of the greater Wichita police force.

Surprisingly, the man that leaps from the driver's side is clean-shaven and wearing a black pinstripe suit. Not what I expected, but I guess it's better than a young punk in a hoodie smoking a joint. The man looks at me, then at Selma, and then back to me. Did I pass the test? Was he expecting someone different than me?

"OK, open your trunk, and I'll transfer it to you."

Selma starts to say something, but I've already hit the switch, and the trunk opens, revealing a space beside our neatly packed luggage. The man grabs a box, approximately a one-foot-square package enveloped in Christmas wrapping paper, and places it in the space on the left-hand side. I use my Mexican blanket to cover it up and shut the trunk. He says something to Selma that I can't hear. I probably don't want to know what they are talking about or how well they know each other. Judging by her reaction, it seems like idle chitchat, but you never know. Not my concern, as I will never see this man again.

Selma gazes over at me and says in the sweetest voice, "Let's go, dear."

How can I resist her request? We drive off, hoping to gain some distance from Wichita.

Chapter 9

After a couple more hours, we decide to stop and find a place to stay just outside of Kansas City. It is amazing when one has unlimited funds how the choice of hotels exponentially increases. We had a fantastic room at the Hilton last night, but tonight we just need a place to crash. I see a Fairfield Inn at the next exit and suggest it to Selma, which she happily agrees to. At this moment, stopping and resting is priority one. Priority two is a clean room. The package pickup back in Wichita seemed anticlimactic and disappointing. I don't know. I was kind of expecting a cloak-and-dagger exchange and narrowly escaping the clutches of the law.

I am curious as to what we picked up back there, though I appreciate the humor of it being wrapped in Christmas paper. Whatever Selma knows about it, she isn't telling me. I need not bother to ask her. I wonder, though, what else she isn't telling me.

"There's the Fairfield Inn. I see it on the right."

"I hope they have a room. Otherwise, you may have to work your charm again, dear." I guess I shouldn't joke about it too much because her charm is starting to work its magic on me.

"Do you want to do the talking? That last bit of driving tuckered me out." She lets out a big yawn.

"OK, let's get the room booked, and then I'll go park while you head to the room."

"Here, let me at least carry my handbag." She reaches in the back seat to retrieve her lifeline bag. I bet she has got food stashed in there in case of emergency.

We walk into the Fairfield Inn and head over to the reception desk.

I say, "Hello. We would like a room with two double beds. Do you have anything available?"

"Yes, we do. Are either of you members?"

"Sadly, no." I really need to get a membership someday.

"No worries. What are your names?"

"Mr. and Mrs. Phil Banks. Here's my card." I hand it over.

We get checked in, and Selma heads off to the room. I go park the vehicle and gather the bags, including the Christmas package. It was Selma's idea earlier to grab a recyclable shopping bag and carry it in there. I guess it does not look too obvious, as I stuff the Mexican blanket on top of it for good coverage. Nobody would ever suspect anything about the contents of the bag. Hell, I don't even know the contents of the bag. I assume there is a warning to handle it very carefully though.

I wave to the receptionist as I walk in, and he points to the elevators to the left. He never looks up from the computer screen, possibly wasting time surfing the Internet. Thanking him, I go over to the elevator and proceed to the third floor. I get out, look on the room key envelope for the number, and, glancing at the chart on the wall, decide the room is to down the hall to the right. The hallway is silent, as most people have retired for the evening. It is an eerie silence, like when in the movies the person is going to get shot from behind before he turns around. I know, I know, don't turn around. The gooseflesh kicks in and I pause for a moment in front of our room door. What happens if I open this door and am staring at the barrel of a gun? Will she shoot me, or will she say something cool first and then shoot me? Should I just open the door and duck or act like I tripped on the carpet? Aw hell, it is what it is.

I stick the key in the door and slowly open it. I look into the room but don't see her. I turn around, and she is standing behind me, having just come out of the bathroom.

"Hello, dear, what took you so long?"

My heart is beating a hundred times a minute. I quickly look at her hands and see no gun. That is a good sign. She has a puzzled look on her face. I ask her where to put the bags down. I notice she has already laid her stuff on the bed closest to the AC unit. I place her bag on her bed.

"Are you staying up or crashing right now?" I question her.

"I could stay up if you're willing to open that bottle of tequila you're always carrying around. But just one drink, OK?" Selma responds.

"Fair enough. I'm getting tired, too."

"I'll go get the glasses if you open the bottle."

How could I refuse. "Sounds like a plan."

Selma doesn't miss anything, no matter how small the detail, or she is keen to always know where the liquor is stashed.

Apart from some episodes of her snoring really loudly from the other bed, we both get some well-deserved sleep. I still find it odd to share a hotel room with a complete stranger. Well, I guess we aren't strangers anymore. We are even moving to the next stage when we learn each other's morning and bathroom habits. I guess when one is forced to be with someone for forty-eight hours straight, one learns a lot about another person.

We wake up about 8:00 a.m., just in time to head downstairs for breakfast. Now I am going to learn how she likes her coffee. She already knows I don't like the stuff.

"So we got more driving today. Yay!" I try to inject some enthusiasm at the breakfast table, but she is having none of that.

If fact, she looks really sad. I mean, the breakfast choices aren't exciting to me either, but they are nothing to get depressed about. Maybe she is getting sick of me and wishes for this trip to be completed sooner rather than later. I am actually starting to get into this routine and settling into the road-tripping lifestyle. I wonder what is bothering her. Should I bother to ask? She is just staring down at her unappetizing breakfast choices. Maybe it's not a good time to enquire why she is silent.

Rachel looks down at her phone. She just received a text message from Lenny and thinks, *It's about time.* The message states: *Arrived in SLC and dropped off the Subaru. See you soon.*

Rachel looks up and smiles. *Finally, that part is going smoothly. I have the utmost faith in Team Two for the work they'll be doing. It's kinda funny that Jim's car will be found in SLC. Much easier for the authorities to piece it together that Jim masterminded all of this. Poor Jim. You really never knew your own wife, did you?*

Rachel thinks an old photo of her and Jim before they were married. *You should have taken the time to get to know all about me and my family. Especially a distant cousin's really intelligent daughter named Selma. Oh wait, you've met her and are currently traveling around the country with her. Sorry, old Jim, there are some things a woman keeps a secret...*

We go back to the room to finish packing and complete last-minute checks before clearing and checking out. While Selma is in the bathroom, I quickly text Aaron to say that we changed driving plans and can rendezvous outside Champaign, Illinois. There is a bad thunderstorm in the day's forecast, and this may delay us for a bit. Selma and I watched the weather at breakfast and agreed to press on as much as we could until the storm got too bad for driving. We decide to take I-70 to I-57 and then into Chicago, coincidentally driving through the town of Champaign.

It is one of those days where I have this feeling that something is not right. It doesn't help that the person I'm with has also been acting strange all morning. If something is going to go down, I can say I have prepared myself for it. I hope that Selma is all right as well and not the one about to pull the trigger of a gun pointing at me.

Hector is going to be disappointed in me. I don't think I can go through with it. I am really starting to like Jim. How can I just up and shoot him dead? I realize he isn't part of the big picture here and I still have to assemble the device, but does Jim really have to die? He knows. I know he knows something is going to happen to us today. He isn't that stupid to figure out something's not right. I can't even look him in the eyes, yet I wanted to tell him last night. I know if I don't do it, Hector will send someone else to do it, and right in front of me. And later take me out in the process. Hector gets pissed when people don't follow his plans to the T.

I take over driving for a bit, and Selma is still as quiet as she can be. I notice she keeps rummaging with the contents of her handbag. I swear she is holding out on me. There must some M&M'S in there that she's not sharing with me.

We get through the greater Saint Louis area and cross the mighty Mississippi River. It looks smaller than you would think. And then the rain starts to come down. It is light at first, but the farther east we go, the storm seems to gain on us, and rain comes down harder and harder. I pull off at the next exit to fill up with gas while Selma goes and buys extra water, snacks, and some sandwiches to ride this out if we need to.

These are the fun times I will remember about traveling with Selma. Sometimes, it's like we are working as a team with gathering rations for each other, taking shifts driving, and helping the other navigating. I look at her when she exits the gas station building, and she is looking at me. We seem to communicate to each other even without words, and smiles go across each of our faces. She is coming closer as I am about to finish pumping gas when some lightning cracks in the distance off to the north. Our spiritual eye contact breaks off immediately, and she bolts toward the passenger door, yelling at me to hurry it up and get inside as she closes the door. I finish up, close the lid, and take my receipt just in time. The winds start to pick up with the rain coming down in buckets, pelting me in the process of getting in the vehicle and closing the door.

I cautiously drive down the main boulevard until I get back on I-70 heading in an eastern direction. The rain is still pouring, the wind has picked up with gusts up to 30 mph, and the sky— well, the sky is turning a real nasty, dark, hideous color. This drive is really getting worse, and I'm thinking we should have stopped back at the gas station. The average speed is slowing down among other drivers, and some are pulling over to an underpass or driving with their hazards on. Selma is looking even more worried at me. I don't think she likes thunderstorms, at least not driving or riding in them. I continue to press on, fighting the pull of the winds and the constant movement of the wiper blades.

Flash. Crack.

That was much closer than the last few. I don't dare tell Selma how close that was, but I see the fear taking over in her eyes. She really fears for her own life at the moment as I struggle with what to do to comfort her. I am waiting for a tornado to start forming around us; that's all we need right now. In a glimmer of hope, I see the sign for the next rest area in two miles. I assure Selma that we will stop there until the storm subsides. She seems somewhat relived though she is, honest to God, scared shitless.

After what seems like forever, I signal to turn into the rest area. It is not that crowded; maybe a half dozen cars and trucks are already parked there. I expected more, but then again, there weren't lots of drivers on the road to begin with in the last hour. I park away from the others in an effort to have a little breathing space and privacy. I tell her to crack the windows a little for some fresh air as I shut the engine off.

Now we wait.

Chapter 10

After having an exquisite dinner at La Tequila Restaurant with Hector as her date, Rachel retires to her place at Number 42 near the plaza center. She opens the door, drops her purse, shuts the door behind her, and proceeds to the office room to turn on the computer at her desk. There, she signs on to the secured website and pours herself a glass of a nice Malbec from Mendoza, Argentina. After a few passwords, she finally reaches the secured email and reads the latest messages from the interested stakeholders.

She needs this device assembled by Selma and ready to work by Saturday. Why is it taking Selma so long to get the pieces together? Are she and Jim sightseeing and stopping at every roadside attraction? It was hard enough to get the pieces into the country without the FBI tracking the shipment or catching on to what was being built right under their noses.

Besides, her cousin had told her the theory of the device and applications, and she certainly had believed Selma that it could be built. She had even fronted the research grant to Selma last year, and the project started receiving favorable results. Thus she had brought in Hector to further the project along. That's why she had taken it to the bosses of the cartels for the final sales pitch. With this sale, Rachel could retire comfortably in southern France, and this was all possible because of the freak chance in meeting her husband, or soon-to-be-dead husband Jim, who had introduced her to the right people years ago at an office party. *I bet Jim never thought that he is the cause of all of this. Look what you started, my love. Look what you have caused. You can only blame yourself.*

As fate would have it, her disappearance had coincided with her partnering with Hector, providing her the means to rise to the position she is currently holding. Now, she has to start eliminating the very people that have been making this all happen. Rachel picks up her second phone and calls Lenny, whom she is starting to develop a sense of trust in.

"Lenny, what are you doing right now?" No hello, no pleasantries.

"Hello, ma'am. I did like you said. I drove Jim's car to Salt Lake City, rigged it with the explosives, and parked it at the address he supplied me with back in Texas."

Rachel thinks that Lenny's voice suggests he is nervous or intimidated by her. "Well done. I can always count on you. We need to get together sometime after this is all done. You shall be rewarded for your service someday." *More like I need to have you eliminated if you messed this up. However, you are really proving yourself more and more useful.*

"That would be fine, ma'am. I would like that. Now, do you need me to do anything else while I'm here? I have the guns and other items you requested and have the perfect location that I'm staying at."

"No, you've done exactly what I needed you to do. Take a break, and see the town and sights. I'll contact you again when I need you. I'm thinking in about three days from now you should be ready in case I need you to implement Plan B."

"Sounds good. I've got my phone ready when you need me. You can always count on me, ma'am."

"We'll be in touch."

"Goodbye."

Click.

91

I glance at my phone to see the latest radar update, and it is not looking pretty. We are the marker that is in the center of a huge red-cell thunderstorm. I don't have a degree in meteorology, but I can honestly say we are screwed. I check on Selma, and she is plainly freaking out, sweating and trembling. I start to worry about her, as she jumps with every crack of lightning and rumble of each thunderclap. Analysis would suggest she does not like thunderstorms. I really hope this area is not prone to tornados.

"Honey—er, Jim, is there going be a tornado? This storm is really bad. Is there going to be one? What are we going to do? I…I'm really scared right now."

She looks terrified, and I think I see her shaking even more. I reach for her hand in an act of support and comfort. "You have nothing to worry about. This storm should pass over in a few minutes." I am lying my ass off.

Selma looks at me for reassurance. "You think so? Will it be over soon?"

"Of course, dear. Trust me," I say as another bolt of lightning lights up the southern sky. Wow, that one was pretty close.

Selma has now gotten out of her seat and, somehow, moved closer to me than she has ever been. I don't know if I should pray for our safety or for more inclement weather, but her being close to me gives me a feeling of euphoria.

CRACK.

A tree about two hundred and fifty feet in front of us gets nailed by a lightning strike and goes down, luckily falling in the opposite direction.

Selma screams in terror. *"Jim, I need you! Help me! We're gonna die! I'm so sorry!"*

Sorry for what? Probably not a good time to ask but definitely something to enquire about later on at some point. I can only offer a shoulder to snuggle against, but I embrace her tight for an extra sense of security. I assume it is working, as she latches on to me really tight.

Rumble. Rumble.

Lightning flashes across the sky. The wind is gusting. I am balancing my phone in my left hand to get the latest weather report while trying to calm Selma down with my right arm. Finally, with a hint of desperation, I suggest we climb in the back seat. No, not for that; rather, so I can hold her tighter and in a more comfortable manner. Despite some interesting maneuvering, we climb in the backseat. I even reach over and grab my illustrious Mexican blanket from the trunk area. We finally get situated, and Selma leans on me. I feel her body next to mine, her heartbeat thumping away as I wrap our bodies with my now favorite blanket. This blanket is the best twenty bucks I have ever spent! Almost immediately, the heat between us grows intense as she clings to me with nearly a death grip. But I am not complaining. All I can think about is someone up in heaven is really pulling for me

The vehicle starts to shake with the wind gusting outside, the lightning is still causing an incredible light display in the sky, and the thunder is loudly rumbling away into the night. Selma only cowers closer to me. Suddenly, I have the urge to tell her that I love her. I don't know why that is the first thing that pops in my head. But it seems like the most appropriate thing to say at a moment like this. I think she feels she is going to die right now. I should really say something cool, like the hero always does in the movies, but I bet the hero never dealt with the freakin' storm of the century that seems to be going on outside. The vehicle is rocking really badly, appropriately by Mother Nature and not by us.

I look down to see Selma crying. Tears are bursting out, and she is really distressed. I am talking a major river of tears flowing down her pretty face and pooling on my shirt. While the wet spot on my shirt is OK, the fact that she is severely distraught is not.

"Selma, I got you. Everything's all right. We'll make it through this storm. We—"

"It's not that, Jim," she snorts. Some of that probably now resides on my shirt.

"Then what is it?" I am confused.

"Jim…" She pauses momentarily to compose herself. "Jim, I need to tell you something. I—"

Another crack of lightning, and she buries her head in my rather soaked shirt.

I hold her head in a comforting sort of way, I think, and she slowly lifts it. She gazes up at my worried eyes and strokes my right arm. She sighs deeply before squaring up to my face.

"Jim, I've been lying to you all along, and I'm truly sorry. Please, please forgive me…before it's too late for us."

The bomb has dropped. This changes the game, or at least makes it more interesting. Please continue, Selma. You have my attention.

She now wraps her arms around my torso, and I feel her heartbeat next to mine as she buries her head in my chest. How I react will reflect the very way we progress from this very point. How do I decide? My choices are either kick her out of the vehicle and my life for lying to me or choose Door Number 2 and see what I win. Or, in other words, see what she is about to say. How does a man make such a decision in the moment of a crisis like the one currently happening right now? Do I choose the red pill or blue pill? Door Number 1 or Door Number 2? The left fork in the road or the right?

You learn early in life it is all about timing. You have to learn to hit a baseball at the right time. You learn to move your body in sync with the club to properly hit a golf ball, and you just know the right moment to propose to your soon-to-be bride. Unfortunately, none of these things matter when you are in the middle of a thunderstorm with a tornado practically beating down on you and the woman next to you is telling you she has been lying to you all along. Talk about some bad timing.

So with all that's going on around us, she drops that bomb. And, mind you, I really think a tornado is near us. I had already stopped checking my weather app because it had been too depressing. The sky continues to look like the Fourth of July with the awesome lightning show. Add to the mix my adrenaline pumping full strength, and it takes a moment for my brain to really register what Selma has said to me. It then takes an additional minute to fully comprehend the true meaning of it. I must have been squeezing her too hard while thinking about it, as she pushes away from my tight clutch and into a fit of confusion, distress, and crying all rolled into one. The trifecta of the worst things any mortal man ever wants to see in the woman next to him, especially when there is no place to run and hide.

"Selma." The adrenaline is slowing down, and I try to speak in a calm voice.

She only cries more. Sometimes, I have that effect on people. I try one more time. "Selma, look at me. Take a deep breath. Focus on my voice. Just relax." Why is it when you tell someone to relax, they almost never do? It seems so pointless.

I try again with a different approach. "Selma, I am not going anywhere. I'm here next to you, and storm is starting to subside." Thank you, God, for not cracking one more bolt of lightning at this very moment. "Why don't we eat some of snacks and get something to drink first." Food and drink are always good conversation-starters. At least, they are for me.

She slowly nods her head but still has a hard time looking me in the eyes.

I reach for the food bag in the front seat. I start to grab a Coke, but having her more amped up on caffeine is probably not a good decision. I grab some salty potato chips instead and a Vitamin water bottle. I try not to glare at her with a judgmental expression, but my poker face is not working quite right tonight. I know this is a traumatic experience for her, but it is also a helluva of time to spurt out revelations of lying and treachery. Do I really want to know the whole story? I want to tell her get out of the car; hell, I want to throw her ass out and get her out of my life. But—and there is always a *but*—I just can't do it. My gut instinct says to listen to her, and when the gut speaks, except for cases when it wants food, the mind must listen. So, listen I shall. I wait for her to start speaking when she is ready.

After feeding her potato chips, M&M'S, and some Vitaminwater, I feel that she now will tell me what she needs to tell me. Besides, we aren't going anywhere due to the torrential rain that continues to fall. At least this random rest area is a more idyllic setting than some random fast-food parking lot.

Selma finally stops crying for a moment and gives the impression that she is gathering her thoughts very carefully. After all, it is based on what she says, and how I choose to interpret exactly what she articulates, that affects us henceforth.

That's a huge burden on her, but hey, I wasn't the one that admitted to lying.

"Jim." She says it so softly you'd think we were lying in the bed at the hotel. Alas, we are not there, except maybe in one of my fantasies. But that is another story.

"Selma." How else could I have replied? I am waiting for her to make the first move in revealing the deep, dark secret she has been hiding. Or is it secrets?

"I...I need to tell you something, but *promise* you will listen to everything I have to say."

Ha, what a leading statement. How does one react, other than the opposite way than the speaker wants you to? I could use a shot of the tequila from the bottle I am carrying before she speaks any further. I am starting to get pissed off at her, yet I gaze into her eyes, and I see hope staring back at me. *You gotta trust her, Jim*, my gut is telling me. Somehow, I get this feeling I am going to have to ride this whole thing out to the end. I still feel like such a sucker that she is reeling in.

"I met Hector in some sleazy bar in Tijuana. I was young and naive, not in tune with the ways of the world, and..." She laughs. "Sorry, I just thought I'd lighten the mood, sweetie."

Hardy-har-har...to bullshit me with a joke, which takes some smarts and guts to do at a time like this. Ah, she called me *sweetie*. I am starting to melt. Wait a minute. I should be pissed off.

"OK, OK. What do you want me to say, Jim? I've messed up, and it's too hard to untangle. I don't even know where to begin." It looks like she is attempting to turn on the faucet to the tears. Every mortal man hates when a woman uses this trick.

Torn among impatience, anger, and a bit of lust, I suggest, "Well, being straight with me for the first time might be a good place to start." I take a chomp on the Snickers I recently discovered in the food bag.

Silence envelops us as we sit in the back seat. Selma jerks away from me, leaving me wishing she hadn't moved so far away.

"Lying isn't exactly the right way to put it. I just didn't tell you everything."

She is eyeing my Snickers like it's the Last Supper. She can't still be hungry, can she? I start to frown at her.

She goes on. "Honestly, Hector wants me to take you out of the picture once you get me to New York City. Boy, what did you do to piss him off? I thought you two were friends from a long time ago." She produces a gun from her handbag, hence why she has been attached to it the entire trip so far. She hands it to me. It looks like a cannon when held in her hand. "Here, take it. It does me no good. I couldn't shoot your ass if my life depended on it."

She hands me the gun, making sure not to point it at me. I clear the gun so we don't accidentally shoot each other, but I do admire it. "Do you know how to even fire a gun?"

"No. Maybe."

"Well, I actually do. Good to know. Now, can we change topics?" I should hold on to it for a while, but I give it back to her after having second thoughts. It is her gun, and she needs it more than I do to protect herself.

"Why is Hector so interested in you, anyway?" I have been quite curious about this aspect; maybe she will shed some light on it.

"Because I'm the only one that can build the device. I call it The Bourbon Box, but Hector thinks it should be called something more clever, like The Tequila Shooter. You know—it goes straight in and messes you up once inside."

"What the hell are you talking about?" Now I feel like the one on trial for being uninformed and, as they say, not reading my emails.

"You really don't know about anything, do you? Like that I just graduated with my PhD from Caltech?"

"Well, you always seemed bright." What, does she have some fancy degree as well? Oh, I guess she does.

"I know I'm supposed to transport the drugs and ensure you get to New York City in one piece. We're supposed to make three stops. By the way, what is the third one? I counted Wichita and Niles. Did Hector tell you something I don't know?" Isn't that the understatement of the year!

"No, he only mentioned those two places to me. How can I assemble the device by the time we hit New York City? It's not possible, or is it?" She is now in deep thought and clearly not thinking about me or the act of omission she has been committing for the last forty-eight hours. She snaps back to reality and looks at me intently. "Jim, there is a bigger picture. The device is potentially devastating to the financial markets in the United States or any other country. You need to think beyond yourself for the next few days because Hector has been playing us and will get rid of us afterward. Think about it hard. Can you do that for me, sweetie?"

Is she flirting with me to get me to go along with her? Or I am hooked and being reeled in?

"Oh, I should probably also tell you: There's an assassin named Roberto out there. I think that's his name, though I can't remember. Anyway, he's going to a shoot you dead soon if I don't do it first."

"Wait, I thought I had to get you to New York City?"

"Yes and no. It's fair game on you after we pick up the second package in Michigan."

"Thanks. Is there any more info about Roberto and when he's supposed to shoot me?" Not the best news I'd heard all day. I should bring out tequila bottle.

"Like I said, sometime after the Michigan pickup. I guess you're not needed after that." She grabs the Snickers bar out of my hand. "I suppose he can drive me if you're unavailable. Oh wait; sorry."

She really did rattle that off in a very technical way with no emotion whatsoever. I guess she is a scientist at heart. Selma, eating the candy bar, continues. "What do we do now?"

"For one, we have to let Aaron know the current update."

"Who the hell is Aaron?"

"The guy that's going to save me from getting shot."

Selma thinks to herself, *Well, at least I told him part of the truth*, as she chews the remainder of the Snickers bar. *I wonder when I should tell him the rest.*

As the weather starts to subside, we both sit in the back seat. I am holding Selma in my arms with my ever lucky Mexican blanket covering us. She lifts her head, and our eyes meet for that moment in time. It truly is a defining event between two people that sends an unspoken message of trust and commitment. We both must see this through even if it is likely that our new "partnership" may piss off the very people who will try to have us both killed.

"So who is Aaron, anyway?" she asks as she stokes my arm.

"Aaron is like me. He fixes difficult situations," I reply sternly because she is rubbing against my arm and I am trying not to laugh.

"What's he going to do?"

"Wait. Let's call him first with an update." I sit up as Selma readjusts herself in the back seat. She grabs another drink of Vitamin water as I reach for my phone.

"Hey, buddy," I say as Aaron picks up on the other end. Trying not to give away too much, I ask Aaron if he has moved since the last time we talked.

"Still sitting here, amigo, waiting on further instructions. Actually, sitting in a bar waiting to hustle somebody at the pool table."

"Good, we'll rendezvous shortly. The storm has finally cleared up. Go get some food, and see ya soon. Selma is looking forward to meeting you."

"Oh, so you've told her about me? What else have you said? Wait, what has she said to you?" he asks with a very inquisitive voice.

"Go grab a burger. I'll tell ya later." I hope he understands I don't want to say everything with her nearby just yet.

"Gotcha, bro. See ya soon."

"Later."

Click.

"OK, Selma, let's take a bathroom break because we got to hit the road."

I stare into her eyes and take her hand. Then I probe her. "I am trusting you, but I gotta believe in you. Are you with me or not? Because you can walk away right now. The choice is yours."

Without hesitation, she replies in a heartfelt but serious voice, "Yes, dear. I am with you till the end of the road."

How can I not trust her after that declaration? I hope I am not wrong on this one.

I quickly walk to the restroom building with Selma next to me. She goes left, and I proceed right. I am in there for only a few minutes and quickly exit the men's room. I wait patiently for Selma to come out. Is she still committed to me after all this, or was she lying to me all along and has now done a runner? A thousand thoughts are being processed in the left side of my brain before I see Selma exit the women's bathroom.

There she stands in a testament to the beauty that I adore about her: both physical and the deeper spiritual sense. She has cleaned herself up a bit, and her makeup is not smeared from the tears of fear shed earlier. She looks absolutely radiant. I am taken in and wrapped up in her every command, though she does not yet know that she has this power over me. Yup, I am falling for this woman. She smiles back at me and tilts her head in such a way that every man walking through the building doors is taken in by her. I quickly block the first guy before he thinks about taking a chance. The nerve of some people; she is with me.

She comes up to me and stops. I put my arm out, and she embraces me before I escort her back to the vehicle. Sometimes, no words need to be said. I finally feel a sense of peace and happiness in these past few minutes, but unfortunately, we have a bigger issue to face in the coming days. Enjoy the moment, old Jim, as it is about to turn south in a hurry.

"What's Aaron like? Tell me about him. How well do you know him?" Selma switches back to serious mode. Must remember her quick transition shifts.

"Aaron is one of my best friends. We have been friends for quite a while, going back to the Army days when we were deployed together on some mountaintop collecting intel that helped our side win the Gulf War years ago." I have a lifetime of war stories to tell, but I keep it brief this time. "I haven't chatted with him much recently, as he is quite busy these days in his private security business."

"Oh, that's right. You served in the Army. I think that's so awesome. What does he look like? Mean and tough like you?"

"He's much blonder and bigger than me, but I guess I'm the smarter one." I let out a hardy laugh at my own joke. "You'll like him, I know it. He has this effect on all women he meets." Hmmmm, she thinks I'm mean and tough?

"You're still my favorite, by the way, or at least in my current top ten list."

We keep on driving, looking at each other and just smiling away, knowing the tide is about to change, and not in a good way. Might as well enjoy the good times now.

Meanwhile, a man is pacing himself behind the red dot blinking on the screen. Roberto has been trailing the vehicle, aka the red dot, for quite some time. It stopped for a while but is on the move again. He thinks he should tell the boss lady the update.

"Hey, ma'am, this is Roberto."

"Yes, Roberto, how are things in your part of the country?" Rachel enquires.

"The target is on the move again; it appears they are on course for Michigan and the pickup of the next component. I'm about three miles from their present location. There was a nasty storm, and we all stopped for a bit."

"Brilliant. This is why I entrusted you for this job. You do know what to do after they stop in Michigan, don't you?"

Roberto confidently replies, "Yes, ma'am, I already have three different vantage points to take out the male."

"Well done, Roberto. The amount agreed upon will be deposited upon confirmation that Jim is dead. I have every bit of faith in you."

"This is what I do. Later."

Rachel hears Roberto hang up. She is paying him a lot of money. There should be no mistakes.

Chapter 11

"I keep telling you, Rachel, you are paying this Roberto fella way too much money for a simple job." After a pause, Hector swigs some high-priced tequila from a glass.

"Nope, he'll get the job done cleanly. We should take out the girl too, but you fancy her too much. Besides, we only need her to finish assembling the device, and then she's a goner, too." Rachel looks at Hector, waiting for her glass to be refilled, as he just refilled his own. "Sorry, cousin, or whoever you are, Selma."

Hector, staring at Rachel from across the table, decides to give her some more from the expensive La Cava de Don Agustín Añejo Tequila bottle.

"I still think we should keep Selma around. She's maybe a little too sassy, but she's proven to be quite useful and smart. God only knows there's not a lot of smart folk around here these days."

"Yes, yes, you like her. I know that. But she's too smart for her own good. Just take her out and be done with it. No loose ends. Isn't that what you told me a year ago?"

Rachel smiles after sipping the tequila. It is really quite good with a hint of smoke flavor, but still smooth. That's why she always puts up with Hector. He may be a bastard, but he does have really expensive tastes. Exquisite tastes like her own that have developed since leaving Jim a while ago.

Hector needs to finalize the deal and the transfer of the monetary payment once Selma finishes building the device and they auction it off to the highest bidder. It was costly to find the different pieces that Selma required when she discussed how the device was to be built. Hector had to contact an old friend in the

Ukraine to ship a part to Michigan through Canada that one normally can't buy off the shelves at Lowe's. Add to that, he had to cash in a favor from the Russian cartel, so now he is even with those dirty Eastern European criminals. This device better work as Selma promised, or there are going to be a lot of dead people in the next few days, including himself.

Hector stands up and walks over to the bar to grab another bottle. Rachel is one step ahead of him and walks over to the sofa and sits on the far end. She slips her shoes off and stretches out. Hector walks back over to the sofa and refills the glasses with a different añejo tequila, one that is more smoky in flavor but still excellent in taste. It should be, for the price he paid for it last week.

"Rachel, my dear?"

"Yes, Hector?"

"How much do you think we can sell the device for on the open market? Will every criminal in the free world want it once we prove it actually works, like your cousin said it would?"

"At least one hundred million, for starters. What do you think?"

"I was thinking more, once they see our little demonstration next week in New York City. Oh, is Miguel ready, by the way? Have you talked to him recently?"

"My business associate is fine, thank you for asking. He's enjoying the tour of our operations in New York City. He's quite efficient in dealing with those petty issues that arise from time to time."

"Ha, ha. You mean how we take out the competition. Yeah, that's why you pay the police, judges, and garbagemen well in that town. Everyone has a price, and we meet all their demands in exchange for cleaning up some of those elimination jobs!"

"You say it so beautifully, Hector!"

"I know, my dear, I know. Speaking of which, I need to open the books to you someday. I think you'll find it interesting where some of the outflow goes these days."

Rachel is not interested in talking about the books but rather an issue that is plaguing her. "It still bothers me that you wanted to keep Selma for yourself. She can really disrupt a lot of things for us, like our association, for instance. What else can she do for you, for us, and the organization?"

"It is of no concern to you. I don't question you for wanting to eliminate your husband, or should I say ex-husband, as you divorced him six months ago with the help from that judge in Arizona. You're welcome for that, by the way. Consider it an early Christmas bonus," Hector retorts and laughs at his own joke.

Still frowning, Rachel composes herself. "Yes, Hector, thank you for that. Now can we stop talking about those two for a while and get back to the real business at hand?"

"Sure, my dear, anything you want. But first, you need to fill up the glasses this time." He shakes an empty glass in his right hand.

"Are you sure about this guy? What time is it? Where's your friend?"

"What do you mean, Selma? I've known Aaron for a long time. He's like a brother to me." I don't know which I am getting more annoyed by: her lack of faith in Aaron or his disregard for timekeeping.

"Then your brother's late," Selma replies with a hint of sarcasm.

We are sitting in the Lowe's parking lot located in the southern part of Champaign. We were to meet Aaron at around two o'clock, and he is already twenty minutes late. He is never one for punctuality, unless it involves food, but it is a stretch even for him to be this late. I should have told him to meet us at the Steak 'n Shake, which I can see while looking out the driver's side window. I know we just ate lunch, but staring at that restaurant for the last ten minutes, I am starting to get hungry again.

I look over to Selma, who seems quite annoyed and bored. I realize we are still coming down from our adrenaline rush earlier, and we still haven't had time to sit together and define what *is going on between us*. It is all so...

Selma looks in my general direction and then screams really loudly.

I am confused until I turn around and see there is a man making a silly face on the other side of the driver's side window. Aaron has arrived.

He is dressed in his typical fashion: cowboy hat, plaid shirt, dirty jeans, and combat boots. You would think the rodeo was in town or it is the semifinals of open-mic night at the local country bar. Either way, this is my buddy standing on the outside of the Escape. Perhaps I should get out and greet him.

Selma is still breathing heavy from being frightened a second time today. He is not scoring any points in his, or my, favor. I should let her catch her breath.

I open the door and give my buddy a big hug, man-style, of course. Yes, there is a difference when a guy hugs a woman (sweet and nice) versus when a guy hugs another man (just a goodwill gesture). For example, the guy-to-woman hug is bear-style but soft and cozy, producing the *ah* effect. When a guy hugs another guy, it is with an arm or elbow so the chests barely touch, thus minimizing the body contact. Long chest contact versus minimal chest contact. Hugging lesson complete.

After the exchange of manly hugs, Aaron looks past me and asks, "Well, are you gonna introduce your girl to me?"

She is not my girl. Well, not yet. I don't even know what we are, but comments like that only complicate this situation more. Well, at least Selma doesn't take it personally, or maybe she didn't hear him. Here's hoping for the latter.

Aaron's eyes follow Selma as she jumps out of the Escape and walks around the front of the vehicle to join us. She really can work people when she wants to or maybe doesn't realize what she does. Naw, I believe she knows exactly what she's doing because she stops right next to me, slides her left hand down my torso, and then puts her arm around my waist. She finishes by glancing up to say hello to Aaron. I smile ear to ear, as Aaron has his mouth agape and is wearing a dumbfounded expression.

"Selma, this is my longtime buddy Aaron."

She unhooks from me and gives Aaron a hug. I count the seconds in my head of their chest contact.

"Well, you're sure a sweet thing." This is the only thing Aaron can muster right now. His head seems clouded and distracted at the moment.

Selma replies with a girlish giggle before retreating back next to me, where she should be, as far from Cowboy Aaron as possible.

"Well, why are we standing around here unless you need something from Lowe's? Let's bugger outta here," Aaron says.

I couldn't agree more. "We can follow you back to where you're staying."

"Unless Selma wants to ride with me in my Jeep," he quips.

"Not on your life, buddy."

"Well, then," he says after getting man-blocked, "I got a better place to go to then."

"OK, this is your show. Lead on, cowboy."

"Just try to keep up, buddy boy." He winks at Selma, gets in his vehicle, and drives off.

We drive through the greater Champaign area, seeing the sights of this small Midwestern town until we eventually hit the University of Illinois Urbana-Champaign campus. We stop near the State Farm Center. I park in the next aisle over from Aaron's car in case we are followed. Selma and I get out and start heading toward the track near the baseball field. Aaron is already parked up behind us and to the right. He sits in his vehicle awhile longer before finally exiting. He ditched the cowboy hat in the truck but he still stands out. He looks like a parent of someone who attends classes here.

As we walk around the outside of the track oval and proceed to the bleachers on the far side, I make a quick observation of the area, and it appears normal. There are students running the quarter-mile track, some are on the field, and some are just milling around. There are also people sitting on the bleachers, chatting and wasting the beautiful day doing nothing. I assumed the bleachers is what Aaron had in mind to meet because that's what I would have picked out. Soon, we'll be like the students already there who are just hanging out.

We walk up the middle section of the bleachers and sit down on the hot aluminum seats. Selma sits next to me with her legs crossed, and I lean back resting on my elbows. If we had cigarettes dangling from our mouths, we would look like the cool kids from school, or at least the oldest ones. I just need to slick my hair back in a fifties greaser sort of style. Selma looks better in the jean shorts rather than the poodle skirt though.

It really is a nice day outside. I guess I can't complain when I have a girl next to me and I am outside and not in a cubicle typing away with eyes straining from gazing at the screen all day. Life is what you make of it sometimes, and it's lookin' pretty good right now. And, of course, Aaron picks this exact moment to walk up and sit down next to me.

"Bro, you're blocking my sun." It is the only thing I can say to keep up my cool-guy image.

He punches me square in the left arm. I guess I deserved that. OK, that snaps me out of daydream mode and back into reality. I kind of like it here though. This university seems really laid-back. Maybe I should apply to grad school here so I can chill out on the bleachers every day. How much are the tuition fees here for an out-of-state student? I ponder the thought of going back to school.

Selma elbows me in the side. I guess I should be listening, as nobody is going to let me relax this afternoon.

"As I was saying," Aaron says, staring at me. "What's your next move?"

"We need to go up to Michigan, some small town near the Indiana border. I reckon about three hours from here. We have to meet the package man between eight and nine tonight. After that, we are to beeline it to New York City in time for Saturday."

"You got everything figured out, buddy. Why did you call me?"

111

"I originally called you for a different reason, but I'll let Selma take this one."

I look over to her. She takes a deep breath, preparing herself. Then she chimes in, "Someone is out there planning to kill Jim, probably tomorrow, and me soon after I assemble the three pieces together and get the box to work."

Aaron has a confused facile expression with Selma's talk of missing pieces and a box. I should fill in the details at some point to Aaron but he seems to follow along anyways.

Something has been bothering me for quite a period of time, but I never could articulate it until this very moment. I turn to her with a very serious expression on my face and ask, "Selma, where is the third piece?"

"Oh, I guess I forgot to mention that part, too. Sorry."

Aaron and I both sigh at the same time.

"We actually have the third piece with us. We've been carrying it with us all along," she says.

"Then where is it?" I shoot back at her quickly.

"It's safe and secure. That's all you need to know for now. Why don't we start making our way to Michigan so we aren't late?"

"Fair enough." She still doesn't fully trust me yet.

"OK, Jim Bob." I really hate when he calls me that. Aaron continues, "Ya'll go on, and I'll follow behind you about three miles. We can track each other with this nifty app after I install it on our phones."

He reaches out, and I hand him my phone. "No making any long-distance phone calls."

Aaron stares at me for a moment and then starts downloading the app and installing it so it is aligned with only the three of us. I guess that joke is no longer funny anymore.

Maybe I should stop showing my age with these stale jokes. I spy Selma looking at me in an odd way; she didn't get the joke either and is now actively searching for gray hairs on top of my head. I guess I probably will have five cool points deducted today. AARP will be mailing out an application with my name on it next week.

While Aaron is configuring the phones, I lean over to Selma and question if she is ready for the pickup tonight. Do you know what to do? Got all the instructions? Is there anything I need to know, e.g., is there a gunman that is going to shoot me dead? You know, the usual stuff.

Selma stays silent and only nods or shakes her head in response to my barrage of questions. Finally, after a moment of stillness, she speaks up.

"I'm going to walk to the other side of the track and make a phone call," she says. "You can watch me the whole time, and I'll wave my arm if I need you all to save me." I think she meant that last part sarcastically, but I better make sure my white horse is ready to gallop in. She gets up and walks away, obviously looking tense and worried.

Aaron watches Selma walk away and then turns to me. "You know, you may not make it to New York City. I will try my best to help you, my friend. But have you thought about just walking away? I heard parts of Alaska are pretty cool this time of year." He chuckles at his own witty banter.

He doesn't ever bother to see my reaction, but he probably surmises I am stuck on this roller coaster ride all the way to the end. It is ironic that the end of the ride is near Coney Island, but I am no longer amused. However, a Coney Island hot dog does sound good right about now. Clearly, I am getting hungry.

I continue to watch Selma cross the track out of hearing distance from us. She reaches in her purse for her phone and starts to make the call.

Chapter 12

"Hello again, Hector."

"Hold on," he replies.

Some glasses clang in the background, and a door slams. Hector comes back on the phone.

"Well, hel-lo, dear, I haven't heard from you in a while. I was starting to wonder if you did a runner with old Jim boy."

Hector seems to be in a good mood at the moment. Maybe it has something to do with his guest that slammed the door in the background. Selma can also hear the suspicious tone in Hector's joyous voice, but she gives him the current update.

"We're ready to pick up the other piece. Is there anything special we have to do on this one?"

"Where are you two now?"

"About three hours away. Just trying to time it perfectly today. We were delayed by a bad storm."

"You two are all right, I take it? Nothing wrong with the vehicle?"

"Yes, Hector, we're fine. Thank you for asking about us. The components seem to be unscathed. And nothing was too shaken up in the near-hurricane storm we experienced earlier on. I'm looking forward to picking up the computer chips tonight so I can start assembling the device. I haven't mentioned about the third piece to Jim. It's best he doesn't know for now."

"Good thinking. Has he been asking questions about the device, though? You know, Jim was always the inquisitive one in the Army unit. *Is he suspicious of what's going on, and have you told him anything?*

"Jim is really distant and quite...how should I say this? To be honest, I find him quite boring. I wish you had teamed me up with someone who was more, you know, interesting. Hector, this trip is killing me, and we aren't even halfway there. I could have flown, you know." *I wonder if Hector is buying it. I hope I didn't overplay it.*

"Ha, ha, I thought you two would be Facebook friends by now!" He still can't tell if she is lying or not, as he is still in high spirits from his last visitor in his office.

"Jim? He keeps staring at me in a stalkerish way. He's disgusting and a good-for-nothing. At least Lenny admitted he was a womanizing bastard. I would have been happier if I was teamed up with him. I don't see why I can't take a train or plane at this point." *Come on, Hector, you've really got to believe that I don't want to be around Jim anymore.*

"Well, fine, my dear, it's almost over. Just get the last piece and put it all together by Saturday. This will be finished, and you can go back to California to your normal life. You'll get what was promised to you in the beginning." *Except that it'll be delivered by a bullet. Accidentally, of course.*

"All right, what do we have to do tonight? Where are we supposed to go? Who is the guy, and what does he look like?"

Hector tells her what she needs to know. He does not tell her that Roberto will be waiting the next day to take out Jim.

I can see Selma pacing back and forth. I can't tell if the phone conversation is going well. I see some college frat boy start walking toward her, and I am ready to leap up and gallop to her safety. Maybe I could hit a couple of the hurdles on the track as I race toward her, but she must have been having a heated conversation on the phone because the frat boy decides to pursue another girl who ran past him on the track. So much for my heroics.

116

"Hey, Aaron, should we be trusting her?" I ask him nonchalantly, as I am bored sitting here just watching her and he is engaged in his third sudoku puzzle on his phone.

Never looking up as he places a number three in a box, he replies, "Why are you so paranoid, Jim? She seems like a sweet gal who knows how to take care of herself. She's got a great body to match, and she's college smart and all that. Whatcha complaining about? Or you two haven't yet…oh, I see what you mean. Yeah."

I turn red and have a hard time covering it up. "I mean, I hardly know her. I was only sent to watch her, which she clearly doesn't need my help with, and only recently she tells me, 'Oh, there's some guy out there that's going to shoot your ass.' What would you think?"

Aaron completes the sudoku puzzle and puts his phone down. "Yeah, women. What can you say? Ha, ha. At least you're having…whatever you want to call it."

Not helpful, Aaron. Not helpful at all.

Selma comes back and walks up the bleachers. Aaron and I watch every step she takes as though time is frozen. We slowly track her progress until she is on the step in front of us. Aaron coughs and turns to watch some coed doing the hurdles. I wait for Selma to speak versus asking the obvious question based on non-verbal communication signs. She only stares at me with a raised eyebrow, as if daring me to ask how it went. I learned years ago to not say anything at all at times like these and this is definitely one of those times. I wait patiently and try not to stare directly into her eyes. She looks like she is going to bite my head off, and Aaron's, too. Aaron is making it a priority to not look at Selma either and continues to focus on the coed on the track. Thanks, buddy, for your support.

"I hope Hector bought it," she whispers to herself just audibly enough that we both hear it. I decide not to pursue a follow-up question. Then, to Aaron, she asks, "Hey, how much do you charge to take someone out?"

"You mean dinner, movie, and drinks? Well, I charge different prices, depending if it's male or female. Probably a hundred or a hundred and fifty bucks, but that depends on how the night is going." Aaron says it in such a serious tone that I almost believe him.

"No, not that! The other kind," Selma shouts back at him.

Aaron still pleads his innocence by not looking at her and gets up and walks away. I am now on my own to face the wrath of the irate woman.

"Where's your friend going?" she barks at me.

"He's fine. What happened with the phone call? Do you know what we have to do tonight?" I ask gingerly.

"I swear I'm gonna kill him if he reneges on our deal." She hesitates as if she has said too much.

"What deal?" I fire back.

"Fine. You should probably know the whole truth 'cause it doesn't make a difference at this point. He's going to pay me five million bucks to assemble the device that we've been running around the country picking up pieces for. We really should start heading to Michigan, as I need that final piece so I can start assembling it as soon as possible."

I discover something new from her every time I turn around. When was she going to tell me about the $5 million? It makes the grand that Hector paid me look like small change. I am so keeping this Ford Escape now, minus all the drugs stashed away in it.

"So how is it going down tonight? What's the plan, boss?"

I listen intently to what she has to say. I keep thinking, If Hector wants to pay $5 million for this device, then how much is it really worth? $50 million? $500 million? And who's going to die to keep it or try to obtain it? I wish there was a wimp clause that paid $1 million to walk away, but it is too late now. Aaron mentioned Alaska. Maybe it is not as bad up there as I have been led to believe. I could get used to the cold. More importantly, what is Selma going to do after she collects her $5 million?

Aaron is out of sight now, most likely already at his vehicle. I phone him quickly to tell him we will be leaving and heading for South Bend. He acknowledges and hangs up. What, is he pissed off at me too? Am I letting a woman get between our friendship? Most of all, is my favorite gyro place in South Bend from when I was a student there still open? All these questions will be answered soon enough.

After a three-hour drive, we arrive at the South Bend city limits. The flood of old memories starts to hit me. One of the best feelings in the world is happy memories. I always enjoyed my scholastic studies at Notre Dame. Going to football games was as traditional as apple pie, except the one year the team was terrible. Meeting the chicks that went to Saint Mary's College next door was always a challenge, a challenge any mortal man who went to Notre Dame took on with enthusiasm and trepidation. Ah, I miss the old college days. It was a happier and more carefree time back then.

I should tell Selma that we are going to take a detour and stop at the football stadium for a few minutes. As much fun as that would be for me, I decide to drive on to King Gyros instead. I know Aaron will be there because this is the one place I talked about constantly to the point that he and I drove three hundred miles years ago just to eat there. At least he loved it and understood why I yakked about it all the time.

As we turn onto Western Avenue, I am already excited, and my stomach is grumbling in anticipation. Yes, Mr. Belly, you remember most of junior and senior year gorging out on gyro meat. Oh yeah, I can't hardly wait to take that first bite once again. I am already salivating like a dog.

"What are you so excited about?" Selma remarks. She must have been watching me for some time.

"You know, I graduated from here, and where we're going happens to be one of my favorite places to eat. I hope you love gyros because that's what you're about to get." I am not giving her a choice. Just eat it and be happy.

"Ah, I had a similar place near Caltech, except it was an amazing vegetarian sandwich place. Fair enough. Seems I have no choice in the matter."

"No. No, you don't."

I turn into the parking lot. I look in the window as we walk to the door and see Aaron already there, scarfing down a famous gyro. I am so jealous.

We place our order and receive the food in a little longer time than normal. Hey, you can't hurry awesome food. We sit next to Aaron and are ready to feast on our yummy gyro platter. Selma is more resigned. She is all in and ordered a gyro out of respect for me; no salad for her today. Even if she doesn't eat the immense portion of sliced lamb meat facing her on the plate, I at least give her more credit for attempting this feat.

Ten minutes later, all is quiet at the table as we are chowing away. Finally, Aaron breaks the silence.

"Well, I'm the third wheel, so I gotta skate out of here. I'll be at Bucktown Tap in Michigan at eight p.m. and start drinking at seven p.m." He laughs and follows that with, "See ya'll later." And with that, Aaron leaves so he can arrive early at the bar to get into position.

Now we can get some alone time to sort everything out. I am already three-fourths of the way done with my platter. She is only less than half but still eating at a steady pace.

"Selma."

She looks up with a piece of lamb hanging outside her mouth. Gosh, I love watching people eat. Embarrassed, she wipes it away and takes a drink from her Coke. She asks, "What is it?"

"What are you thinkin' about?"

"How I'm going to spend all the money, for one. Why you're asking me when my mouth is full of lamb is a close second."

I have to ask, "Does your device work? Is it really going to do what Hector wants it to do?" I really am out of my league because I still haven't figured out what it does, but I know it is worth a lot, and I mean a lot, of money.

Whatever poker face she has, she is figuratively playing her cards close to her face. She reaches for another fry and replies, "Jim, I hardly know you, yet I trust you. It would be great if you would do the same for me. The device will work. I have until Saturday to assemble it and make sure it works. I really need you to be patient to allow me to complete it. After that, Jim, the sky's the limit. I haven't given up on you yet despite your ongoing dilemma."

She winks at me before taking another bite of lamb meat with tzatziki sauce. That's all I can ask for, at least for now.

Chapter 13

Nothing beats small-town America. We arrive at the bar around 8:15 p.m. We haven't eaten since our huge gyro platters earlier this afternoon. We are not that hungry, but a small appetizer or two will probably set us for the evening. Besides, having a beer or two might be a better way to ease into the night, for today has been a roller coaster ride of emotions.

We walk into Bucktown Tap and clearly feel the division of those who are local, those who are not, but either way they come here to drink. Most of the bar patrons are watching the Detroit Tigers game, and it looks like they are winning 5-2 in the bottom of the fourth inning. Well, at least the patrons will be happy and distracted, and nobody should take heed of two strangers coming in for a drink as something to munch on. Unless you are the guy that is supposed to deliver a package to the two strangers.

I make no acknowledgement of the fact that Aaron is also sitting at the bar. We've been through this before, maybe in a foreign country, so I simply ignore him, and he does the same. It is good to know we have each other's back in this middle-of-nowhere bar. I can barely make out the argument he is having with the drunk next to him about who was the batting champion in some random year. He is really blending in like he comes in here every night. Aaron is the quintessential barfly

On the list of important decisions to be made this evening, Selma is trying to decide between the potato skins or the buffalo chicken quesadilla. I am glad she is not bothered at all about what will transpire tonight. Maybe I am just overreacting because I feel in the air that something is amiss, or maybe it is because the planets are not aligned. Either way, I shouldn't drink too much because I really need to be ready for anything, even the extra-spicy shredded-beef nachos we just received. Good choice, Selma. I never saw that one coming.

The baseball game is starting to wane in entertainment value as the score remains the same and another inning goes by. Aaron enlists another drunk in his sports smack-talk circle, and they are currently arguing some useless 1960s baseball trivia. Selma keeps checking her phone for the latest news or possibly what's trending on Facebook and Twitter. She is obviously not a baseball fan. I am haphazardly watching the game but keenly observant every time someone new walks in the bar.

After another thirty minutes, I finally pick out the mark. This guy that just walked in screams, "Hired goon someone paid to do a job like this." Add to that the fact that I can see the gun bulging out from his imitation leather jacket. He must have arrived via a motorcycle, maybe a Kawasaki Ninja 1000? Why else would one wear a fake leather jacket this time of year? I mean, Selma is still in jean shorts and I have a short-sleeve shirt on, a bit on the casual side, I might add. It's still hot outside, and this is Michigan; the rest of the country must be in a heat wave or an extreme drought. The old El Niño is really kicking it up this year. I guess some weather person might get that joke.

The hired goon looks around the bar and spots us immediately from the crowd of fifteen people. Judging from the other couples in the bar, I would have picked out our table, too. We look like we don't belong in this town and, more importantly, we look too tense to be a normal couple. We made it too easy. Next time, I will put out a large whiteboard sign that reads, "Mr. Hired Assassin: this table!"

I am watching this guy, and he is watching us. He orders a draft, pays for it with cash, throws a buck in the tip jar, and immediately walks toward our table. I must work on disguises next time or at least grow a beard or something. He sits down next to Selma, as I would probably have done, and says nothing. Not what I would expect, but he is sizing us up for whatever reason. At this point, I would reach for my gun, but alas, I have no gun. Selma must have been thinking the same thing because she is holding something in her handbag and it is bulging out in the direction of our male guest. He looks down, sees the predicament he is in, and resigns himself to say a greeting.

"Hello. You must be Selma," he says in a slow, Southern-ish drawl. What accent is that? I can't tell if it's Carolinian or Honduran. It is a real mishmash of a lot of places, some I have never visited or would rather not to remember.

Selma says, "There's a reason why you're here. Are you gonna make this easy or difficult tonight?"

This is her show; she is calling the shots. I bet half the people in here are packing a gun, though I don't want that theory proven right now or any other night I am in attendance. This guy must have had a gun pointed at him before because he is not flinching one bit. That may also mean he is not alone either. I immediately start looking around the bar for an accomplice. I try to signal to Aaron, but he is doing shots at the bar, probably of the cheap house whiskey if he is buying, and we will receive no help from him at the moment. I guess I never thought that the guy would be bringing backup, or a gun, for that matter. I just assumed he was going to hand over the package like the last one and be on his merry way.

The guy is still staring at Selma, dead-eyed and without blinking, and she is still pointing the handbag with a loaded pistol at the man's abdomen while his hands are still on the table where we can see them. I am waiting patiently and studying him, hoping he won't pull out a gun and shoot me dead. For some odd reason, he is still grinning. That's annoying the living crap out of me at the moment.

I finally break the silence. "Well, are you going to hand it over?" I ask. Honest and blunt is sometimes the best course of action.

Without blinking or looking at me, he replies, "I am not dealing with, amigo. You can be gone. Just leave me and the lady alone."

"The fuck I am." The English language at its finest.

He continues. "She seems to be handling the situation better than you. Why don't you go get us some drinks or some pretzels?"

He takes another sip from his draft beer, his eyes never leaving the sight of Selma or the handgun in the purse. He checks her out from head to toe one more time, clearly assuming she is not going to shoot him. I start to say something, but then I see something I did not see before out of the corner of my eye. The guy at the dartboard looks over one too many times. I found this guy's backup, or I am at least willing to bet on it. This must be the second shooter. I call over to Aaron, who just happens to be returning from the bathroom and wiping his hands on his pants to dry them.

"Aaron, why don't you go play darts," I say, grabbing him as he walks past our table.

"Gotcha." Aaron walks over to the dart player and has words with him. I don't think the words are in a friendly manner, like, "Do you want to play a game of 501, double out?"

"OK," I say as I turn to the guy at our table, a little more confident. "What's it going to be, amigo? Your move."

I wish I had more time to really think about what I had just said. The man, still not bothered with the gun pointed at him, decides to make his move despite his backup being compromised. He reaches for the gun in Selma's bag. A clever move, as pushing down on the gun prevents it from firing upward into his chest cavity. However, he never anticipated the next sequence of events.

I scream at Selma. She lets go of the gun and reaches for the empty beer glass parked on our table. She wails the guy's head with the glass. The guy wails in pain. The bartender and three other patrons immediately jump into the fray and restrain him. Selma plays the female card, pleading innocence and claiming that the guy was being ungentlemanly. She reaches into his pocket to retrieve the computer chips that she says are hers. How she knows where they were located is a mystery to me. The manly bar patrons and bartender throw the guy out of the bar and flex in a show of support for the distressed woman in jean shorts and offer her a drink of choice. Selma just smiles and winks at the men and tells them that she has to go check on her man. They groan and make various rude comments, most likely, if not all, directed toward me.

I am still sitting, openmouthed, trying to comprehend what the hell just happened right in front of me. In the end, I can't really complain. We got fed decent nachos, though a little spicy; nobody got shot despite the numerous amounts of handguns likely present in this particular bar; and the guy surrendered the second (or third) piece that Selma desperately needs to assemble whatever device. Most important of all, the Tigers hold on to win the baseball game, so everyone in the bar is happy and excited. They could care less about the events that transpired just ten minutes ago surrounding an out-of-town man arguing with a female and some stolen Russian computer chips designed to power a really awful device. I say it is about time we cash out and leave this bar. I look for Aaron, but he is walking back in. He obviously had been outside escorting someone off the premises.

We leave the bar but are ever vigilant that the guy and his accomplice may still be lurking about. Face it: there are not a lot of places to go at night in this small town, so we could be walking into another ambush. My only thought is to get out of this town and hightail it to a bigger one to figure out our next plan of action. Aaron and Selma cannot agree more. This whole situation keeps changing with every moment and every new person we encounter. I am starting to doubt whether we will even make it to New York City.

We head toward the vehicle, and I know I have lost some face with Selma. She is stuck with me on this adventure, but I just sat there and watched while she glassed a complete stranger in a bar. I really don't know this woman at all. But as the alpha male in this team, I feel I was supposed to smash the glass over the guy's head or stab him in some awesome way. If there is a cool way to stab a guy. Anyways, I need to do something soon to prove my manliness and rack up some cool-guy points.

We agree that a late-night diner outside of South Bend will suffice. That will not be that far of a drive, and I will feel more comfortable being in an area I know. We say goodbye to Aaron, and I escort Selma to the passenger side of the Escape. The moon is shining brightly, and the air is warm with a slight breeze from the south. Here is my moment to say something nonchalant as I open the door for her. I grab the keys out of my pocket and go to click the unlock button for the doors with the fob, except that I fumble in my nervousness and drop the keys right near her feet. Smooth. Real suave way to impress the lady.

Now, here is an interesting scenario. Person A drops an item on the ground and must retrieve it. Person B sees the dropped item and feels compelled to bend over and pick it up. Here lies the problem: both Person A and Person B bend down toward the item at the exact same time and then bump heads, causing an even more awkward moment.

This is exactly what happens when Selma and I look at each other and both go for the dropped keys. We each rub our heads in the sore spots from the collision, but neither one of us manage to grab the keys. I put my hand out to motion her to freeze so I can grab them.

Attempt Number 2 to retrieve the keys. I stoop down to pick them up and see a shiny quarter approximately twelve inches away from the keys under the vehicle. I become fixated on the quarter because there is pool of water also underneath the vehicle. I laugh inside at first at the thought of being a cheap ass for trying to grab the quarter. Then, however, I am no longer laughing. Rather, I feel uneasiness and anxiety slowly creeping over me with each second. I struggle to comprehend why I am seeing a reddish blinking light reflect off the water puddle and the shiny quarter.

I grab the quarter anyways, along with the keys, and stand up with a blank expression, causing Selma to look at me with confusion. The night has just gotten more interesting.

"Selma, we need to talk. As in talk right freakin' *now*."

I think I am scaring her even more. "What…what is it, Jim?" she stumbles.

I look around one more time in case the two guys are waiting for me to get in the vehicle and watch it explode. I have no idea what the red blinking light is doing under the vehicle that we have been driving cross-country. It really is quite unnerving and downright creepy, and I know that Selma is reading that on my face.

I phone for Aaron before he hits the highway. Luckily, he stopped off at a gas station in town to pick up a Coke and some chips for the drive.

"Aaron, could you turn back around and meet us? It's like really important."

"Sure, be right there."

No point in worrying Selma any more than I have to. I ask her to walk over to the gas station store across the street, or at least away from our vehicle.

"Jim, tell me what's going on!" she demands. I ignore her pleas, but I do it with a smile.

Aaron peels over and parks next to me, though I am shooing him away. He ignores me. I guess karma is even now, as I ignored her and now he ignores me.

"What's up, Jimmy boy? Do you need help navigating back to the highway?" Aaron cracks a joke directed toward my impeccable navigational skills.

I simply say, "Red flashing light." No other words are needed.

Aaron is still laughing at his joke, then stops with a confused look. The light bulb finally shines brightly above his head, and his changed expression says it all.

"What...where?" In a more serious tone, finally.

"Underneath." I point to the vehicle.

Unnerved, he immediately goes into drill sergeant mode and starts barking commands to Selma and I. "Selma, drive my jeep over there," he says as he throws her the keys and points to a vacant lot across the street. She catches the keys and doesn't drop them, unlike me.

"Jimbo, you got a flashlight and a screwdriver?"

Luckily, I was already anticipating he was going to ask for a screwdriver but didn't have a flashlight. I whip out my multi-purpose tool and hand in over. Who carries a flashlight around anyways? "Just use your cellphone," I suggest, and so he does.

"OK, I'm going underneath to check things out. You stand guard and shoot anyone who comes by."

He hands me his gun from his shoulder holster. Aaron has a gun. Selma has a gun. Am I the only one not packing these days? At least I still have my blackjack in case of close-combat fighting. Oh wait, I never pulled it out, but I guess you don't when the girl next to you glasses somebody. I take the gun out and square it up in my hand. I actually feel better with a gun in my hand, just like the old days.

I see Selma is parked across the street and is OK for the moment. I motion her to stand back and try to motion for her to lock the car doors, but I don't know the international gesture for that.

"Jim!" Aaron shouts at me from under the Escape.

I stoop down to look at him. He looks back at me and smiles.

"You've been tracked by somebody the whole time!" Aaron is holding a small metal box with some wires and a red-colored light that is still blinking. He hands me the box, crawls out from under the vehicle, brushes himself off, and turns toward me. "I got an idea!" He snatches the box back from me. "We throw this device on something going the opposite direction of our way. I dunno....a 18-wheeler rig or a train maybe?"

"It's not gonna work," I say with a staunch conviction anticipating what he is going to say.

"You have no faith and no sense of humor, Jim."

"If anyone asks my opinion, I think it's great," Selma adds. When did she return to the scene?

Aaron adds, "Of course it will work, and it will buy us time. That's the beauty of it. By the time they figure it out, we'll be in and out of New York City." Now looking at Selma directly, he states sternly, "That is, if what you say is true about the device-for-cash exchange and I, of course, take my consultation fee."

Selma looks offended but replies, "Of course the exchange will happen, but I really could use some stress-free time in the next two days to actually finish the programming and assembling."

I realize at that very moment that I am not needed in this anymore. I will just let them decide what we should all do from now on. Wait a minute. Before I surrender all my voting rights, I look back to Aaron, "So you think throwing the tracking device on a westbound train is going to buy us enough time and throw them off the track, no pun intended?"

"Not only will it do that, but you two will be taking the train eastbound to New York City. How funny is that?" Aaron really amuses himself sometimes, even if no one else laughs.

"So let me get this straight. We are going to drive west toward Chicago tonight, where Selma and I will take the Amtrak to NYC tomorrow morning. You will take the tracker device and wait at the rail yard, where you will place it on the next westward train. Selma will call Hector and tell him she's got the computer chips and we are now heading to NYC in time for the exchange on Saturday morning. Hector—and we are assuming it was him who had the tracker device installed—will be watching the tracker and see us going west versus east and think something is wrong. After the phone call, we will ditch the phones in Lake Michigan or something. The assassin, what's his name?" I ask Selma.

"Roberto. And he's pretty good, from what Hector says," Selma replies.

"Yes, Roberto." I pause and then continue. "He'll think we're doing a runner and chase after us, calling Hector in the process. Hector will think we betrayed him and fly out to some major western city like Denver or Salt Lake City hoping to track us down, assuming he's buying all of this. Does that sound about right?"

Aaron adds, "You forgot about the part where you buy me a steak dinner and a drink. Maybe two drinks, now that I think about it. And while you're at it, why don't you buy Selma something nice too? Perhaps a scarf or a necklace."

"I think a necklace would be nice, for starters. I assume the dinner is automatic, as I'm starving right now. What about you, Jim? Have you finally digested your gyro and are ready to eat again?" Selma is clearly provoking me, as we just had spicy nachos about an hour ago. Surely she can't be hungry already? I think she wants to go sit somewhere and is teaming up with Aaron to get her way.

"Well, Jim, time to break the bank. I'm starving too!" Aaron says. This man can always eat, especially if someone else is footing the bill.

"All right, all right, both of you. You'd think you two were in cahoots with each other. Should we try to leave this one-horse town again and hit the road? There should be a Texas

Roadhouse off of I-94 right when you exit Michigan and enter Indiana. Is that OK for everyone?" I ask sarcastically.

"Sure," they both chime in unison. They are working together. I knew it.

At least the steak was great, even though I was not that hungry. I reflect for a moment after the last buttered roll is eaten and last bit of a well-done filet mignon is chewed. Nursing a cold draft of Labatt Blue, as it was a drink special, I turn my head to the other two at the table. They are actively engaged in some silly nonsense discussion about who their favorite character is on *The Big Bang Theory*, or at least that was where they were at when I actually start listening.

It seems odd that I was leading a different life not even three weeks ago, a boring one at that, and now I am caught up in some cross-country thriller with this beautiful woman and my best friend who helps me out from time to time. I really shouldn't be complaining, should I? Most recently, I feel like I really am always one bullet away from death, one exploding car away from my doom. All I need is Selma to poison me at some point, and I will have achieved one of the top ways to die. Oh, they are laughing and joking about some episode from season two, or what it season three? I don't know, and I don't really care. All that matters is that for this brief moment at the steakhouse, we are just three people sitting here enjoying a night out among friends. It is like the calm before the storm, and it is about get nasty real soon.

"Earth to Jim, *heellllloooo*?"

"I'm here, what's up?"

"We were starting to get worried about you or thinking you were plotting a way to get out of paying the check." Aaron laughs. He is holding the bill, waiting to pass it over to me.

"It's all good." I put down a nice crisp hundred-dollar bill, courtesy of Hector, with plenty left for a most generous tip to the waitress. I smile at her as she comes by to collect. "Here ya go, dear. Keep the change."

She winks at me and throws her hips to and fro one more time as she walks away from the table, or maybe I just imagine it. Selma starts calling me again, and I snap out of it.

"Jim, what are we going to do next?"

A most interesting question indeed. "Well, my dear, we are going to Chicago."

Aaron throws in, "Let's get going, you two. We still got a lot to do." He puts on his hat and walks toward the door.

I wait for Selma. We walk together through the first set of doors, and she stops, turns around, and kisses me on the cheek.

"Thanks for dinner," she says and throws in a smile to complement the batting of her eyes. "And thanks for *everything* so far, you know, what you have done."

Suddenly, the evening got even better.

Chapter 14

We get in the vehicle and head off to destination: Chicago. Aaron is already well on his way to The Windy City, as he waits for no one, not even me. I decide to take it easy and drive the rest of the way in a relaxed and carefree manner. Not because I had two beers and am worried about being pulled over but rather to reminisce about Selma's nifty way of saying thank you for the dinner and everything.

I casually glance over and see her staring back at me. I try to quickly look back to the endless road of I-94, but I fail in not being noticed, as I get caught gazing at her. I hear her let out a snicker, and then she proceeds to ask me a rather random question, especially for this time of evening. Why not? I need something to keep me awake.

"Do you want to know what I am assembling? Surely it must have piqued your interest at some point by now."

I play it smooth. "Naw, your business is your own." Head focused straight; eyes on the road.

She doesn't believe it for one instant and screams, "Bullshit!"

I cave way too fast. "OK, OK. You got me. I'm a little interested. But don't start throwing out technical words, or you'll lose me."

Selma thinks how to phrase her answer. Before she can start, I continue. "But I wonder if my chances of staying alive are increased by the more I don't know." I think that's what I mean.

She ponders that for a second. "Yeah, you may be right. Though you must be a little interested, given it's worth a lot of money. And haven't you any idea how *we* are gonna spend it?

You know, I do enjoy traveling around *with you*! Besides, our next road trip should be out West, don't you think?"

"I certainly agree!" Hmm, she emphasized the *with you*. That's a good sign. Wait a minute, what did I just agree to? Was it the next road trip out West or spending the money with her?

"What do you have in mind?" I throw in just to see what she replies.

"Well, we may have to have a serious talk over dinner at a fancy restaurant about that at some point. But listen up. We have to get through this weekend. And I have something that's really important to share with you, so buckle up and pay attention."

"I'm all ears." I set the car to cruise control.

"OK. First, you probably want to know why we've gone through the trouble to pick up these three pieces. Well, Hector seemed to trust you somewhat, but not much. He also needed to make a drug delivery to Dallas as a routine shipment, so that part was a bonus. He thought if we kept the number of pieces unclear or what they would be used for, you wouldn't be interested. We initially planned that you thought it was a part of the smuggling operation and thus didn't put a lot of thought into it."

"So are there actually three pieces or not?"

"Oh yes, there are three pieces. As I said, we have had one of them with us the whole time." She looks toward the luggage in the back. "It's actually the laptop computer in my luggage. It was modified and rebuilt back in my lab at Caltech months ago. I've been working on it for about six months, but I needed two other specific, we'll say, 'unique components,' to make it work. Well, that's the hardware part. The other part is the programming, which I have been working on for quite some time."

I have to frequently check the highway up ahead to make sure this drive is going along smoothly. However, I would rather pull over to the side of the road because I really want to listen to what Selma has to say.

She pauses for a drink from a water bottle and then continues. "A mutual friend introduced me to Hector last year and gave me the opportunity to pitch the idea. Coincidentally, Hector was looking for a way to rip off the financial markets. I'm not talking tens of thousands either. He was shooting to steal tens of millions from Wall Street. I didn't really think it through at the time, as I was looking for investment backers to get my ideas from the drawing board to reality. After all, this is the dream of most scientists: to find a financial backer that fronts all the costs up front."

"Ironically, the original idea was to streamline routine stock trades to the point that if a person was a second ahead of the game, they could conceivably make that fraction-of-a-price change more in the split-second difference. So, Jim, say that the stock price was forty-five dollars and fifty cents at a particular moment of time, say 2:02:30pm. Now, as the price fluctuates throughout the day, being a split second ahead of the game makes all the difference in profit."

"Sure," I say, not knowing if I really understand what she is saying but continuing to listen.

"So, for example, if the price rises to forty-six dollars at 2:02:55p.m., then the purchases we made during the fraction of the second could make a difference if you could get your purchase in before that second changed. That is the principle of the device I'm building. In essence, to beat the clock."

"And your programming could make the device do that if stock prices shifted higher or lower?" She had definitely piqued my interest.

"They later discussed if I could manipulate it to do this or that, and every time I modified it to their requests. I firmly believed it would react faster than either way the price fluctuated," she confidently replies. "Finally, Hector was convinced and willing to front the whole investment and offer me a specific monetary contract. He was more concerned in the profitability of the device in the secondary market and seemed confident in me that I could build it to what he specifically wanted to market to his customers. Jim, I kid you not. He was literally throwing money at me at a time when I needed cash to pay off bills and student loans to survive. I thought he was truly generous, and he never thought of me in any other way than business. He made it clear to his associates that I was not to be touched, hit on, looked at funny, or messed with in any way."

Selma laughs for a moment. Did I miss a joke or something? Should I be laughing or not?

"So, that night you saw me in a compromising position onstage: well, I hope you got a great view and enjoyed the show because that's all you'll ever get." She pauses for a moment to see the expression on my face. "Well, unless you play your cards right...Jimmy." She winks at me.

I start to say something, but I can't form the words and sputter like a buffoon. Nice going, Mr. Smooth.

"Moving along. Like I told you, it was partially a setup to appeal to you, but it was also a celebration of sorts for me. I cracked the daunting programming dilemma earlier that week and was ready to test the new superchips that Hector promised I would have in a couple of days. He told me that these illegal

Russian chips had cleared through customs via Canada, and they would be ready for pickup later this week. These computer chips are really experimental technology. I didn't care if they were stolen or not at this point, but they'll make my device do what it's supposed to do."

"And what is that?" I am afraid to ask.

"The programming is the heart of it, but it's these Russian computer chips that do it at a much faster rate than anything we could obtain here in the US, legal or illegal."

"Do *what* faster, exactly? What do you mean?"

"Weren't you listening to me a few minutes ago?"

"Well, I was, but I thought you were kidding about it."

"No, the device can manipulate the stock market. You know, change the stock prices arbitrarily so we can buy when it's programmed to be lowered and sell at the higher price. You know, Economics 101."

"You really weren't bullshitting me?"

"Jim, I don't kid around, and yes, it will work, which leads to the first pickup the other day. The item was a sophisticated antenna. A very high-powered antenna designed to send the signal that will hack into the central stock exchange computer to implement the program. The antenna is quite technologically advanced, and I don't know the origins of it. I suspect China or South Korea. Anyway, it operates on frequency-hopper communications technology."

"What is—?" I start to ask, but Selma cuts in. "Frequency hopper is changing frequencies randomly a fixed rate per minute. As long as you are synced up with the receiver, data can be transmitted without the fear of being compromised because it keeps changing the frequency that it is being transmitted on."

"Hard to track, I suppose."

"Yes, Jim. Score one point for getting that one."

I think she is making fun of me, but I continue to listen.

"Combine this with the over-clocked, high-tech computer chips, this device rocks. It's blazing fast and undetectable by anyone or any government. At least, this is the theory I pitched to Hector and his associates. There's nothing that can track the signal or isolate it, as it is too damn fast. Obviously, it will be way faster than that old-fashioned stock market-programmed ticker, and thus we can manipulate a price drop or rise before it's updated. It's really that simple, Jim. Well, I think it is in a nutshell, but I'm the one with the PhD who created it, so I just assume it's simple and easy to understand. Thoughts? Comments? Questions?"

I am still in shock at what she has just told me and realizing I am in three layers deep and way over my neck.

"I get the feeling you're having moral issues with me and my device right now," Selma says. "You probably can see the potential for what Hector and his associates could do to the stock markets or whomever he sells it could do in the next week or so. Besides make a ton of money overnight, the device, if used properly, can also bankrupt millions of people in the process."

I have to pause for a second, at least for dramatic effect. I finally respond, "However, next Saturday, you're selling it for a cool five million. Though Hector will obviously sell it for twenty times that price. Enough for you and *maybe another person* to leave the country and retire in Central America or somewhere tropical."

"Yes, I'm selling it for five million and want to take the money and run. So I ask you, Jim, do you have any moral issues *now*? Is there anything that you'd like to discuss with me at this very moment?"

Morality was never my favorite subject in school, by the way.

"Jim, do you hear what I am saying to you?"

I am still driving a two-ton-plus vehicle with the cruise control set at 72 mph down a busy highway at night. So my initial reaction is of hesitation, and she reads it right away. Possibly what gives it away is the fact that I hit the brakes, causing the vehicle to slow down. It is a tough decision to gamble everything you have for a potential sure thing. I feel like I have bought a lottery ticket and four of five numbers have hit and I am waiting patiently for the fifth ball to come up to see if I have won the entire jackpot. Except that I may have to enjoy the jackpot in Panama or Argentina, but that's a minor detail in the bigger picture. At least Argentina has incredible steaks with a little chimichurri sauce and tasty Malbec wine to wash it down. I do like a well-done steak served with a glass of Malbec. How hard is it to learn a language like Spanish, enough to get by in a foreign land?

She is still looking at me for a definitive answer, a sound commitment, or some reassurance that I am willing to gamble my future with her. Except here I am, thinking of what world-recognized red wines are coming out in the autumn from the Mendoza valley vineyards.

"Wow. I don't have a reply, yet I reckon I should. How do I respond and still have a clear conscience about all of this? I mean, wow, manipulating the stock market…but…retirement in the tropics or South America…I'm struggling here, Selma. Throw me a lifeline, because I'm drowning."

Now is the very moment that defines how Selma and I go forward from this point. And what perfect timing, as our exit is coming up fast. The very next exit, as a matter of fact. I still have time to walk away and take my chances that Roberto, Hector, or a host of others don't track me down and shoot my ass dead. Or Selma, for that matter. She could still shoot me and then have a shot of bourbon at the next bar she comes across before driving the Escape to New York City. Or what about Aaron? He could be super jealous, take me out of the picture, play the macho card with Selma, and off those two immigrate to the sunny beaches of Patagonia in two weeks hence.

It is in this fit of madness racing through my mind that I am driving through the streets of Chicago. OK, the suburbs of Chicago. I really should slow it down at this time of night. All we need right now is for the police to be sniffing around our luggage in the back. I stop the vehicle on the side of the road and cut the lights.

"Selma, my dear, give me something tangible that does not make me get out, throw the keys to you, and walk away."

Selma reaches over to my right thigh, strategically places her hand above my knee, and says, "Jim, I...er, we, are doing the right thing. You have to trust me on this one. Trust your gut instincts. It'll eventually make sense in the end. Good always triumphs over evil, doesn't it?" She goes silent for a second. "Are you with me, Jim? I need to know right this minute. I need you to complete this assignment with me, and I need you to be with me...afterward. I can't complete this without you, and I want you next to me all the way through to the end. You'll just have to trust me on this one."

She is grasping my thigh really tight, but her right hand is in her handbag. I hope she is grabbing a tissue and not the handgun, but who can tell at this moment. I study her eyes from across the vehicle and see the one thing that had escaped me before but is now clear in my mind. I now know how I am going to answer this question.

"Without a doubt, Selma. Yes, I'm in this with you until the end."

I have a sneaky suspicion I know what she really intends to do with the device, but she probably doesn't want to ruin the surprise for me. Here's hoping, at any rate.

I start the engine and continue to drive in the greater Chicago area.

Chapter 15

Roberto is driving along the highway, keeping close to the red dot on the screen but far enough away so they don't pick up on him. He has been shadowing the woman and the two guys since yesterday and is ever ready to receive the word to take out the target: Jim. However, with the second male in the mix, he wonders if boss man wants him eliminated, too. It will cost extra, at least an extra five grand. *Seventy-five hundred if they want the Roberto Special, ha, ha.*

Roberto would laugh at his own joke, except that the target vehicle is not heading east like it should be after the pickup. Rather it is going the opposite direction, west. West, as in heading-toward-Chicago west. Has the plan changed and he was not informed? Why are they going to Chicago when they are supposed to be heading toward New York City? *Should I call boss man and let him know? What should I do? Just keep following them, Roberto, that's all you gotta do.*

They sat in the restaurant for a long, long, time. How long does it take to eat a steak dinner? Roberto thinks to himself. *Man, I could go for some decent food these days, and that steak is starting to sound really tempting. Hector would shoot me himself if I lose sight of these three targets. Besides, they're up to something. I can just feel it.*

OK, I see them exiting the steakhouse. The one male is heading off by himself, and the other guy and the girl are slowly walking toward the Ford Escape. Wait a minute, the red dot's moving! It should be standing still, as the Escape is not *moving. Why is that? Unless they found the tracker and the first male is carrying it with him. I need to call boss man right now. They must have figured out the tracker device, and I bet they're planning to do a runner. I told Hector the other day not to trust the female. He should always listen to what I have to say. It's me that's out here following them, not him in his comfy bar with his women and expensive tequila. I'm going to call him right now, and I hope I interrupt the bastard. Serves him right. I better get a bonus when this is finished.*

Ring. Ring.

Hector picks up on the third ring. "Hola. What is it?" There are some muffled sounds in the background.

"Boss man, it's Roberto." Pause.

"Well, what is it? I'm busy. What is it?" Hector shouts into the phone.

Good. I interrupted him. "I've been tracking the target, and they changed direction." *Phew. He's not gonna like it.*

"*What* do you mean, they changed direction? You better explain right now, Roberto…"

"They picked up the second item earlier and then started to head to South Bend but changed it up, and they are heading in a westerly direction, toward Chicago." Roberto is breathing rapidly.

"*What? What* do you mean, Chicago? Why?"

Roberto is talking really fast now. "That's not all. The tracker is pointing to another vehicle. I saw it with my own eyes. It's the vehicle with the second male."

"What the hell is going on, Roberto? I told you specifically to follow the vehicle with Jim and Selma. You better have not lost them. So help me…"

"I'm only telling you what I'm seeing."

Hector pauses for a moment. "I'll call ya back."

Click.

145

Boss man sounds pissed, Roberto thinks. *Good for him.*

Hector is sitting is his club watching the blonde girl onstage dance away while drinking a straight reposado tequila. *This is a very nice reposado. Quite spicy but delicious, unlike Sandy or whatever her name is dancing onstage. She simply will not do, as her dancing is, how shall I say, amateur at best. Maybe she's better suited to waitress or bartending, as clearly the crowd is not cheering her on. Oh well, I ain't paying her. This is her audition.*

The phone rings.

Who's calling me now? Oh, it's Roberto. What the hell does he want? His instructions were quite simple and clear: follow Jim and Selma with the tracker, and await further instructions. How difficult can that be?

Picking up on the third ring, he says, "Hola. What is it?"

After hanging up on Roberto, Hector ponders what exactly is going on, other than the plan and everything else is going to shit at the moment.

What in the hell is that bitch doing? She's double-crossing me and running off with Jim and that other guy. Roberto, you better not lose sight of them, or I will drive up there and shoot you myself. Selma better pick up the phone right now and explain herself.

Hector immediately phones Selma.

"Hello?" Selma whispers.

"Selma, my dear, how are you doing? Is everything all right?" Hector says in a strained voice.

"Oh, hi, Hector. What's up?"

"I haven't heard from you in a while and wanted to see how things are going."

"Fine. Just fine. We picked up the computer chips from your friends earlier. They weren't playing nice right away, but I managed to convince them to hand them over. I got the computer chips safe and secure." Selma pauses to catch her breath.

"Excellent. Will it be ready by Saturday? Do you remember where to go in New York City? You remember the various places I showed you last month when we flew out there for the weekend? I'll pass along detailed instructions to the specific place once you arrive."

"Yes. Yes, I remember it all, Hector. I'm going to start assembling it, and it will be ready as planned."

"Good to hear, Selma, good to hear. Say, where are you right now?"

"Right now? We are...we're in South Bend looking for a hotel room. Jim is, has, er, tried one place, and they were, er, booked. We are trying another hotel next door."

"Has Jim been all right to you? You know, he's done what we needed him to do. I'll tell ya what: I can put you on the next flight, and you can just fly out to New York City. I'll even put you up in a swanky Midtown hotel. I can even meet you a day before the Saturday meeting."

"No. No...that's all right. Jim is fine. I can deal with him; I've gotten used to him. Besides, he's doing most of the driving, which gives me time to program and finish the assembly. He keeps telling me he doesn't mind. After we find a hotel, I'll tell him to take a break and go grab a beer at the bar tonight because I'm tired. I always tell him to bugger off so I can concentrate on working on the device, and he does. He's good about that. He hasn't been asking too many questions about me or what I'm working on. He just drives and plays horrible music on the radio." Selma snickers.

"Are you sure you will have it ready by Saturday? This is a big deal, Selma. This is serious. I don't want it to turn ugly. There are consequences if you fail to deliver as promised. Do you understand me?"

"I understand you perfectly clear, Hector. I really do, and I won't fail you."

"Fine then, see you on Saturday. Stay in contact. I want to hear regular status reports."

"Goodbye, Hector. Good night." Selma hangs up.

As Hector puts the phone down, Sandy strides down the steps from the stage but slips and stumbles before gracefully regaining her balance. *That could have ended poorly.* He looks up to her and half-heartedly smiles. Though clearly embarrassed, she smiles back at him. Hector motions her to sit at his table and flags the ever-present and attentive waitress to get them a round of drinks, pronto.

"So my dear," he says to whatever her name is. *Sandy,* he thinks. "What do you want to do for Hector?"

Sandy starts to say something but then Hector stops her and tells her, "Go to the bar. Leave. Leave right now."

Sandy gets up and scuttles away in a hurry. Hector immediately phones Roberto.

Answer, dammit. Come on, Roberto. Answer the phone now, or I swear, I will...

"Yes, boss man."

"What's going on right now?"

"I'm following them. They're in two vehicles, and the tracker is with the lone male. They're just outside Chicago."

"Take them out tonight or in the morning. Do it as quickly as possible. Both males. I repeat, only the men. Don't harm Selma under any circumstances. If she's shooting back at you, then disarm her, but do not shoot her. We need her alive. Do you understand me, Roberto? Are we clear?"

"I understand. Boss man...I...er..."

"Yes, yes. You will be paid accordingly. I even have a female here I think you'll be interested in as a bonus. Anyway, do not harm Selma. Got it?"

"Yes, boss man. Should I abduct her then?"

"No, leave Selma alone but watch her closely. Encourage her to travel with you per my request but don't make a scene. I'm sure she can be persuaded if you encourage her accordingly. Remember, we only need her alive. Her ability to walk is not important." He adds, "Oh, Roberto. Don't make it a messy scene. OK? If the police are involved, you're on your own. Got it? Call me when you complete the job, or don't bother calling ever."

Hector hangs up the phone.

I knew boss man would want me to take both males out. He'd better pay me good, and this female better be worth it, too. This is it. I'm leaving for Southern Mexico after this job. Screw boss man. Ah hell. I gotta call my buddies right now.

Roberto picks up a radio and switches to Channel 47. He puts the call out to the Latin Counts, his old gang in Chicago. Pedro, who is a lifelong member, picks up the call and, as they weren't doing anything tonight anyway, agrees to assist him for a small convenience fee, of say, in the ballpark of around two grand. Roberto agrees and tells them to meet him near the rail yard on the South Side, their old hangout from years ago.

149

The Latin Counts eventually arrive, and Roberto explains that he is tracking this hombre driving a jeep. They need to ride tandem to where this dude is hiding out with these two other people that Roberto is also interested in. Coordinate it, and don't lose sight of the first male are Roberto's instructions.

Meanwhile, back at Hector's club, Hector picks up the phone and calls Rachel.

"Rachel, we are going to the alternate plan."

"Well, good evening to you, Hector. Nice of you to call. What's up?"

"I'm having Roberto eliminate your ex-husband and his friend tonight. Don't shed a tear now."

"Why should I? You're doing me a favor. Something I should have done years ago." Rachel plays her poker face and masks any emotion in her voice from Hector.

"Heartless bitch," Hector empathically calls her out.

"Who do ya think I learned it from? Besides, is your girl gonna complete our device by Saturday? Did you forget to tell her you're personally gonna shoot her after she shows us it works?"

"No, I haven't told her. Thanks for asking. By the way, do you have a buyer lined up for Saturday?"

"Of course. I met with him last week. Charming fellow. Old European chap. You could learn a thing or two from him!" Rachel laughs out loud.

"Anything else, funny girl? You got the airline confirmations set as well?"

"Yes, dear," Rachel replies sarcastically. "You know, sometimes you are worse than my ex."

"I've had enough of your attitude for one evening. Goodbye, Rachel."

"See you soon, dear."

The phone rings in my front pocket. I reach for it while driving and quickly throw it to Selma.

"Hey, Selma, can you answer this? It's Aaron calling me."

"Sure," Selma replies but puts in on speakerphone. "Good afternoon, this is Jim's phone. How can I help you?"

Aaron chat away, "Hello, babe. Good. I actually want to talk to you and not Jimbo. Listen, when was Roberto supposed to make the hit on us, and what vehicle is he driving?"

"Oh, he was gonna do it after we made the pickup in Michigan. I'm not sure what vehicle he drives these days. I assume an Escape like ours."

"Fine. Thanks, sweet cheeks. Now be a dear and hand the phone over to Jim."

Selma turns off the speakerphone and hands the phone to me.

"Jim, listen. Roberto is out there, and he may try to ambush us. I don't know. I have the tracker in my vehicle, so he's most likely following me. I'm ditching the damn thing pronto. I need to get off the highway and try to take a different route. I have this gut feeling I'm being followed but don't see the same vehicle following me. It's a strange feeling though, and I just know it. I assume you're approximately three to five miles behind me, so keep your distance. It's better to be safe than dead. Go find a hotel for the night and call me back."

Aaron hangs up. I hold the phone for a second and then put it down in the central console.

Selma is impatient. "What was that all about?"

"Nothing. He wanted to thank me for dinner and to tell me he enjoys your company." As I finish lying to Selma for no real reason, I see the next exit sign coming up in my peripheral view. "I've decided to take a different way, Selma. Call it gut instinct. Please be a dear and start looking for a hotel, will ya?"

"OK. Is everything really all right?"

"I hope so. I really do. Hey, why don't you start checking out hotels near the airport, perhaps the Marriott or something?"

Aaron drives through downtown Chicago in hopes of drawing Roberto toward him and away from the other two. *What I really need to do is ditch this tracker device in Lake Michigan and let Roberto go after it. But I gotta stick to the plan, and the plan calls for me to put it on a train heading westbound in hopes to draw everyone in that direction for the next few hours or, if we're lucky, days. However, it's never that easy, and driving to the rail yard will be more efficient than the lake option. Besides, by my best estimate, I should have a three-mile or about a seven-minute lead on Roberto. Just enough time to plant the device on a train and drive off, leaving Roberto to chase a ghost halfway across the country.*

Coming up on the rail yard, Aaron stops the vehicle about twenty feet back from the guard fence. He looks around to make sure there are no other vehicles around and walks through the open gate. Trains are moving to and fro, even at this time of night, and Aaron is looking for a specific train to plant the device on. When he sees it eventually, he knows it's the right one. He takes one last look at the shiny metal box with the red blinking light and starts walking toward a slow-moving train that is heading west. He watches as the train cars go by one by one. He takes one last look around, left and right, and then proceeds to chuck the device into an open car. The box lands perfectly and slides toward the back from the motion of the car. *Perfect.*

Aaron walks back toward his vehicle, glancing around to make sure one last time there are no witnesses. When satisfied that there are none, he starts up the vehicle and drives off.

Roberto wonders why the red dot on the screen is showing up in the rail yard. *Is it a trap? Are they going to ambush me in a secluded place? I better be on guard for anything.*

He sees another vehicle pull up ahead and stop, so Roberto decides to wait to see what plays out. He observes a man get out of the vehicle carrying a metal box just like the tracker device planted on Jim and Selma's Ford Escape.

This must be the other male that entered the picture. Should I take him out right now? I've got the perfect shot and no witnesses. It's too easy, but wait—this guy can lead me to the other one. Possibly. My job is to kill both of them. Tough decision, indeed.

OK. The guy threw the device on the train. The tracker dot on the screen is now moving again. So that's the ruse: to make us think they're heading west. Ha, I foiled their ploy. These people are a bunch of amateurs. I should shoot him and take him out of his misery for being out of his league. He's double-checking, looking for me, but I'm camouflaged by this other train. This is too easy. He knows I'm here, or so he thinks, but he can't see me.

Ha, ha, here I am! He's looking around one more time, thinking no one saw him, but I certainly did. I watched the whole thing, and you, my friend, are guilty as charged. And now I have your vehicle plate and make/model, which makes it even easier to follow you. You're going to lead me straight to the other guy, Jim, and then it's payday for me. I really am awesome at my job. Hector should be so lucky. Alas, no killing tonight, as I really need to find the other two.

Roberto switches the radio again to Channel 47.

"OK, fellow Latin Count brothers," he speaks into the private channel. "The male is heading back to his vehicle and will be driving off soon. Start the shadowing and handoffs with the motorcycles first and the cars secondary. Try to pinpoint where he's heading. I want everyone to follow his vehicle for a couple of miles and guess where he's heading. I want the motorcycles to speed up and be ready to follow when he passes their position. Everyone talk on the radio and continuously provide what road they are on and what direction the target is going. I bet he's heading toward the airport, but that's only a guess. Come on, guys, talk to me now."

Pedro is on his sixth vehicle exchange tonight. *This is way too easy money*, he thinks to himself. He handed off the vehicle driven by the gringo earlier, and now he has moved into position in case the target vehicle goes down the airport hotel road.

The radio squawks that the vehicle is approaching him: "He's in a normal jeep." *How discreet is that?*

The vehicle passes him and turns onto the hotel road. *Which hotel is he going for—Holiday Inn, Hampton, Courtyard, or Marriott? He just passed the first two, and it appears it's going to be the Marriott.* He radios in the hotel and parks a few minutes after the gringo in the Escape arrives.

As Pedro walks in, the guy is booking a room and at the same time asking about train schedules for tomorrow on his phone. He nods to the guy when he looks over to him, and Pedro waits patiently in line to book a room. Pedro takes his time asking for availability as the male goes toward his room. Then Pedro decides the room price is too high for his budget, apologizes, and walks out. He returns to his vehicle and radios in the latest update to Roberto.

"It looks like they're taking the train in the morning, Roberto. Sounds like the guy is interested in the morning train times, or at least, that's what he was talking about on the phone."

"Excellent, Pedro. I can always count on you. Meet me at the Waffle House down the road, as I have another job for you all."

"Good. I'm starving right now."

"See you there," another caller on the channel responds.

Chapter 16

Knock. Knock.

I look through the peephole while holding a gun at my left-hand side—Selma's gun, for the record—and see Aaron in the field of view. I am still in position to shoot in case it is an ambush. I slowly open the door, checking left and right down the hall. Aaron walks past me, heads to the fridge to grab a beer, opens it, and starts chugging. Selma is sitting on the sofa in more relaxed attire also drinking some alcoholic drink, just not a beer. Aaron tips his hat toward her and then turns to me. How rude. He never offered to get me a beer. My own beer, for that matter.

"The good news is that I ditched the tracker device. The bad news is that I may have been followed." He takes another swig.

I lock and bolt the door, then return to the sitting area, grabbing a drink of my own and joining Selma on the sofa. "What makes you think that? Oh, did you by chance buy the tickets for tomorrow morning?"

"Just a feeling, bro." Aaron clangs the beer bottle to mine. "Anyhoo, I got the tickets booked for ya'll. I'll take our phones and ditch them as well. You guys will get on the train, and I'll meet you in NYC by Saturday. Somehow. Some way."

Selma chimes in, "Sounds great. I hope this plan works. Do you have the PAYG phones for us?"

Aaron reaches in his right coat pocket and produces a flip phone. He tosses it to Selma, a little short, causing her to lurch forward to grab it. He smiles, and she starts to blush but looks at the phone attentively.

"A flip phone? You've got to be kidding."

"Hey, that's all ya need. Go buy a more expensive one next week."

I pipe up, "Where's my phone?"

"I only got ya'll one phone. Share it." Aaron goes back to the fridge to resupply himself with a new beer. "Leave the new SIM card in there for now. Hold on to your old SIM card, as you may be able to use it again someday."

"Hey, who's going to pay for all those beers?" I say sarcastically, trying to divert Aaron's attention.

Aaron quickly replies, "You! And that's not all you're paying for. Wait until you see my bill!"

"All right, get outta here before you start charging us an evening rate. See ya in the morning, reckon around eight."

"Good night you two. Don't stay up too late." Aaron winks toward me, walks out the door, and heads down the hall to his room.

"Selma, what should we do now?" I ask as I wink at her.

"You can start by refilling my drink." She adjusts to a more comfortable position on the otherwise uncomfortable sofa. I bring over another beer, hand it to her, and sit on the opposite side of the sofa. I may be too exhausted for deep conversation, but always up for anything else.

The next morning, Selma and I pack and prepare to depart. Aaron meets us downstairs for breakfast. It's a quiet breakfast with not much small talk. Both Aaron and I are suspicious of everyone and think it best not to say much, except, of course, to comment on the lack of decent sausage at this hotel chain.

The three of us finish up breakfast and head back to our rooms to clean up and check out. Aaron is rather quick and heads downstairs to check out first. The plan, which we discussed earlier, was for us to arrive downstairs exactly ten minutes after him and check out also. I have not received a text from Aaron in the last ten minutes, as he must be putting the bags in the car. I assume all is clear from his silence and that he is departing for the train station.

I stand by the door waiting for Selma to finish up checking the room for any remaining items. When she is satisfied that she has checked the bathroom twice as well as the closets and under the bed, Selma gives the OK that she is ready to depart.

"Are you sure, Selma, that you have everything and that you've checked everywhere?"

"I'm good. Ready to go, and stop making fun of me. That's not very gentlemanly of you," she replies in a stern tone.

"Then let's go, Mrs. Banks!" I have a chuckle at the phony names we have been using throughout this trip.

We check out, neglecting to comment on how much alcohol was drunk from the mini-bar. Thus, we pay the extra forty bucks grudgingly and thank the front-desk clerk for being so attentive to our drinking escapades.

I look over to Selma, my wife in fake name only, and enquire, "Ready to go, wifey?"

Selma never misses a beat and with quick wit replies, "Sure, hubby, take us outta here."

She gives me the final nod, and I start up the vehicle and proceed onward to the train station as well.

Pedro arrives in time to see a male and female load up a black Ford Escape and drive out of the parking lot. He is frustrated because he knows his ass will be in deep shit if he screws this up. He radios in that the two people he has been watching are leaving. He thinks for his own safety not to mention how he missed the single gringo leaving.

Aaron arrives at the train station, making a nondescript entrance. He thought ahead to apply the necessary enhancements to slightly change his appearance. They may be only subtle changes, but they should fool the casual observer or dim-witted gangster. He thinks to himself that these changes will give him an overall upper hand over said gangsters. He knows that someone is out there waiting to take them out, and Jim and Selma need to get on that train at any cost.

I won't let you down, my friend, Aaron says to himself as he walks up to the counter and asks for the reservation he made last night. "I have booked two tickets. One for me and one for my wife, please."

The clerk, still half-asleep from a rough night the previous evening, looks at Aaron and asks, "What name is it under, and how are you paying? Cash or credit card?"

We drive toward the Amtrak train station, a little nervous about what is about to happen. Maybe nothing will happen, and we will joyously get on the train and ride off heading to the East Coast. I probably should not kid myself and prepare for anything. Hopefully, Aaron will have our tickets ready, and it should be an easy process getting on the train. What Aaron does with the faithful Ford Escape after we depart is beyond my control.

The best way to stay alive is by staying one step ahead of the enemy, in this case Hector and his henchmen. All we have to do is check in, grab a train seat, and off we go to our destination, New York City. It sounds pretty easy, and sure, that is what happens in the movies. However, there is this minor point about a killer out there waiting for us in the shadows. I am sure he has my name etched on one of his bullets.

I take the exit and park toward the back of the Amtrak parking lot. I glance over to Selma, and she has a worried and muddled look on her face as if to question what will happen next and if we are safe. I don't know what to say to her, but I have to protect Selma at all costs and believe deep inside Aaron is willing to make the same sacrifice.

"Don't let me down, Aaron old buddy," I whisper to myself. "I know you understand loyalty and honor. Let us get on that train safely, and fate can take over from there."

We enter the train station and unload our bags on a bench next to us, the same bags of clothes that desperately need to be washed, as they have been on this road trip for four days and counting. It has been a rather strange trip, I ponder. Me and Selma were barely acquaintances, and now we are tied to each other for survival. I only hope there are no serious issues today, as earlier this morning, I woke up next to Selma, and that, in anyone's book, is an awesome way to start the day.

I scan the station to and fro. Finally, I spy Aaron in the crowd and casually guide Selma toward his direction. Selma has done a good job with the request I gave her this morning. She is wearing her hair up and sporting some really thick sunglasses in a vain attempt to somewhat conceal her identity. As for me, I am wearing a cheap Gilligan-style hat to cover my hair and lose some cool points. I am not sure if my attempt is better than Selma's, but any deception is better than none.

Aaron stares at us for a second, not sure if he wants to acknowledge that he knows these two silly-looking folks in front of him or not, but reaches out his hand for a firm handshake that passes the tickets in one direction and keys to the Escape in the other. Phase one is complete, and I never say a word to Aaron, only head nod as an acknowledgement of a greeting and a silent thanks for everything. We casually walk away, heading to platform 7B to await the next train headed to New York City.

Roberto and his old gang members are staring at every couple that walks past them.

They've got to be here somewhere, but where? Every white male and white female couple looks all the same to me. How am I supposed to pick out guy I was hired to take out? And what about the lone-wolf gringo. Where is he? Roberto's thoughts are getting the better of him.

Aaron gets a morning paper and a bagel sandwich. He is hungry, and it is the perfect disguise. *Unless I was in New York City, then it would have to be a lox and cream cheese bagel, otherwise, I'm happy with this overpriced buttered poppy seed bagel.* Aaron is still watching Jim and Selma, but he is also searching for anyone who is watching for Jim and Selma. So far, no one seems to look out of the ordinary, but it is still early in the morning. *Roberto or his gang of friends is bound to show up sometime today to crash the party.*

We produce our train tickets and board the train. We head to our cabin located in car Number 4. It is rather quaint accommodations, but it will suffice until we reach our destination. I have never traveled via Amtrak, but I am sure it will be fun and relaxing.

161

Selma, on the other hand, hopes she has time to finish assembling the device. *As long as Jim doesn't distract me too much*, she thinks, and then lets out a silent chuckle.

Roberto and his team keep scouring the crowd looking for Jim and Selma. He knows they are here somewhere, and, if they escape, Hector will not be pleased. The train is about to depart while Roberto is frantically walking up and down the platform.

As the train blows its final whistle and starts to move, he thinks he sees Selma, or at least a woman that looks like the Selma he remembered from the club months ago. She was laughing and joking at Hector's table, telling him how much money he and his organization would make on their return on their investment. Roberto specifically remembers Selma's amazing green eyes, and he swears he just saw those eyes on a woman with an ordinary-looking man in one of the cabins halfway down the train. He isn't sure if it was them, but he has to make a choice soon. Then, he sees those eyes and her face, and though can't see the eyes directly, the face looks like the one that had smiled at him earlier this year.

"That's got to be her. I know it," Roberto mumbles to himself, still gazing at the train as it starts to move.

Selma brings out her laptop to start working while Jim begins to situate everything in their private cabin. She pauses as the computer is booting up and causally glances out the window, removing her sunglasses and putting them away. She studies the faces on the platform as the train slowly moves and jolts when she sees a familiar face.

No, it can't be. That's...that's Roberto's face. I would recognize it anywhere.

She immediately elbows Jim and begs for the phone to notify Aaron.

Aaron walks about the train station platform trying to find the man that Selma previously described over dinner the other night. *It should be easy looking for a gunman in this crowd*, he thinks as he stares at every person who walks by that gives him a second look. Nobody has that suspicious and nervous look about them.

The train's departing, and I should be going. Gotta get rid of the Escape. He is glad he remembered to get the keys from Jim.

Aaron almost trips over his own shoelace and walks over to a bench to tie it. At the same time, his phone starts ringing.

Oops, I forgot to change the ringtone and lower the volume. Wow, that's really loud. He had bought these PAYG phones yesterday and hadn't had time to reset all the settings. Everyone around him can hear it ringing as he desperately tries to answer it. A man standing nearby and staring at the departing train turns his head toward his direction as Aaron is trying to answer the phone and, at the same time, attempt to tie his shoelace.

Aaron picks up the phone call on the third ring as the train leaves the platform. As he answers, a bullet is fired toward him. He immediately drops the phone and ducks for cover.

Selma only hears the sound of a gun being fired and then the sound of static as the phone on the other end is dropped.

Oh my God, is Aaron alive? she thinks.

Roberto's immediate thought is that the other guy, the one whose phone is ringing really loud and really annoyingly, must be the second male. This one is bent over trying to tie his shoelace, and Roberto rushes to withdraw his gun as the adrenaline starts flowing. He fires a shot, but he aims too high. He fires a second shot, and the male goes down like a sack of potatoes ripped open. Direct hit. Points scored.

The crowds of people around him are screaming, and hysteria grows louder as people panic, running for their lives. Which is why Roberto never sees the bullet fired or knows that the return fire from Aaron's drawn gun hit him until the pain in his chest grows worse. Roberto looks down and sees the blood spurting from his chest. That is the last thing he sees before he crumbles to the ground dead. He never got his bonus, but he will never have to worry about what Hector thinks of him. Ever.

Chapter 17

"Aaron, are you still there?" Selma screams into her cheap PAYG phone, hoping and waiting for a reply.

The train departs the station on its way to New York City.

"He's dead. Aaron's dead. I know it." She starts to cry.

"We don't know that, Selma. Aaron's a tough guy. He'll be all right, just wait and see." I am so lying my ass off to her.

"*What* do ya mean? I heard the gunshots loud and clear, and then the phone drops out, the line goes dead. Oh my gosh, I'm so sorry, Jim. He was your best friend." She cries even louder.

I am starting to get annoyed by the falsehood Selma is spewing out. "He ain't dead, stop saying that. Don't you have that device to build?"

Tears run down her cheeks. "I am soooo sorry, Jim."

"I can't take any more of this. I'm leaving for a while. I'll be back…eventually."

I get up and storm out of the cabin, heading to front of the train, most likely where the bar is located.

Selma wipes away the tears as the cabin door slams shut. It wasn't her intention to make Jim upset, but now he seems pretty pissed. *He must be in denial, and I should leave him be for the moment.*

She turns toward the window and stares out, looking at the rows of corn passing by. Field after field of corn. *All that corn. I really can't think straight right now, but I've got to get to work on that damn device. Aaron is dead. I know it, I can feel it, and I am starting to believe it. Why isn't Jim crying or showing any emotion over his friend? Doesn't he care about Aaron? I thought they were close friends and army buddies? Why isn't Jim upset?*

The more she thinks about it, the more she starts to cry.

Jim finds the car that houses the bar on this train. Without saying anything else, he blurts out to the bartender, "Maker's Mark, double straight."

The bartender clearly knows this type of customer. No other words need to be spoken; rather, a simple nod will suffice. He pours more than is required, as clearly this is not the time to measure exact pours. He pushes the glass in front of Jim and only responds, "What cabin number so I can start a running tab?" Again, times like these require only minimal words.

"147. Phil Banks," Jim responds without even looking up.

"Not a problem, sir." The bartender is already pouring another double as Jim finishes the first and slams the glass on the bar.

I have seen this type all too often, the bartender thinks. *Either his girlfriend dumped him, or it's a death in the family. Either way, I hope he remembers to throw a couple of bucks in the tip jar.*

"What's up, sir, if I may ask?"

Jim reaches for the second glass in front of him. "You'd rather not know."

"No problem."

"Just charge it to the room."

Jim takes the second glass and goes to sit at a table that is currently unoccupied.

Moments later, Selma walks into the bar car. She sees Jim staring out the window and decides to proceed to the bar. She asks the bartender for a gin and tonic, make it strong, and charge it to cabin Number 147 under Susan Banks. The bartender laughs to himself, as this could be the showdown between these two people.

She takes her drink and hesitantly goes and sits across from Jim. He never flinches. She takes a sip.

Finally breaking the silence, Selma asks, "Look at me, Jim."

I hesitate, but then slowly turn my head toward her. I take a deep sigh and another sip from the glass before asking, "What do you want?"

"I want you to tell me what you're feeling."

"I am feeling nothing."

"What can I do to help you?"

"Absolutely nothing."

"Jim, I'm here for you. Can't you understand that?"

"Selma. You are smart, funny, beautiful, blah, blah, blah, but right now, I need some serious alone time."

Selma's shocked facial expression tells all. "Jim...Jim..." She is at a loss for words.

I only glance at her before taking a large gulp from my glass. I want to say something, but my eyes can't quite meet hers. My eyes show no emotion, and I go back to staring out the window.

"Jim, I'm leaving now and going to bed. Come back to the cabin when you need to. Good night." She then kisses me on the top of the head and walks away.

I only close my eyes for a moment and then open them to find Selma gone. I take a last sip from the glass and silently say a toast to Aaron, a salute in his honor.

After a while, I get up and head toward our cabin. I don't even know what I can say to her right at the moment. Perhaps she is already asleep. I can only be so lucky. Too bad Aaron wasn't so lucky. *Sigh*.

The train rolls on toward Cleveland.

"What…where the hell am I?" Aaron awakes, unaware as to what his current location is at the moment.

He slowly opens his eyes and sees nothing but white. Upon closer inspection, he first sees the tubes connected to his arm, followed by the white sheets. Everything else also looks like a hospital room.

I remember now. That bastard Roberto shot me, above all, when I was bending over to tie my shoelace. Go figure. Well, it saved my life. Thank you, unraveling shoelace. I responded in kind by putting the first return volley straight into his chest. Too bad that he got a lucky shot and plucked me in the left shoulder. Imagine if I was standing up versus hunched over. The bullet would probably be taking residence in my heart or chest or a major organ. Thanks again, Mr. Shoelace. OK, what do I need to do to get out of this place?

Aaron scans the surroundings and makes a mental note of what is going on with him in the hospital room.

OK, I have a heart monitor and drip bag. Mostly likely attached to an alarm if disconnected from me. Must disconnect both of them. I sure as hell hope there is no guard outside my door. I did, after all, kill a man, even if that man, Roberto or whatever the hell was the bastard's name, shot me first. I know,

I know, tell it to the judge. Must escape first, then worry about other stuff second. I am disconnecting the drip cord right now. This is really gonna fucking hurt like hell.

Saline squirts all over the bed and floor.

Down the hall at the nurses' station, the alarm goes off.

"Oh shit, what's going on right now?" the nurse on the midnight shift asks. *This is supposed to be the easy shift, and all I have to do is just check every half hour to make sure patients are still alive, or at least breathing.*

Where is that police officer, Bob, with the horrible seventies mustache that keeps asking for extra cream for his coffee? "Proper cream, and not the fake stuff," he keeps repeating. I better go check, as he's supposed to be stationed outside the blond-haired guy's room. He most likely went for a smoke break or another cup of coffee. I ain't giving him any more cream. Or sugar, for that matter. She snickers at her own joke.

The nurse gets up and quickly walks toward the room with the alarm. She enters the room, slightly out of breath from being slightly out of shape, and sees the tubes disconnected and saline all over the place. She looks around but sees no patient at all.

Where did he go? I ain't cleaning that mess up. They must need it for evidence, and the dayshift can do it. She resets the alarm but knows there will be a lot of questions asked in the morning.

Aaron rips the tubes from his arm. The alarms start buzzing away. He grabs the clothes that are sitting in a pile on the chair. *No time to change. I've got to escape immediately.*

169

As the nurse starts frantically heading toward his room, he has no time to run, so he hides behind the door. When the nurse opens it and steps in, Aaron bolts behind her while she is staring into the empty room. *This is all too easy, just like in the movies.*

Aaron heads straight for the stairs and is out the doors even before another alarm, a much louder one, starts to blast like a Klaxon horn in the background. He starts to pick up the pace and goes into a full run, while getting dressed, and escapes into the night.

Aaron doesn't even have a cell phone to call anyone. *Hell, I don't even know where I'm at or what street I'm on. What was the name of the hospital I was at? Come on, man, remember something.*

He finally stops running and downgrades it to a slow trot. A car approaches him. *Is it the police looking for me, an escaped fugitive on the run? Could it be one of Hector's henchmen looking to extract vengeance for killing one of their own? Or could it be someone who lives in this neighborhood returning home for the evening?*

Aaron can't take a chance, as two of the three scenarios promise to have a bad ending. He isn't playing the odds tonight and starts to cross the road to run down a side street. The vehicle doesn't follow him, so he is safe for the time being. *Boy, to be without a mobile phone of all times, not to mention no money and no gun. I am a man with no identity walking the streets of Chicago on a brisk Thursday evening. At least it isn't raining.* Aaron looks up to the heavens to make sure he didn't just jinx himself.

I wake up on the sofa in the cabin with a wool blanket covering me and a flat pillow moderately supporting my aching head, which is pounding away. At least I didn't wake up still holding the bar glass. I start, or rather poorly attempt, to speak, but the morning cottonmouth makes it difficult to formulate words. My vision is less hazy as I start to look around for Selma.

She is not present, or at the very least, I cannot see her. I call her name and get no response, but then I hear water running. It takes a few minutes for my brain to engage, but I accept she must be taking a shower. It's too bad because I really need to drain my bladder. Talk about bad timing to be hogging the bathroom, Selma. I try to lie back down to wait it out and to ease the pressure on the bladder, but sooner or later, the bladder will prevail.

Selma steps out of the bathroom wearing just a towel, and her wet hair only adds to the amazing view for the early morning. She blushes when she sees me with my mouth open and staring and retreats to her feminine innocence.

"Oh sorry, I thought you were still asleep, and I didn't bring any clean clothes with me into the bathroom." She is still red in the face, and the water is turning to steam on her body. She will be dry in no time.

"That's quite all right. Sorry." Now I am the one who feels foolish for being caught gazing at her. Was she just going to get dressed in front of me while I slept? That is too much to handle at the moment, so I ask to be excused and rush past her and into the bathroom. In this very moment, only the call of nature surpasses the other call of the wild.

Once I am finished, I call out, "Is it ok? Are you dressed?"

"Hold on, give me one more minute," is the response returned I get through the bathroom door.

I patiently wait in the bathroom, wondering if I hadn't asked and just exited the bathroom how things might have played out. But my stomach growls and aches, and it distracts me from pursuing any more thoughts about the previous matter.

"How 'bout now?"

"OK."

I open the door and then triumphantly step out of the bathroom. Selma is sitting on the couch with her computer running the startup program. She tilts her head up for a second only to say good morning and goes back to doing whatever she is doing. I return the greeting and decide that Selma is in work mode and it is best not to disturb her. I announce that I am going to take a shower and will remember to bring a change of clothes with me. Selma murmurs a slight acknowledgement. I stare at her one more time and turn around toward the shower and a hope of a cleaner self. I close the door and start the water.

Selma only smiles and lets out a giggle for a second while glancing at the bathroom door with the knowledge that teasing Jim proved to be a success. Now the fun is over, and it is back to work for her on some serious programming. She begins typing somewhere near the five hundred-thousandth line of computer code.

After the refreshing shower, I think for one moment that maybe I should walk out of the bathroom wearing only a towel to surprise her, but she may freak out and scream. Maybe that's a bad decision, so I decide to play it safe this time. I am now showered, dressed, and ready to grab a bite to eat. I open the door to find Selma with a cart of room service and vigorously typing away on the computer. At least she thought to order for the both of us, I hope. It looks like there is enough food for two people, but traveling with her over the last few days, I should probably ask and not assume. I've seen Selma's breakfast eating habits.

As I am lost in thought, I notice Selma looking right through me and wearing an odd grin on her face.

"I ordered breakfast for the both of us. Thought you might be hungry."

Thank you, Lord, she is a godsend. "I hope you left me some bacon."

"It was tempting to eat it all, but I spared you a piece or two." She takes a bite from a strawberry and continues. "Though if you took any longer in the shower, I would have eaten it all!"

I crack a smile. "Then I better dig in before there's nothing left."

"Good timing, as I am on my break." She hands me a strawberry to start with and a glass of freshly squeezed OJ.

Chapter 18

Sitting on a park bench hurts after about an hour. Sleeping on a park bench and staying on one side because the other is recovering from a bullet wound hurts beyond belief. That is how Aaron feels on the fresh Friday morning in a random Chicago park. *Well, nobody bothered me, and nobody stole my shoes and I have no wallet to take, so everything is all right.*

He sits up and stretches out, feeling the tightness in the side that was closest to the bench. He will file a complaint with the mayor of Chicago when he has a moment about the awful benches in this fair town, as they are not comfortable to sleep on.

A mother and her baby are close by, as apparent by the proximity of the kid's rather loud wails and screams for such an early time of the morning. The mother has not spotted Aaron yet, but she may decide to change direction in a hurry once his presence is known. He might as well act friendly and use some cowboy charm versus scaring her by appearing like a stalker or serial killer.

"Good morning, ma'am. Can I trouble you for a moment?"

The woman is startled and starts to freak out, but a second look at Aaron and she is hedging her bets on her safety.

"Good morning. My, my, you appear to have had a rough night." She is still checking him out and decides he is safe, for the moment.

"Yeah, you don't know the half of it." Aaron smiles at her while he tightening his chest and arm muscles. "But definitely a rough night for starters."

"Then why don't you share your story, as I have all day. I could use someone interesting to talk with!" She smiles back at him.

Aaron tells her of how he and his buddies were out celebrating somebody's birthday. As it happens, he might have drunk too much, but he is quick to point out the worse state of the other guys. Aaron rattles off more bullshit, and the woman is just eating it up. He mentions a bar fight, running from the police, and the fact that, at some point in the evening, a knife was brandished in his face. He is almost confusing himself as he makes up the imaginary night of debauchery and mayhem. She loves every detail as opposed to her otherwise mundane life of mothering and daytime TV.

The woman seems intrigued, given Aaron is more interesting to look at than a wailing kid. "So, you got a name?"

"Why, it's Aaron, and what's yours, pretty gal?"

She blushes. "Karen."

"Then howdy, Miss Karen. Listen, I need a favor to ask of you."

"Sure, Aaron, what do ya need?" She looks him up and down one more time.

"My buddies thought it would be funny to leave me here passed out and take my wallet, keys, and cell phone. Luckily, they left my clothes, but I'm not from around these parts. I need to make a phone call to get me back to where I should be. Do you have a phone I can borrow? I would be so much in your debt, Karen." He winks at her at the last part.

Karen is hooked like a trout caught by fly fisherman in a small creek somewhere in Montana. She produces a phone out of nowhere and slowly slides it to Aaron, making sure she pauses momentarily as she brushes over his strong right hand.

We are laughing away, enjoying the breakfast and each other's company. It is good to just be ourselves and not worry about life's problems, mortgage bills, or the depressing five o'clock breaking news. We are just Jim and Selma, a man and a woman taking the train to The Big Apple, where we hope to receive a payout of $5 million so we can flee the country and live out our lives together. This always makes great tableside chatter, but then I glance down, not at Selma's legs, but at the phone that is buzzing away next to us. That's odd, as these phones were only activated the other day, and nobody knows this phone number except one other person.

"Selma, hand me the phone. Quick."

Aaron is still smooth-talking Karen when he finally gets her phone. She makes a joke about no long-distance calls, but he is welcome to put his number in her contacts. He produces a smile that melts Karen upon seeing it. *Wow, I wonder what her homelife is like? Then again, maybe some things I don't want to ever know about.*

Aaron punches in a phone number he activated two days ago. It is easy to remember because it is one digit off from his. *Come on, Jimbo, answer the phone, damn it. Answer it.*

I flip the phone and hit the Answer button. "Hello, who is this?"

"Who in the hell would be calling you, Jimbo?"

"It—it c-c-c-an't be. Y-y-you're s-s-s-upposed to b-b-be *dead*," I stutter.

Selma puts her hands over her mouth.

"I ain't dead, or else I'm borrowing an angel's phone."

"What…anyways, what the hell happened? We thought you were shot…died on the platform."

"I am alive and would love to discuss my funeral arrangements, but I could really use your help. Pronto."

"Aaron…I…we…are sooo relieved. You're alive. What do you need us to do?"

"I could use some cash."

"Selma, wire some cash to a Western Union."

Selma gets on it. "Aaron, where are you?" I ask.

"Karen, sweetie, where are we?"

"Uh…Chicago?" I hear a woman's voice in the background

I blurt out right away, "Buddy, whose Karen?" questioning who Aaron's new friend is.

"Man, don't go there."

Aaron finally pinpoints the approximate location and relays it to me. I pass it to Selma, and she informs us there is a Western Union about five blocks away from his location in the park. Aaron asks Karen where the liquor store that Selma told him about is, and she is all too happy to drive him over there.

I ask Aaron, "Is five hundred bucks enough to cover you for the time being?"

"Better make it a grand."

"Consider it done."

"On my way to pick it up. Thanks, Jim, I owe you one. Will call you back in two hours."

"No problem, bro, no problem."

Hanging up the phone, I glance over at Selma, who looks so reassured she could cry. I wonder sometimes if she would shed tears for me.

Selma finishes up with breakfast and refocuses back on her main task at hand. Her attention is diverted over thoughts about Jim.

OK, it is time to get serious on finishing this device so we can be done with any more association with Hector. We can collect our money and be outta here. Oh my gosh, this is the first time I've thought we. Am I really growing closer to Jim? I know that he likes me and I like him, but this is so complicated, and, with all that's going on, it's definitely not the best time to start a serious relationship.

We are both in this together, but am I falling for the idea of the relationship, or am I falling in love with this guy because we have been stuck together for the last seven days? Or am I just happy with him and should be content with that? Is this what a relationship is supposed to be like? Wait, wait a minute, why am I thinking about us? I really should be concentrating on this device. Must get this done. No distractions. No worrying about relationship status. No serious flirting with Jim. OK, maybe some innocent flirting and a lot more teasing. OK. Back to work. Build it and build it now.

I put the dirty clothes in some plastic bags along with Selma's to be laundered and returned later today. It is a good thing, as I am down to my last clean shirt. After that, well, I wouldn't be very attractive or smell nice, to say the least. And the permeating odor of dirty used socks fermenting the entire cabin is not the way to attract Selma either. I am trying very hard not to distract her, as she is busy and in work mode, aka, do not disturb.

I believe what she is doing is important yet dangerous because people have been killed over this device already. She really wants to forget it all and run away with me. How does one react when one hardly knows the other person that they are supposed to run away with and are associated with only because they both experienced an adventure together? I mean, Selma is a great gal, the best thing to happen to me since I met Rachel. I try not to think of Rachel anymore. It just goes back to unanswered questions and the missing-person case that will never be solved. Selma entered and became a part of my life in the last week, and I should be happy that we are fostering a relationship, if that's what you call it these days. Besides, where would I ever find another woman like her? Church? The workplace? The bar scene?

A woman like this doesn't come around very often, at least, not in my life. I should just accept her and all her faults: intelligent, sexiness, and sassiness. Yeah, so many faults, how can I possibly tolerate her any given day? Why would anyone be with such a woman? She probably even makes more money than me. So what? After this job payout, we will be set up for life. That is, if there is a *we* after this is all said and done. On top of it, she does own a gun. What more could a man want in a woman?

Selma looks up for an instant to see me looking at her, flashes a smile, and goes back to assembling the device. She must feel me thinking about her. I hope my staring at her is not creeping her out. I should leave her alone for the time being and let her finish in peace and quiet. I start to ask if she needs any help but then stop because, clearly, I already know the answer to that one and would just look more foolish than I already do. Maybe I should ask something else, like if she needs anything.

"Do you want something to drink, a bottled water or juice or something?"

"Yes, Jim, a bottled water would be great."

I see a twinkle in her eyes, even if it is only about water. Maybe she is really parched. At least I feel I am being supportive and earning my keep. Gosh, she is hammering away on the keyboard. She obviously knows what she is doing, and her expert programming skills are quite evident.

"I'm going to get you one. Be right back."

Translation: "I should take my time to leave you alone to work without distractions."

"OK, thanks. Don't be gone long."

Translation: "Take your time because I really can't be interrupted at this crucial moment."

I feel for a second as though she really means it. Nah, it is all in my head. I turn to leave the cabin, trying not to slam the door on the way out.

Finally.

Selma lets out a big sigh in relief. *Now it's the final assembly. There's no turning back. First, I have to connect this wire to the motherboard, and that should enable the antenna to work on this device.*

Selma flips the computer back around and tries to boot it up again. She starts the program, and the diagnostic test shows a pass on the antenna with a range of approximately two thousand to three thousand feet. *Not bad. So far, so good.*

She toys with the hard plastic container that houses the Russian military-grade computer chips. *Wait till I install these puppies. Then this whole thing will be humming. So how am I going to do this demonstration on Saturday? I need an access portal to a financial institution.*

Recalling some of the potential meeting locations, Selma does a radius search of the nearest financial portal. In this case, it appears to be a Chase ATM at a bank building about two blocks away. *Perfect. I should be able to hack that system and show the feasibility of how it will work. Hector and his potential buyer will be pleased. They will see that it really works.*

Selma checks to ensure Jim is not around. *OK, girl, this is the most important programming, so don't screw it up. It has to work, and the tiny microchip can't be detectable to even Hector's computer geeks. Jim will be so proud of me that this extra piece will render the device inoperable and fry it in twenty-four hours once it's activated. And the beauty of it is that it's unstoppable. The hackers or whoever is poking around won't be able to shut it off, and Hector will watch his dreams fade away as the program and the motherboard on the device destroy themselves.*

Selma then encrypts the only other copy of the code and uploads it in three separate parts to the cloud disguised as an image that to most people would look like gibberish. *I'm doing it for Jim, as Hector was never going to use my device for the furtherance of society but only to immensely profit off of it. Sorry, Hector. Jim has won my heart and my talent, and now it's time to prove it to him.*

She brings up the hidden program called Tequila that she has been working on for quite some time and piggybacks it on the device's main program in the 478,147th line of code. *By the time they figure it out, the program will be initiated, and there will be no turning back. Brilliant, Selma. Absolutely brilliant. If you ever thought badly of me, Jim, for what I told you about my device, I hope this makes up for all of it. I want Jim and I to look forward to the future together that we will make. OK. OK. Focus on the task at hand.*

I'm ready to install the first computer chip. Time to be serious. No more thoughts of Jim, though it's tough not to think about him these days. Especially when he's walking through the door and carrying my water bottle and an energy bar. How thoughtful! Thank you, Jim. You just made my day.

"OK, Jim, I appreciate that, but I still need to be alone, as this is a critical time."

"*No problemo,* Selma. I will continue to meander up and down the train. Good luck. Make us proud. I'm going to the engine room and try to get the conductor to blow the whistle, ha!"

The door shuts.

The first chip is installed. Let's see what happens now.
The computer screen flashes and boots up immediately. So far, so good. Here goes test número uno. Let the games begin.

Selma hits the Enter key, and the screen lights up in a beautiful pattern of computer code, *Matrix* style. Well, close enough.

OMG, what is happening on the screen? I didn't expect this to occur so soon. Hector will be pleased to see this.

Selma types a few more lines, and then the computer moves at a faster rate than expected. First, she scans all the networks currently operating on the train. *OK, forty-seven different ones.*

Now she tries to isolate the secured ones, which narrows it down to thirty-two.

Hmm, who is idly surfing the 'net, and who is doing something interesting, like checking a secured e-mail or a secured bank account? Aha, I have two lucky people checking a secured financial account. Let's start with the IP address 125.010.090.117 and see what happens.

Selma makes a few more keystrokes and then lets the device and program do its magic. *Excellent. I'm hacked into their account*, she thinks as the financial information mirrors on her computer screen. She looks at the portfolio and makes a transfer to a bogus offshore account she had set up earlier. *Transfer of $9,949.00, and they will hardly miss it.*

The computer screen reads: *TRANSFER COMPLETE*

Selma stops for a second to see if she can hear an "Oh shit!" from down the hall or somewhere in this car. Surprisingly, she hears none and proceeds with the test.

She quickly logs into the secret account and sees that the balance has increased by $9,949.00. *Well, that was easy. Let's see what the other person is checking on.*

She shuts down the account that she just hacked into and attempts to penetrate the second one. Just as she starts the same procedure and entry into the second account, she stops and pauses to reflect.

Why am I testing on random people's accounts? I should go for a bigger prize and see what else I can do. Besides, I should be trying to hack the NYSE, as that is what I was really paid to do. Hmm, but I'm too far from one of their relay servers. I should have some fun and see if I can hack one of Hector's accounts.

Selma looks through her notebook to find the page that contains Hector's information just in case he decided she wasn't smart enough to program the device on her own. She is going to prove it to him by withdrawing $100,000.00 from his offshore accounts to get his attention. *Better yet*, she thinks, *I should delay the transfer until Saturday at midnight just for laughs.*

183

Too bad I don't have that bitch Rachel's account number, or else I would take a withdraw from one of her accounts as well in honor of Jim. Call it a payback gift to him. All right, here we go. Let's see if I can set up the delay and the transfer out of one of Hector's accounts.

Selma increases the range on the antenna to maximum, as she needs to ping a tower long enough to make the transfer. The antenna picks up a relay tower from the nearby city of Pittsburgh, Pennsylvania.

Perfect. I have sixty-three seconds to break into his account, set up a transfer to the offshore account, and have it delayed for Saturday at 11:59 p.m. I pray he or someone doesn't check his accounts, especially the transfer section, every day. OK, here we go.

She boosts the antenna range and initiates the program. The Russian chips kick in, and she types away as fast as she can. At forty-five seconds, she is finally through to one of Hector's Grand Cayman accounts, and after fifty-nine seconds, she hits confirm for a transfer of $100,000.00 to be transferred at 11:59 p.m. on Saturday. She logs out of the account and shuts down the computer, as it is starting to overheat. *Damn those Russian chips; they never could develop a proper cooling system.* She puts the computer and her notes away just as there is a knock on the door. As she closes the bag, she sees the grenade in the bag. *Well, there is my insurance policy.*

She hears his voice. "Selma, it's Jim. Can I come in, or do you need more time?"

"Come on in. I can't wait to see you." Selma is beaming and super excited; she can hardly contain herself.

Jim opens the door and sees her sitting on the couch with everything shut down and neatly put away. *Though I appear suspicious and guilty of something, or maybe I feel that way as I unwind from working too hard. Either way, I can't stop smiling away at Jim, who looks so confused at me.*

He asks, "So how did the test go? Does it work to your liking?"

"Test went awesome. Say, I'm getting cabin fever. I need to get out of here. Let's celebrate. Where is that bar car again?" She takes Jim's hand, wanting him to lead her to the bar.

We exit the cabin and walk down the hall. I tell her it isn't that far, only two more cars to walk through. I start to tell her a funny story about when I was walking around and heard this guy yell out, "Oh shit!" or something like that. He sounded really pissed, and I just scooted on past his cabin in a hurry. I didn't want to feel the wrath from the man behind the door.

Selma just laughs and laughs like I am a comedian or the funniest guy she has ever met. It makes being with her all the better.

Aaron collects his $1,000 from the Western Union window at the back of the liquor store. The temptation to buy a bottle of bourbon is pressing in his mind, but he needs to get out as fast as possible and somehow get to New York City in less than two days. The Western Union clerk looks at him apprehensively, but everything matches up, including the very detailed description of the person who is collecting the money without an ID.

"Do you want small or large bills?" the clerk asks Aaron.

"A mix of twenties and fifties will suffice," he replies.

The clerk deals with people like this all the time, so it isn't really a concern whom he pays the money to. *I'm just doing what the instructions said,* the clerk thinks silently to himself

185

and counts out the money into Aaron's hands. Aaron nods his head to the clerk and wishes him a nice day. He leaves the store, bypassing the enormous bourbon selection, as tempting as it is to spend some of this newfound wealth.

Karen is surprisingly still waiting for him outside. She lifts her head from her cellphone and asks Aaron where he is heading next.

"I really need to get my car, wallet, and cell phone back. Do you mind giving me a lift to the train station, hon? I can give you gas money if it's out of your way." Aaron knows that Karen seems to melt every time he calls her *hon* with that cowboy accent.

She bats her eyes. "I can do that for *you!*"

He only has to appease her for a just a little longer, and then he knows he will have made her day while he will be off on his merry way.

Karen's minivan turns right out of the liquor store parking lot and heads for the train station downtown. Aaron is already planning his next move. Twenty minutes later, the minivan pulls up to the temporary parking in front of the train station. Karen puts the vehicle in park but leaves the engine running. There is an air of awkwardness, as neither party knows what the social graces book dictates the next move to be. Aaron is itching to bolt and run, whereas Karen would not mind the moment to last a wee bit longer. Finally, the tension is broken by her son waking up and crying, possibly because it's feeding time. Karen lets out a disappointed sigh, as her fantasy adventure for today is about to end. Aaron tips his hat to her and extends his hand. Karen's hand slowly progresses toward his until they meet.

Upon her hand touching Aaron's strong masculine one, she can also feel a piece of paper. Is it his phone number? She opens her eyes and slowly moves them from his eyes toward her hand, where she spies only a folded up $50 bill. Aaron senses the disappointment in her and starts to ask if she needs more gas money. Karen lets go of his hand and just waves, signaling the $50 bill is fine for reimbursement.

Aaron throws a wink at her as he tips his hand toward her. "Thank you, Karen. I won't forget you."

The minivan door slams shut, and off he goes toward the station.

Karen pauses until another car starts beeping its horn, ready to take her spot. She looks back at her son and starts forward, driving off toward home. "At least today was interesting, and I did make fifty bucks," she says to herself and wonders what tomorrow might bring.

Aaron is finally free of the woman he has wasted too much time on today. He walks over to his vehicle where he parked it the other day. He retrieves the hidden spare key under the back wheel well and opens the car door. Using the key, he unlocks the glove box and gets his wallet, emergency set of keys, and, more importantly, his backup phone. Relaxing in the familiarity of his vehicle, Aaron sits back, puts the $950.00 in his wallet, and adds the spare key to his key ring. He is still holding the phone and stares at it for another five minutes before he finally opens it and makes the call.

"Yeah, this is Aaron," he says when the call is answered.

The person on the other end does not seem bothered or surprised to hear from him. "Why are you calling?"

"I want to see you tonight."

"Fine. Maybe we should catch up on events and such. You've been out of contact for quite some time." The caller hangs up.

Aaron puts the phone down and starts the engine. He knows what he needs to do next and drives off, heading toward downtown.

Hector sits in his office. The bar is doing rather well this week, and other business is picking up slowly. He hates to leave the club to his bar manager to run in his absence. The new singers and dancers and the new house band have proven to be decent returns on investment. He continues to look at the other financial books, often wondering if anyone working for him is skimming off his profits, when the phone rings.

Hector picks up the phone to immediately hear the voice of a woman screaming, "What, you weren't going to call me?"

"No, Rachel, I've been busy. I do have a business to run down here."

"You mean that front to launder your drug money? Oh yes, how soon I forget."

Hector hears her laughter after she finishes her last sentence but ignores her glib remark and instead refills his glass. After a long pause by both parties, Rachel starts up again.

"So are you ready for our little trip? Are you still flying out to New York City on Saturday morning? Will you be sending a car for me?"

"I have an early flight on Saturday. Yeah, I'll come get you eventually, but I have to acquire the hardware for the meeting first. Then we'll swing by the bank to fill the briefcase. How many buyers have you lined up, by the way?"

Rachel gets a little more serious. "Don't worry about the buyers. I still have three very interested and two more to contact. Leave this to me, and I'll have them in a bidding war

188

well into next week. Are you sure your smart gal will have the device ready?"

"Spoke to her earlier today. She is in the testing phase, and everything is working like a charm."

"All I'll say is that it better work like she said. We're betting everything on this. I can't believe you talked me into this, but here's hoping. Where's my cousin and my ex-husband right now? More importantly, where is your guy Roberto?"

Hector pauses for a moment to take a drink. "She's traveling toward New York City. Should be there tonight. Roberto hasn't called me back, but he operates like that sometimes. He should have taken care of your ex, in case you were wondering."

"He better have. We don't need Jim in this anymore. Can you call Roberto one more time?"

"Sure, for you, I will. But he probably won't answer."

"We can't leave anything to chance on Saturday, can we?"

"Absolutely not, dear."

Click.

Hector calls his bar manager to the office. He shows up faster than expected. *At least he shows some respect.* Hector lays out the instructions for the weekend and expects no trouble over the next few days in his absence.

The bar manager gives every kind of reassurance and will call if there are any problems. But there won't be, he keeps repeating to Hector. Hector seems satisfied that he is entrusting the right man with the job. He passes a stuffed envelope to the bar manager, and the bar manager acknowledges it accordingly. Hector dismisses him and asks him to get the girl who auditioned earlier, Sandy, in here right away. The man hurries to track down the girl Hector wants to see.

Meanwhile, Hector places a call to Roberto, but the phone just rings and rings.

Chapter 19

Aaron is wandering around the downtown streets of Chicago. He tries to blend in like any other person he passes, local or tourist. He finally finds the building he has been looking for after an encounter with an amazing street vendor who sold him a tasty Chicago-style hot dog. One can never argue with authenticity, especially from a street-food vendor. Life is good sometimes.

Aaron walks into the public library and goes to the second floor where the computer lab is located. He signs in and gets computer Number 12 for free for a half hour and $3.00 an hour after that. He isn't going to be here longer than a few minutes at best. Aaron gets on the computer and clicks the OK button to consent to the standard computer lab agreement. He brings up Google and logs into one of his many Gmail accounts. This account is very special, as few people, apart from e-mail spammers, know it. He sees the message he has been waiting for and opens it. It reads:

Buckingham Fountain, 7:00 p.m. Wear something decent.

Well, OK, that was easy. Why didn't I just get told that earlier when I called? Everything has to be so complicated these days.

He looks at his watch. He has just enough time to drive to his apartment, shower, and change clothes. Aaron logs out of the Gmail account and the computer and proceeds to tell the receptionist he is all finished. He then goes to his vehicle and drives back to his apartment. On the way, he orders a taxicab for pickup at his apartment at 6:30 p.m. to take him to Chicago's favorite fountain.

Sitting in the train bar, Selma and I are having a great evening. I assume that any more drinks after the last round will either turn this night into something really great or something really awful and regretful in the morning. "Perhaps we should slow down on the drinks," I say in a fatherly tone.

Selma ignores me and yells out for two shots of Jack to be delivered to the table and some pretzels. I give up, resigned, and laugh.

"OK, we're supposed to arrive in a couple of hours. We can go back and take a nap, but what do we do when we arrive?" Selma asks with slightly hazy eyes.

"We can get a hotel room close to where we're supposed to go tomorrow afternoon for the meeting." I try to say it in a soft voice, but after a few drinks, there is no such thing as a soft voice.

"Yeah. Then we can go out and see what The Big Apple has to offer. Let's go downtown near Broadway. Come on, Jim, pleasssssseeee," Selma replies enthusiastically.

"Fine. Do you want to see a show? Go to dinner? See a band?"

"Oh, go on and surprise me, Jim. I dare ya!"

"You're lucky if you get a street hot dog. It's Friday night. It might be tough to get a restaurant reservation. How about a pizza instead?" I throw at her.

"Or a deli. I could go for an awesome Reuben sandwich, you know, from a proper New York deli. Come on, Jim, we've got to go for that. I don't need some fancy place. Come on, Jim! Reuben! Reuben!" She starts to chant it. I swear I hear others around us chime in for support.

"Fine. We'll go to a deli; er, get a Reuben sandwich; and just let The Big Apple direct us throughout the night. I'm sure we can find some dive bar in this town to have some more drinks and actually listen to a band."

"I love it. I love it, Jim."

"Me, too. Now, about that nap…"

"Pay the check, and let's go."

"Bartender, check please. Charge it to the Banks' cabin, and throw in a tip for yourself."

The taxi drops Aaron off right in front of the famed Buckingham fountain. *It really is an impressive fountain, especially when the lights are shown on the water.* Aaron stares at it for a few moments, as he is early for the 7:00 p.m. meeting. He reflects back that this has been a crazy week with Jim and Selma and the incident with Roberto. He then realizes he has not had a proper moment to himself. He is finally glad it is all about to come to a close by the end of the week.

Aaron is dressed to the nines in his usual cowboy regalia. He has the 5X cowboy hat, genuine black leather cowboy boots, and the enormous buckle, which he actually earned on the Professional Bull Riders circuit years ago, to finish off the outfit.

He is not surprised when he spots the men in black suits coming forward on his front left and front right on the other side of the fountain. He also knows that it means only one thing: that there are two additional men behind him.

He says to himself, *I hope they're enjoying the fountain view as much as I am.* He turns around, and there are the men, sporting dark sunglasses that match their solid-black suits and snakeskin boots.

"If you would like to come with us, Aaron, your guest is waiting," the man on the left utters.

"Do I have a choice?" he cracks as he walks with them toward the limo parked on the street. People around them make way, wondering if some celebrity is in the area.

Aaron casually walks up to the limo but feels the heavy hand of one of the bodyguards on his right shoulder.

"All due respect, can you hand over your piece? We'll keep it safe until the night is over."

Aaron sheepishly hands over the Glock .45mm in his shoulder holster to the bodyguard that is bigger than he is.

"Sorry, sir, but one more thing. Can you pass over your boot knife as well?" the bodyguard asks.

"You guys don't miss much, do ya?"

The other guard responds, "We're going to scan you now in case we did miss something. Just try not to make a scene, Aaron. Trust me, it's for your own good that you cooperate."

Aaron stands there nonchalantly as the guards pat him down thoroughly. They find a hidden Gerber knife and confiscate that, too. Satisfied that they have stripped him of any dangerous weapons, they open the door for him to climb in the limo.

"Well, hello, cowboy!" the female greets him with a sassy tone.

"Hello, Rachel, my dear. Good to see you as well, ma'am." He tips his hat toward her before removing it.

"I've missed you so much. You haven't called me in days, and I was starting to get worried that maybe Roberto's bullet finally found you."

"That's because I've been babysitting your ex-husband— or should I say, soon-to-be-dead ex-husband."

They share a laugh as one of the bodyguards passes him a champagne flute. Rachel and Aaron clink glasses and stare into

194

each other's eyes while the limo driver takes them to one of Chicago's famous upscale restaurant for a romantic dinner on this warm Chicago evening.

Chapter 20

In the nightclub, business is booming, as people are spending Mexican pesos and US dollars interchangeably for drinks and other things. Hector is ecstatic, though he much prefers the strong US dollars coming in from the US tourists versus the deflated pesos from the locals. *Money is money, though. It really doesn't matter what currency. It all will mix in with the drug money and get laundered the same way.*

The band is drawing in a strong crowd tonight, as the dancing girls add to the vibe for the pumped-up males in the club. Good, the guys drink more and buy more expensive drinks. This equals more of their money feeding their alcohol buzz and more spending. *Maybe I should hire more girls to entertain the crowd. It makes it so much easier to launder the money from the illegal businesses.* Hector watches from his private booth and thinks, *This is a great night. What could possibly change it?*

His assistant, the bar manager, knocks on the door, and one of the girls in the room gets up to answer it. The man enters the private suite, passes one of the girls, and quickly looks at the other two beautiful women sitting seductively on the sofa waiting for further instructions on what to do when Hector turns to the assistant. He is still gazing at the women when he passes some interesting news to Hector.

"*What* do you mean, he's dead?" Hector yells.

"I'm telling you, boss, that's what was passed along on the phone earlier. Roberto was shot dead in Chicago yesterday morning."

"And who told you this?" Hector demands.

"The guy—sorry, I can't remember his name—is from the Latin Counts gang. There was a shootout at the train station earlier in the day. One guy was shot in the shoulder, and another was killed. The guy that was shot escaped police custody and is currently wanted by CPD." The bar manager looks fearful that the boss man is going to shoot the messenger at this very moment.

"And they confirmed it, body and all?"

"I suppose so...I...don't really know. Sorry...boss."

"No, no, you're all right. There's someone else that's going to be really sorry though." Clearly, Hector is livid and aims to take it out on someone tonight.

The bar manager sees the writing on the wall and starts backtracking toward the door, sensing hatred and revenge in Hector's eyes. He makes a quick plea to scamper from the room. "Boss, if that's all, I'll go back downstairs to check on the bar. There's...uh...a possible fight brewing or something."

"Yes, yes, that's fine. Go." Hector is preoccupied with what has transpired. "Girls. Leave. Now."

The three girls get up and hurriedly exit the room faster than the bar manager did. They all know what happens when the boss gets angry and don't want to be around to feel the wrath.

Now that the room is clear of everyone, Hector begins to pace back and forth. He is furious that his best assassin is dead, Selma is most likely playing him, and old Jim is still alive. Who else is messing with him? What the hell is going on? He picks up the phone and immediately calls Selma.

Selma hears her phone ringing and decides not to answer it, given she is enjoying the most incredible Reuben sandwich

197

from Ben's NY Kosher Deli in Midtown Manhattan. "OMG, the sauce with the meat, it's pure heaven."

I couldn't agree more, as I am finishing my sandwich, along with the kosher dill pickle to wash it down. "You may be awesome at the programming stuff and all the techno-geek stuff, Selma, but I can still pick the best places to eat anywhere, even if this place doesn't require a tie or a reservation." I smirk at my own achievement with picking this place. Selma only signals in agreement with her head, as her mouth is full of kraut and pastrami.

It is time to switch to a serious tone after finishing the pickle and downing the last sip of Coke from the bottle. "So Selma, what's our plan for tomorrow? Is ole Hector really just gonna hand over the briefcase full of all that money?"

"I'm hoping so. I trust him. Why, should I not?" Selma has a piece of kraut hanging from her chin. I knock it off with a flick of the napkin.

"Suppose Hector has other motives, one being to take the device and shoot us, for instance."

"Hector wouldn't do that!" she exclaims.

"Five million dollars is a lot of money. I've seen people do strange things to others for far less."

"Hector wouldn't. He trusts me, and I trust him."

"He won't need to trust you when you're dead, dear."

"Do you really think he'll renege on the deal?"

"Without a doubt. Have you told him about the shootout in Chicago? Have you told him about us?"

Selma ponders that for a few minutes as she finishes her delicious sandwich. She finally retorts with, "What about us? What do you mean, Jim?"

My expression is probably a tell. "Well, do you think he should know the game is changing? Alliances have been forged?"

Selma smirks back. "Sorry, I was messin' with ya. No, I haven't told him about us, and it's none of his damn business. Moreover, I don't want to talk about Hector anymore tonight. I want to talk about you and...me." She smiles a gratifying smile at me. I look fuzzily at her, and then the bell strikes and I finally get the message, loud and clear.

"Why don't we leave here and go get a drink or two? What do you say? I can tell you all you want to know on the way." I stand up and clear the trash from dinner and gather it in a neat pile to be thrown away.

Selma stands up and joins arms with me as we depart the deli and hit the streets of Midtown Manhattan. She immediately bombards me straightaway with a series of questions about me. I am all too happy to talk about myself but am hesitant to reveal anything from my past or about Hector in grave detail.

The maître d' says, "Hello, Miss Rachel. It is a pleasure to serve you and your party this evening. Your favorite table awaits you and your...*guest*," he says in a snobbish tone toward Aaron.

Aaron starts to lurch forward but is blocked when Rachel's guiding hand meets his and squeezes in a request to stand down. Aaron stares dead-eyed at the maître d' as they are escorted to their reserved table for a relaxing dinner.

The restaurant is quite busy tonight, especially since it is a Friday night in the big city, but Rachel is well connected here, and when she walks into a place, tables that were booked are usually made available for her. Aaron takes one more glance at Rachel, who is dressed in a stunning fashion: her four-inch high heels complement her tight-fitting little black cocktail dress that certainly accentuates her best, if not all of, her assets. Her darkish auburn hair is tied back in a way that certainly promotes a you-know-who's-in-charge look. Aaron's cowboy attire, though appropriate in Texas, does not fit the manly look of the Midwest style of Chicago's finest gentlemen's apparel. It doesn't matter though. Everyone is checking out Rachel, and Rachel is footing the bill. Aaron is just along for the ride.

The table they are seated at is in a secluded part the restaurant, far away from any others and cozy enough for the evening's conversation and/or actions to stay private. Aaron gets the chair for her, and as she sits down, he guides her left hand for support and classy effect. He removes the cowboy hat but has no place to put it until the attentive waiter takes it and puts it up and away. Crisis averted.

The waiter comes back and offers to take their drink order. Rachel orders her usual vodka martini, with Tito's Handmade Vodka, of course, but Aaron decides on a manlier drink, Blanton's bourbon, and while they are at it, make it a double, straight up. Feeling satisfied with his drink choice, Aaron gazes at the woman he knows all too well, especially in these high-end social settings. Rachel always loves to be wined and dined at only the best places in town, and it's hard to argue with that. Since last year, she has shown him the best in life with what money can buy.

The drinks arrive, and with food orders taken, there is a little downtime before the first course. After the clinking of glasses and cheers, the alcohol starts to work its magic over the two of them. Rachel asks Aaron about the adventures that he has been entertained by in the last few days. He discusses the incident at the bar and the discovery of the tracker device before finally talking about what Rachel really wants to hear: the shootout.

"It's a crazy, fucked-up feeling. You know, killing someone. But you get used to it after a while. Hey, I look at it as he was trying to kill me first. I'm the better shot, after all, as I'm the one alive telling the tale."

Rachel is enthralled by it all, even if it is testosterone-laden. "But Roberto was great at his job. A classic hit man. Hector used him countless times, and Roberto was always successful. That means you must be even better if you took him out. I mean, wow, Aaron."

Aaron is not quite sure how to take that, but resigns to taking it as a compliment. "And so I had to escape the hospital and rip the cords right out of my arms. Fluids squirting everywhere—"

"Excuse me, sir. Your salad is ready," the waiter interrupts.

As her salad is placed in front of her, Rachel asks, "Go on. What did you do next?"

The waiter leaves. Aaron returns to the point he left off from. "I ran, ran into the night, before finally stopping and sleeping on a park bench. It was cold, I tell ya. I was still in a lot of pain."

"That's crazy! I bet you were freezing. My poor Aaron." Rachel blows him a kiss from across the table.

"And you know the rest...here we are." Aaron raises his glass to hers and takes a big swig of the smooth bourbon.

Rachel switches her tone. "So how's the device coming along? Has she completed it yet?"

Aaron is munching through a forkful of chicken Caesar salad when Rachel asks him about the device. He pauses to finish chewing, as it is a big piece of chicken, yet quite tasty.

Rachel stares back impatiently waiting for a reply. Aaron swallows the tasty bite quickly and continues.

"Yes, the device. I was waiting for you to ask about it. All I can say is she seems dedicated to completing it. She kept talking about getting a big payout from Hector, and we were all going to split the proceeds."

"Oh, how thoughtful of those two. Lucky you."

Aaron bluntly asks, "You guys are going to kill them, aren't you?"

Rachel puts down her salad fork and stares into his eyes. "I'm not going to kill them. No love, we thought it best that you should do it."

Aaron is taken aback. "Both? Both of them?"

"Of course, they trust you. Is that a problem? You know, now that I think about it, it should be time for Hector to retire, too."

"You think so? I may need you as backup if this is what you want."

"Don't you agree, hon? Take out the competition? Ha, ha. Hector would never see it coming. Well, maybe he has, but we have to do the other two first. Agreed?"

"Sure, why not."

The entrées arrive. Perfect timing indeed. Aaron has been looking for a proper steak for quite a while, and tonight is the night. Not the second-rate stuff they had at the steakhouse the other day. He smiles as he cuts into the first piece of a Grade-A filet mignon, perfectly seasoned and cooked to a turn. Ah, just like heaven.

He sees Rachel across the table enjoying her perfectly cooked salmon over rice. Aaron relaxes for a moment as everything comes together for them and the life they have created together. He had never thought this crazy double-agent stuff with Jim and Selma would actually work. Above all, he had never thought that he could pull it off without old Jim ever suspecting anything. Aaron had gotten over feeling sorry for Jim after he had hooked up with Rachel last year at Jim's expense. His life has gotten a lot better since the day he met and ran off with Rachel. *Sorry, Jim, old buddy. I won her over, and you lost. That's the breaks.* Rachel has been the best thing that has ever happened to him, and he is not about to give up so fast on this awesome life.

"Waiter, can we get another round of drinks?" Aaron calls out.

Rachel only beams at Aaron with her soft, sultry eyes. It was those same eyes that used to stare uninterestingly at Jim day after day during that horrible marriage all those years ago.

Chapter 21

We leave the deli with the incredible memory of a most delicious Reuben sandwich. Why, it only rivals the deli in Ann Arbor, Michigan, Zingerman's, that I visited years ago. I remember that I had to drive up to the University of Michigan campus one semester during my junior year when Notre Dame was playing an away football game against Michigan. As I recall, that was one heck of a Reuben sandwich, too.

Selma elbows me. "Are you all right?"

"Oh...sorry. I was just thinking of my college days at Notre Dame."

"You better not be reminiscing about those college coeds," Selma replies sternly.

"What...no...I was thinking about this sandwich place in Ann Arbor."

"And that's all you better be thinking about!" Selma lets out a hardy laugh.

We continue to meander around the New York City streets and carry on the discussion about our university days but are constantly interrupted by street vendors of every sort. These are not just normal vendors either; rather, these are professional hecklers selling everything under the sun. One wants to sell us hot dogs with a hundred different condiments. Another is trying to get rid of an assortment of watches, gold and silver chains, and even event tickets. The tickets for the stage production *Rock of Ages* are actually tempting, but the show starts in five minutes. We are even shown a car waiting on the street to drive us to the theater down the road. Not sketchy at all, to say the very least!

I have had enough and flag down a taxi for us to get away from the very persistent ticket salesman.

"Where to, Mac?" the taxi driver demands as he starts the meter.

It is my turn to take control. "Take us to Broadway and 112th Street."

Selma grabs my arm in excited anticipation as we drive off, attempting to conquer The Big Apple. I look over my left shoulder and see Selma. I then look forward to see the taxi meter is running really fast. It is already up to ten bucks. What the heck? But I pause for a moment to ask myself, why do I even care? So what? Here I am with Selma, and we just had a great meal, and why should I look like a penny-pinching punk? Some battles are not worth it, and this is the one time I should not be a jerk.

I turn my head to the left again and see the city skyline lit up. The energy of the city glows brightly from all the people and activities as we drive on by heading to our destination. I sit back and take this moment in.

Minutes later, we arrive at our destination, and the cabbie yells back to me that it is $32.00 and some change. I pull out two crisp $20 bills and tell him to keep the change. The cabbie obliges and wishes us a good night as he whisks away to his next fare.

We both stand there on the corner for a few seconds enjoying the evening silence. I thought of this place to go by hoping my memory served me well and that it is the same place I remembered from years ago. Taking her arm, I defend my choice, stating, "Now, this is just a hole in the wall, and it's dark and usually low key." I further add, "But it's got a great vibe. You'll see what I mean."

"Sounds perfect. What are we waiting for? Let's go inside."

The place is exactly as I described, except for forgetting to mention the saxophone player belting out some sweet-sounding notes in a solo. The musician plays with a blue light shining down upon him while standing on a small stage. There is a wooden stool behind him, but with the smooth melody that the sax player is performing, he is standing up for added effect.

Pointing to the left, I motion Selma to a booth over on the left of the stage, and she nods in agreement and proceeds to walk over to it. Selma goes in first, and I pause to catch the eye of the musician and tip my hand him. The sax player acknowledges me but, in reality, would probably prefer a tip for the glass jar in front of the stage.

Though it is really dim lighting in here, the waitress manages to find us and asks in a thick New Jersey accent what we want. I thought about asking for a friendlier waitress but decide to cease with the wisecracks and let Selma order first. It is also easy for her to decide, as this is the kind of place that doesn't do fancy drinks. Nevertheless, I pray for Selma to keep her drink choice simple. After thinking about it for a minute, Selma blurts out her choice of a rum and Coke, whereas I go for the old standby and choose a Jack and Coke. Going for broke, I additionally ask for some popcorn or pretzels. The waitress, with one eye cocked, only replies, "Sure." Selma and I look at each other and laugh, as we have no idea what we might get or not get, but we ain't gonna complain about whatever the waitress may bring us.

The saxophone player continues with another musical piece before taking a long overdue break. The waitress returns with the two drinks that look the same, and I fight myself from asking her which drink is which and how does she know. She also plops a white paper bowl filled with salty yellowish popcorn in front of us, much to my relief, and asks us if we want to start a tab.

"Sure, that'll be fine," I fire back with a look of "Please leave us alone now and only come back when the drinks need refilling."

The waitress is about to say something in a harsh reply but decides against it and turns around to check on her other tables. Which is good thing, as I thought she was going to ask for a credit card, and I hate to leave a credit card behind the bar, especially in a place like this. I always thought that it was a really bad practice to randomly hand over a credit card to a complete stranger, especially a stranger with as unique an accent as hers. Furthermore, to have the credit card sit unsecured behind a bar, blah. I would rather just cash out on every round to the annoyance of the waitstaff.

We both raise our glasses, clink them together, and toast to a wonderful night. We start to take a drink, and we both almost spit it out on each other. It is an odd feeling when one orders something and it tastes completely different from what you were expecting. We look at each other, laugh, and then switch the glasses.

"Ok, toast, part two. Let me toast to a wonderful evening with an even more wonderful woman, who happens to be sitting next to me."

"To the wonderful date next to me," Selma replies in kind. "He always knows the best places to eat. Cheers!"

"Ah, that's what a Jack and Coke is supposed to taste like. Much better, though no offense to your rum drink!"

"I was thinking the same thing, except for the taste of a rum and Coke."

"We're gonna play this taste-test game every time we order a round, aren't we?"

"You should order a beer for the next round, though that might throw off our waitress!"

"Hold on, I need to go tip the sax player."

I pull out a fiver, but then reconsider and pull out a $10 note. I excuse myself and walk up to the stage. The sax player is playing away but watches me with one eye. I make it known I am adding to the tip jar and turn to walk back to the table. The sax player points to our table in acknowledgement and whittles off an extra piece of music for us. Selma claps happily.

The scene is perfectly set now in my mind: the dimly lit bar, the jazz music playing in the background, and the two of us experiencing it together. We've got drinks (the right ones now), we've got food (well, overly salty popcorn), and I've got the beautiful gal next to me. After one more sip from my drink, I slowly turn to her, barely seeing her in the low cocktail lighting, and ask her a question.

"Fine, dear. Is there anything else you'd like to know that I haven't already told you?"

She pauses and then responds, "Alrighty then! Do I get to ask anything? What areas are taboo? Oh, this is going to be fun. I have so much to ask you, I can't think where to begin."

"No holds barred. In fact, I dare ya!" I just upped the ante, or the alcohol is starting to speak for me. Uncle Jack always has that effect on people after a few rounds.

"Well, I don't want to get in a fight later on, so I'll keep it easy for now," she replies, showing her willingness to play it smart.

"Whatcha got?"

"Ok, we'll start with the category 'Fun Times' for two hundred dollars. So, I know you have a passport, or else you have a fake one, because I met you in Mexico, obviously. Where have you traveled anywhere else outside the US, or have you ever lived abroad longer than a month?"

Phew, I think. I was not sure what she was going to ask. Wiping my forehead with the drink napkin, as I am sweating and blame it on being hot in here, I put the napkin down and answer the first question.

"I grew up here and there and lived in a lot of places, including Hawaii. I have visited and lived in different parts of Europe for a good many years." I go on about the fun of traveling abroad when one doesn't speak the language and having to get by with a lot of gestures. I talk about the excitement of visiting a foreign land as a tourist and what I have faced, both good and bad. I also spoke of living in a foreign country for years and finding that one tends to visit and see more of the sights than a local ever does.

"I get it. You have no qualms about getting up, leaving the US, and living, say, in the Cayman Islands or Costa del Sol, Spain." Her glass is empty, and she flags the waitress down for another round of drinks. I always enjoy a woman who takes charge and can order drinks. Then again, what man wouldn't.

Selma continues. "I have only been to a few places outside the US, and it has been mainly Mexico on various vacations. Clearly, nothing compared to all the places you have visited or lived in. I was just wondering how difficult it would be, but you don't seem to think it's tough at all."

"It's a piece of cake. Give me a *Frommer's* or *Lonely Planet* book along with a map, and I'm your guide." Out of nowhere, I give her right thigh a tap to stress the point. OK, it was more than a tap on the thigh.

"Moving along." Selma is quizzical about the gesture but doesn't mind it. "Question two: how did you get involved with Hector and his organization?"

"Ah, the questions are getting tougher already. I was hoping it was going to be like, 'What's your favorite food?'" I take a bigger sip from my drink in hopes of stalling before answering.

"Nope, and wait till the next question. You'd better start preparing yourself." And it's she who taps my left thigh this time.

"OK, OK. You partially know why I got hooked up with Hector and his associates. He led me to believe he can help me find my missing wife. All I had to do is help him on this job, which happens to be you, and he promised something…a lead or a guy he knows…something. However, I did know Hector from way back when, but that was another time that I would rather not speak of just yet for now."

I am still hesitant but decide to go on a different tangent. "My buddy Aaron and I served together in the army way back when. We kept in touch, but I never got involved in his business dealings or questioned what exactly he did for a living. We meet from time to time for a drink, relive old army war stories, or hang out for a weekend.

"So when Rachel disappeared and I exhausted everything I possibly could do to find her, Aaron came by one day and knew a guy from our past that might have been able to help me out. I was at the end of line and ready to move forward, though those were the darkest days. I mean, that's all one can do in these situations, and, well, a trip across the border sounded more interesting than what I had going on at the time. You know: drink too much cerveza and tequila, eat some greasy food, and watch some crazy shows that you always hear about. What guy would pass that up? Moreover, if I remember correctly, I did all those things, including watching the crazy stage show."

Selma changes a few shades of red even in this low lighting but maintains her composure. She still finds my ribs and places a stinging elbow to my unguarded rib cage on the left side.

"Hey, I really enjoyed the show. It was very artistic!" I reflect back for a second and try to remember if I actually tipped her that night.

"Yeah, yeah, that was still a lot of fun to do, believe it or not. I didn't think that one day that I would run off with one of guys in the audience, but there was this local Mexican guy that the other dancers talked about that tips really generously..." She elbows me in the ribs one more time, but softer, as I was better prepared for her physical ribbing. Though I probably deserved one of those times she ribbed me.

Selma switches to a more serious tone. "So what are you going to do with the information that Hector gives you after the exchange is complete tomorrow?"

"Hmm. I've been thinking about this for quite a while, and I honestly think Hector is bluffing. I don't think he has anything for me, and I also think my chances of walking out tomorrow alive are pretty low." I drop the doom and gloom but not the mic. It is time for another round. Waitress, please make it a double.

The drinks arrive, and the sax player starts his next set. Selma quietly asks, "Jim, last question. Are you ready for this one? I've been saving it all night."

"I'm all ears. Unleash it on me."

"Ok. Here it is." She pauses for dramatic effect. It would be great if the drummer did a drumroll while she asked the question. "What are our chances of me and you staying together?" She hurriedly takes a gulp from her drink.

Interesting question. I reply in an instant, "A hundred percent." I slam the glass down on the table for effect.

"That's a pretty bold number. What makes you think I want you that bad?"

"Easy. For one, you're sitting here with me, so it's looking pretty positive. Two, we're in this thing together, come whatever tomorrow brings. And three…"

"Yes, what's three?" She begs to hear the third declaration.

I take her hand slowly and, without breaking eye contact, utter the following: "Because, Selma, I believe in you and trust you, especially with my life, whatever happens tomorrow. Do you trust me the same way? If the answer is yes, then we really need to devise a survival plan. Or this will literally be our last night."

A long time follows, a second short of eternity. Selma has neither withdrawn her hand nor flinched. The music and background noise seem to go silent, frozen in time. My face is expressionless, but deep down I am waiting for the answer from her, as there is no time to phone a friend.

Finally, Selma leans forward to kiss me, hard and with passion. I am not expecting such a reaction and flinch but soon am drawn in and match Selma's reply. The waitress starts to come by but turns around to go bother another table. The sax player is blowing a beautiful love song away on the saxophone, even better than a Kenny G song.

Finally, we break our bond of trust but only to replenish air in our lungs. "Selma, I'll take that as a definite yes!"

With an expression of desire that only a woman can give, Selma answers, "You sure can. Now, about this plan? What do you have in mind, exactly?"

"I was thinking—" I start to say before Selma cuts in with, "Why don't we leave and take a taxi back to the hotel so we can discuss it?"

"Check, please!" I raise my right arm in a vain attempt to flag down the ever-friendly waitress.

The sound of the saxophone still echoes softly throughout the bar.

Chapter 22

Hector sits behind his desk in his office with a glass of tequila situated in his left hand. His right hand grasps the latest financial statements showing profits in most areas and losses in a few others. Sitting across from him is Sandy, his newly hired financial adviser, accountant, and secretary.

Sandy says, "If you look at these three dates, you'll notice that they're close to what you bring in on an average. I saw the pattern, investigated it, and pinpointed it to one guy that coincidently was the only one who worked all three of those days. I feel, boss, that he's the one skimming from you."

Absolutely brilliant, this girl is, Hector thinks. *Here I had her working in the bar and club when clearly her talents are more suited to administering and tracking the accounting books. Just think if she never told me she had an accounting degree.* He looks across the table to her, and she tries to be confident but actually is really nervous. Hector just nods his head. Sandy sighs in relief that she can demonstrate her talents she went to undergrad for many years ago.

"Sandy, you're incredible. I'm all too glad to discover your true skills and talents and put them to better use. Why didn't you say sooner that you had years of schooling in accountancy and were a genius when it comes to numbers?"

"I...honestly, I didn't think anyone would...take me seriously."

"Well, I'm proud to have you on the team. You're well worth it, and I hope you approve of your most generous salary."

Sandy blushes over how much Hector is paying her. Way more than she was expecting, but she is not going to complain.

Hector is still ecstatic about how she has saved him from this dirty bastard robbing him blind. He adds, "I will put one of my trusted guys on watching your back and issue an order to the rest of the organization that you are not to be messed with unless they want to answer directly to me. You got that? Anyone harasses you, you tell me immediately, and it will be dealt with accordingly. Is that good enough for you? I don't want anything to happen to my ace accountant."

Sandy knows all too well what "dealt with accordingly" means, as she has already seen too much since taking this job. However, the money is great, and she feels safe that no one is going to mess around with her. In fact, most of the guys in the club step aside and look away when she walks by.

Hector can't believe that someone is cheating him out of thousands of pesos and dollars. Sandy showed him the books and what she analyzed over the last two days. That was her conclusion, and she feels quite confident about her decision. Hector will have a chat with that guy right now.

"Thank you again, Sandy. Go get yourself a drink. You have an open tab already established at the bar. You've done good work."

Sandy thanks Hector again and scampers off. He watches her leave, pauses, and then picks up the phone to call in his trusted bar manager. He is knocking on the door two minutes later with another drink for Hector, just in case.

Hector tells him to enter and asks him to put the drink down over to the right. He explains the problem he is having with the bar manager's cousin. "Your cousin is stealing from me. Are you in on it too?" he asks.

"I don't know what you're talking about, boss," the bar manager pleads.

"Well, what am I going to do with him and, more importantly, with you? Surely you must have noticed something." Hector is baiting him.

"Honestly, boss, you've known me a long time. I would never cheat you out of anything." He is almost to the point of crying as he pleads his case and for his life.

Hector walks over to directly stare in his eyes. "You, I believe. Your cousin, I don't. Bring him in now, and put him in the basement with the two guards that are standing behind you. You got that? I am trusting you will not disobey."

"No...no, Hector—I mean, boss—please be merciful to him. He has a young wife and two kids." The bar manager makes one last plea and then walks out to bring in his cousin. The two guards follow closely behind him.

Hector picks up the phone. Miguel answers on the first ring. "Yes, boss?"

"Get in here immediately. Put Jose on the door in your place. I have two of your guards with the bar manager to go get his cousin. Can Jose handle it on his own, or does he need additional help?"

"Jose is fine. I still have one other guy on the club floor watching and keeping the peace. He can always provide backup for Jose."

"Good. I need you for a specific task. Shouldn't take you too long."

"On my way, boss."

Thirty seconds later, there is a knock on the door. "Come in, Miguel. Have a seat." Hector hands him the drink that was sitting on the right-hand side of the desk.

"What do you need, boss?'

216

"I need you on my team tomorrow. We're flying out to New York City. You have a problem with that?"

"No problem here."

"Excellent. We have to close out a problem that has been giving me a headache for weeks now. Plus there is going to be some monetary transactions that may or may not take place. I need you on your best game all weekend. Do you understand me, Miguel? We will arrive early Saturday morning in New York City and be taken by an associate to pick up the necessary hardware before the meeting. You will be able to obtain anything you require to……"

Hector takes a break for a moment and then continues discussing the plans of the operation. "I need you to kill Aaron, plain and simple. Do you remember him?"

"The cowboy?" Miguel questions.

"Yes, that's the one. Also, do you remember the guy that was here last week with the really smart woman?"

"I think so."

"Good. All three should be showing up together at the meeting on Saturday. I found out that Aaron just shot Roberto dead the other day. Take Aaron out first. I don't think Jim should be too much trouble after that. Don't harm the woman though. We still may need her before the day's end. But eventually, you will be disposing of her as you see fit."

"Sure, boss. I can do it," Miguel replies nonchalantly, as if he were just told to shoot ducks or something.

That's what I like about Miguel: obedient and no fear. "You will be repaid in kind. Plus I will throw in a first-class trip for you when this is all done."

"What time do I need to be ready?"

"Be here at seven in the morning. I also need you to take care of something for me right now."

"Sure, what do you need, boss?"

Hector explains that it was discovered recently who was skimming from him. He first wants Miguel to get a confession from the male and then extract repayment.

"I will leave it to your discretion, but make sure you keep him alive. He just doesn't need to the ability to walk at the moment. I figure he is in it for about five thousand in pesos and dollars. Get him to pay double the amount. Have a chat with his cousin, the bar manager, too. He can help pay some of the money back."

"No problem, boss."

Miguel walks out of the office and heads downstairs to the basement. *It's all in a day's work*, he thinks as he brings out the brass knuckles. Sometimes, his job has its rewards.

Chapter 23

It begins on a warm and breezy Saturday morning in New York City.

Selma opens the curtains to let some light in the hotel room. I beg her, in my sleepy voice, to close the curtains or the light will melt my skin. If only I were actually a vampire and we were in a horror movie because I sure feel like the waking dead. Selma obliges my request, and I look over to see her smiling back at me. However, with the flick of a wrist, she reopens the curtains one more time before closing them again, much to the chagrin of my now blinded morning eyes.

I chuck a pillow at her and score a direct hit. She jumps back on the bed, and we begin to tussle, a game where both participants are a winner. After a period of time, I roll on my back with Selma cozying up next to me. I cannot think of a better way to start a Saturday except for the blinding-eye thing, which I have already forgotten about. With Selma held tightly in my left arm, I assume she also agrees.

Next priority. "When are we going to get breakfast?" I ask nonchalantly.

"Whenever. I kinda like it here at the moment."

I squeeze her even tighter. Selma changes her mind in an instant. "Well, I guess I'm hungry and could really use a shower, too. Do you want to go first, as men are usually quicker?"

Not quicker in some things, I think silently, but I say, "OK," and plant a kiss on her forehead and finally beeline it to the bathroom.

Selma sits up and reaches over for her phone to check her missed calls and text messages. She quickly screens the messages and doesn't see anything of real importance, so she moves on to the voicemail. Staring back at her is an icon noting one voicemail message she dreads having to play. She types in her passcode and listens to the message. It is from Hector, telling her that he is looking forward to the meeting today at 5:00 p.m., and he will contact her later with specific instructions.

Jim yells out from the bathroom, "OK, I'm done in here. You're up, Selma."

Selma puts her phone down and plugs it in to be recharged. She takes a deep breath before facing Jim again, possibly to hide her nervousness about today.

Selma walks into the bathroom as I am coming out, smelling fresher and cleaner than before. "I hope you left some hot water for me!" she exclaims as she starts to disrobe in front of me and my wandering eyes.

"I didn't know there was going to be a show. I think I'll stay a bit longer." I start to lean against the vanity, vying for a good seat.

"Shoo, shoo! Get out so I can get clean!" Selma barks at me and throws her T-shirt at me, which flies off to the right.

"Ha, ha! You throw like a girl!" I laugh as I pick up the T-shirt and hand it back to her.

"Yes, but I play like a woman."

Well, she's got me there. I shrug my shoulders and let out a disappointing sigh, hoping to catch one more peek before the door slams closed in front of me.

I walk over to put on some clean clothes and pick up my phone for a check of any new messages. Aha, I received a text from Aaron. Boy, do I feel better that he will be there with us guarding our backs.

I read the message: *Jimbo, I can meet up with you at 3:00 p.m. at Trinity Church. Let me know.*

I respond: *Sounds fine. I hope you've got the stuff we need today.*

Aaron looks at his phone to read the last message from Jim. *OK, he still believes me. Rachel should be pleased. Sorry, pal. Rachel can do things that you just can't do.*

Aaron smiles, thinking about what some of those things are. It is what it is. He puts the phone away to gaze at the woman across the breakfast table from him that made all things possible in his life, including the late-night flight and limo ride to this exclusive hotel in Midtown Manhattan. Well, at least the world that has been created with Rachel includes fine dining, excellent wine, and the proper lifestyle.

She is still reading the morning newspaper and has hardly touched her specially prepared breakfast omelet from the finest chef at the Hilton Midtown. It is a shame to see good food go to waste, but after today, money concerns will be even less of an issue. They will probably have their own private chef at their Grand Cayman retreat. On second thought, it better be a female chef just to keep Rachel in check. Aaron takes a bite from his onion bagel with lox and cream cheese. *Mmmmm, I could get used to this every day.*

Rachel is reading about the financial markets and the closing prices for the end of the week. She is more interested in how her clients, the ones that she has aggressively lined up, are going to pay her for the device. She will be taking all of it once her partnership with Hector is terminated, thanks to her hired boy, Aaron. She looks across the table to see Aaron biting into the bagel with the salmon. *Oh dear. I hope he brushes his teeth to get rid of that fishy onion smell because it is not going to dissipate from his breath on its own.*

She really likes her obedient boy—er, man. *More of a man than Jim ever was, but I need not worry about Jim for too much longer. His best friend will take care of that soon enough, and I should get rid of Jim's new squeeze too just for the hell of it. Because I can and want Jim to have no happiness, even in the end. But if she's so smart, then why is she with Jim anyway? Oh Jim, why weren't you so much better all those years ago? But you never seemed to ever want to delve into the crime syndicate. The benefits and the money were way better, and I had to leave you to make life awesome for myself. I guess I was the smarter one after all. You can't even exploit your gifted brainy girl to make it better for the both of ya'll. Well, it won't matter in a couple of hours anyway. We'll be rid of you sooner rather than later.*

She lets out a laugh and glances over to Aaron, but he has just belched, and the smell of fish permeates the air around the table, heading in her direction. *Oh Aaron, really.* Rachel lets out a deep breath in disgust.

They finish their breakfast and the stimulating, or lack thereof, tableside conversation, and get up to head back to their massive suite. Aaron takes Rachel's hand into his as they strut across the shiny marble floor of the lobby. As they approach the elevator, Rachel leans over to Aaron, plants a kiss on his cheek, and tells him she needs to make a call and will meet him in the suite momentarily.

"You could make the call in our suite while I take a shower."

"As much as I want to join you on your offer, I'll take this call outside. I'll meet you in the room as soon as I can, darling."

"OK, see you when you're done." The elevator chimes, Aaron jumps in, and the doors close as Rachel already heads in the opposite direction.

After a few phone calls to various clients that are interested in the newest toy on the market that may be for sale today, she is pleasantly content that she will be able to sell it once Selma demonstrates that it works. *The little hussy better make it sing, or else I'll lose my credibility with all these billionaire crime bosses. Damn it, all I need is the one transaction, and I'm done with all this crap. That island retirement with Aaron is looking better and better by the day. I better find out what my "partner" is doing right now. I must assume he's plotting my own demise.*

Rachel phones Hector. He picks up on the third ring. "What do you want?"

"Well, good morning to you, too."

"We landed about five minutes ago. What do you need?"

"Is the demonstration still scheduled for today?"

"Yes, yes. Arranging the details right now. She and her new boyfriend should be meeting us around five p.m. You do know what to do, don't you?"

"Trust me. That part will be a pleasure, and I won't even charge you extra."

"Whatever. Just be ready," Hector says. "You got the clients ready when this is finished, don't you?"

"What's the matter? Don't you trust me, dear?"

"Do what needs to be done. Goodbye."

Click.

Rachel stands there with the disconnected call. *Oh, you better believe I'll do what needs to be done, my friend.*

She turns around and walks back to the elevators, readying herself, mentally and physically, for when she reaches the room where Aaron is waiting patiently for her.

Hector sits next to Miguel in the first-class section of the American Airlines flight from Houston to John F. Kennedy International Airport. For Hector, sitting in first class is old hat, but for Miguel, he is living up every moment. He orders three alcoholic drinks before Hector advises him to slow it down. He then starts flirting with the stewardesses and discusses with the cute one about meeting up with her Sunday. Hector plants an elbow to Miguel's abdomen, and he gets the message to tone it down a notch.

Hector wonders, *This is my best shooter? Getting plastered on a morning flight and macking on every woman that walks by? For Christ's sake, it's not even noon yet. You better be on your game come 5:00 p.m., amigo, or else you're a dead man because I'll shoot you myself.*

Hector takes the call from Rachel just after turning his phone back on after landing. He has to elbow Miguel once again to keep it down with his latest attempts to score with the other stewardess from first class as they line up to deplane. Hector finishes the call with Rachel as they start to debark.

"Let's go, Miguel, time's a wasting."

"Sorry, boss." Miguel can't stop from letting out a laugh.

This is going to be one crazy day, and I pray I survive it, Hector thinks to himself as he grabs his carry-on from the overhead storage compartment. Miguel follows suit, and they walk onto the ramp and clear the gate heading to baggage claim to find the syndicate limo driver waiting for them.

Chapter 24

Rachel had her breakfast downstairs, and then Aaron decided to serve her something that hadn't been on the menu when she got upstairs to the suite. Afterwards, he is dressed and ready to go as Rachel heads toward the bathroom and, more importantly, a shower.

"Sweetie, I'm heading out to go find some hardware for this evening. Let me know what you're up to, say in a couple of hours," Aaron says, applying the finishing adjustments to his cowboy hat.

"Yes, dear. May sure you get the extra surprise gun for Jim. I'm sure he'll love what modifications you've added to it for him. Or what you've just done to me."

She starts to let her towel unravel, and it opens, causing the towel to fall gracefully to the floor. Aaron takes in the eye-candy shot as much as he can before departing the bathroom, lest he be delayed any longer.

Rachel still has that come-hither look but also resigns herself to turn on the shower spigot to start the hot water flowing. Aaron says goodbye as he closes the door to the suite and checks the lock twice to make sure it is securely locked.

Aaron thinks about the hardware he has to find in this town within three hours before the final meeting later this afternoon. He starts to think about the look on Jim's face when he's handed a loaded gun that fires blanks. *A going-away gift to you, old buddy. I thought you'd appreciate the irony in firing blanks.*

The elevator doors open, and Aaron reaches for his phone to call upon his old buddy from Brooklyn: Mad Dog, aka Jason Redding. Mad Dog, Jim, and Aaron had all been US Military Intelligence Corps sergeants that had kept America safe from all enemies foreign and domestic. It also meant they had been the worst three NCOs to mess around with, as they had been a tight-knit brotherhood. *Ah, those were the days, when we outdrank everyone in the bar and still woke up the next morning on four hours' or less sleep to run two miles and then pull off an eight- to twelve-hour shift. We worked together, we played together, and we got thrown in jail together. Those were the days, my friends, but alas, times have changed. I hope I get to Mad Dog before Jimbo does, or at least can convince him this is a joke on old Jim.*

Aaron dials the number for Mad Dog. "Who is hell is this?" is the answer he hears.

"Wake your dead ass up and speak to me with some respect, Mr. Mad Dog," Aaron barks back.

"Why, if it isn't Aaron, the son of a bitch who still owes me twenty bucks. Thirty, if you add interest. How the fuck are you? And why in the hell are you calling me at this ungodly hour?"

Aaron looks down at this watch and notes that it is noon. "I thought it would be fun to wake your dead ass up on this Saturday morning, or is it afternoon, and I wanted to make sure you're still alive."

"What do you need, bail money? Are you in jail again? Were you hitting on a seventeen-year-old? Did her old man find you before the police did?" Mad Dog chuckles obnoxiously.

"Actually, I like them a lot older these days, and I'm in your wonderful town right now, by the way," Aaron replies.

"Well, get your ass over here and have a drink. I may even give you a clean glass. Hey, bring some food. I haven't eaten yet."

"I actually need a favor from you."

"Shoot."

"You're close." Aaron describes the hardware he needs for the moment while Mad Dog listens intently. Mad Dog thinks on it, as the phone is silent, then he replies, "Yup, no worries. Where are you at?"

"Midtown."

"Here's my address. Can you be here within the hour?" Mad Dog adds, "Oh, with cash? No offense. I don't work on credit anymore."

"Make it thirty minutes. And do you want dollars or pesos?"

"Hardy-har-har. Real funny, wiseass, though I do feel a hankering to go down to Mexico for a weekend. Make it dollars there, amigo."

"Fine. See you in thirty minutes or less."

"Yup. Mad Dog out."

"Selma, I've got to go out for a little bit," I state rather harshly trying not to give any clues of what I'm up to.

"OK, but be careful. I've got to put the final touches on my project." She winks at me.

"Yes, you need to make sure that thing works. Remember, it's all or nothing today. Though our chances of surviving the night are even worse than the fifty-fifty chance the device currently has."

As I leave, I call up my old army buddy Jason Redding, aka Mad Dog, who happens to live in Brooklyn. When he answers with a grunt, I smile and say, "Mad Dog, you up?"

"Jim, what's up?"

"Hey, hey, Mad Dog, what's going on with yourself? I'm in town right now. Wanna meet up?"

"You know, the same old stuff. Listen, I got to meet a client in a little bit. Did you want to stop by later on this afternoon?"

"No can do. I got a big thing later today. Maybe tomorrow, if I'm still alive."

"That bad, eh?"

"Yup."

"Well, good luck. I'll give ya a holler tomorrow."

"Later, buddy."

Hector and Miguel are riding in the back of the limo on their way to Manhattan. Miguel eyes the fully stocked bar next to him, but Hector gives him the evil eye and Miguel decides sobriety is the better choice. Hector reminds the driver that they need to stop off in Brooklyn and recites the address. His attention turns back to Miguel, and he says, "Now, you know what you have to do, correct?"

"Yes, boss. I am to carry the backpack to the house. The man knows I'm coming by and is ready for me. He will show me several different guns, and I am to choose only three handguns, two for me and one for you. You want a six-shooter, and I can get anything I like, but they have to have silencers on them. I am not to say anything else and only give him the envelope in the backpack." Miguel checks the backpack to make sure the envelope is still in there.

"Not a word. Nothing. No chitchat or sports talk. Nothing. And make it quick. We still need to buy ammo for the guns."

"Yes, boss."

The limo driver signals to Hector that they have arrived at the address. Miguel waits for the driver to open the door for him, but the driver is still sitting in the driver's seat. Miguel just opens the door himself and gets out, carrying the backpack.

Ten minutes later, Miguel comes back and climbs into the limo. They take off, heading to a sporting goods store to buy ammo.

"Mad Dog, you son of a bitch, what's up?" Aaron gives him a huge buddy hug.

"Aaron, get your ass in here." Mad Dog waves him in the house and checks the street one more time.

Aaron follows Mad Dog inside. The house is sparsely filled with furnishings. There is a slightly worn chair in the corner, a beanbag chair in front of the TV, and a folding table used as a kitchen table. *Who has a beanbag anymore?* he wonders.

What Mad Dog lacks in furniture, he makes up for in electronics: PlayStation, Atari, Sega Genesis, Xbox, computer laptops, satellite receivers. They are all scattered about in front of the seventy-inch curved TV screen. *I bet watching football games is freakin' awesome on this beast. Too bad he has to root for the Jets or Giants.*

"Bro, you want a beer?"

"Sure."

One can of some cheap brand is thrown at him, and another is thrust into his hand. "So, my brother not from the same mother, why are you really here?" Mad Dog motions for them to sit down at the folding table.

"We are gonna hit the jackpot tonight!" Aaron grins, quite excited.

"Serious? Are you robbing a bank or something?"

"Naw, nothing that illegal. Well, that's debatable. But me and my woman, Rachel, are gonna retire to some tropical islands tomorrow!" Aaron chuckles and takes a swig of the beer.

"Rachel? What is it with you guys finding women with that name? I thought Jim's old lady who ran off last year was named Rachel, too."

"Well, Mad Dog, you're right, except you're not gonna believe this shit: it's the same freakin' woman!"

"Whoa, that's some crazy shit! What does Jim have to say about all of this? Man, I would kick your ass if you did that shit to me."

Aaron leans in. "He doesn't know. And, my friend, I hope it stays that way, if you know what I mean." The look on his face states he is not joking around.

"Holy shit…what do you mean he doesn't know? He was devastated when his old lady just up and disappeared. We all kept thinking she was kidnapped or that he killed her and buried her. Shit, I suppose I'm relieved to know that he didn't chop her up."

"It turns out Rachel is a high-ranking member in this— how do we say—organization. She's not the happy-go-lucky girl we all remembered from their wedding many years ago. Jim never knew anything about the true Rachel. Can you believe that?"

"Dude, this is way too much to take in. You're crazy, Aaron, you know that? Come on, I'll go get what you came for anyway."

Mad Dog goes to the back bedroom and returns with a brown paper bag. "You know, next time, give me advance notice." He hands over the bag, which contains two handguns and two clips of ammunition. "The Glock is a mighty fine-looking gun, but the bullets are all dummies or blanks, whatever you want to call it. I assume whoever has it won't have much time to inspect the gun closely. Your gun, on the other hand, has two extra clips, so happy hunting or whatever you're going to do. I'd rather not know. I hope you get a good laugh out of it once the shooter realizes the gun is firing blanks."

Aaron tips his hand to Mad Dog and hands him $1,000.00 in cash, twenties and fifties, stuffed in a plain white envelope. He says goodbye to his old buddy and walks out the door.

Mad Dog watches Aaron leave, returns to the living room, and sits on the beanbag chair thinking about what he has just heard.

Chapter 25

Selma sits back and admires her creation.

It really is a work of genius, and I am so proud of myself, she thinks to herself. *It will work well for the demonstration, and then, surprise, it should explode within two or three days, sooner by remote, if needed. I hope it explodes in Rachel's or Hector's face, but the key is that it never works again for anyone, ever. While anyone can try to rebuild the device with the right components, it's the programming and my own algorithms stored on this flash drive that are the secrets to the whole thing. They are the brains behind it all, the soul of the device. They're what make it sing.*

I walk into our hotel room. Any expression of unease I have on my face quickly changes upon seeing Selma sitting back all relaxed with a big grin on her face.

Somberly, I say, "I was hoping you were done, but I can leave if I'm disturbing you."

"I don't think I can make any more alterations or additions. It'll either work or it won't. They'll either kill us or they won't." She switches off the device, as she has already switched off her emotions.

I frown upon hearing that. I was hoping for something along the lines of "It works better than expected. We'll collect the money, and we'll move next week to a tropical island to drink piña coladas."

Selma must sense the air of frustration in the room and changes the topic to something more lighthearted and pleasant. Deep down, I still feel that we are walking into our death sentence. She seems to feel that either all will prevail in the end or we will be dead and it won't matter anymore.

Selma blurts out, "So Jim, are you rooting for the New York Jets to win tomorrow?"

"Why would I do that?" I snap back.

"Sorry, I really don't know anything about football."

"Ha, ha. I would never be a Jets fan, or at least I wouldn't admit it. I'm actually a Detroit Lions fan at heart, even if they haven't won a championship since 1957. Which this is, coincidently, how I feel right about now—you know, Selma, lack of victory. Lack of a championship. It's third and long, and we are down by two points…oh, never mind."

"Come on, let's stop moping around here and go walk around the city. We're in New York City, after all, and we had a great night last night!"

"Did you forget we're supposed to meet Aaron at three p.m. at Trinity Church in Lower Manhattan? What time is it now?"

"Almost one p.m." Realizing the time, Selma says, "Oh shit, we better get going then, I suppose."

"But there's one thing I want to do first." I shake nervously.

"What's that?" Now she seems confused by my odd behavior.

"OK. We may never get a chance like this again, so I should take advantage of the two of us being together alone in this room. So Miss Selma, I have a question for you."

Selma seems unsure what will be the next words coming out of my mouth, but she replies, "Go ahead…I think."

I stare intently into her eyes and whisper, "Selma."

"Yes, Jim," she replies hesitantly.

I pause for an eternity and then reluctantly raise my hand. I start to stumble for words but still manage to ask, "Will you?"

"Will I what?" She looks to see if I am going to pull something out of my pocket. Isn't that how it is supposed to go? "What, Jim? What is it?"

"Will you be my girl? You know—go steady, wear my lettermen jacket, and all that?" I now release the laughter that I have been holding back for so long.

"That's...that's so wrong, Jim."

"Well—"

Interrupting, Selma is quick to the punch. "Why don't you rephrase your question tomorrow and wait for my answer then?" She kisses me passionately on the lips before going off to pack up her device.

I just stand there befuddled before cracking a smile.

As Selma packs up the antenna, her phone goes off with that obnoxious ringtone. She knows immediately that it is a text message from Hector. At the time, she thought it would be funny to set Hector's ringtone to "Rico Suave" by Gerardo, but now she finds it really annoying. Maybe it's that she finds Hector annoying as well.

What does he want now? Is he going to renegotiate the deal? Man, that bastard isn't gonna pay us at all. I've been such a fool. He's been stringing me along the whole time.

Selma picks up her phone to read the text message: *Wall Street Wine Merchants, 4:00 p.m. Ask for the Glenlivet package on the shelf. Please respond.*

Selma texts back: *Jim and I love Scotch. Good recommendation.*

235

She wishes she could send the middle finger but has not figured that one out yet. She starts to put her phone down but receives a reply: *So you are bringing a friend to the party?*

Now she is infuriated. Selma looks down at her phone. She receives one more text: *I didn't know you two were friends.*

Oh, that Hector! Selma thinks and throws her phone down.

Hector just sent the last text and found it quite amusing. *That should piss her off for a while. OK, enough fun. Now on to some serious business.*

He calls out to Miguel, who is busy eating a burger across the table from him at some proper pub in Lower Manhattan.

Despite still chewing the remains of bacon, cheese, bread, and beef, he manages to reply, "Yes, boss?"

"I need you to take a walk soon," he says as he slides a small tracker device across the table to Miguel. Miguel picks up the device and puts it in his pocket.

"You remember what to do with it, right?" Hector questions Miguel. Roberto was much better at knowing what to do. *Give Miguel time*, Hector reminds himself, *he'll figure it out or die trying.*

"Yes, boss. I am to go over to the New York Stock Exchange building and walk up to the door. It should be closed, but I'll attempt to try the doors anyway. I'll wait a few minutes before throwing this device in the bushes closest to the front doors or a trash can nearest to the building. If a guard comes out in the meantime, I will ask to use the bathroom in the building and plant the device there. Either way, the tracker device must be as close to the building as possible. Got it." Miguel goes back to eating the burger and fries.

"Did you set the frequency?" Hector asks all the questions with attention to detail about even the small bits.

"Yes, boss. I'm doing it right now." He takes a crumbled piece of paper out from his pocket and sets the tracker to the number written on the piece of paper. He shoves the paper back in his pocket.

"Excellent. You have been paying attention. Now finish your meal and get going. Should take you ten minutes to walk over there, five minutes of messing about, and another ten minutes to walk back. I need you back here at three p.m. sharp, no later. Understood?"

"Yes, boss." *I got two minutes to enjoy this burger before he starts hounding me to leave. I better enjoy it while I can, especially since he's paying for it.* After practically licking the paper clean and slurping the last bit of Coke, Miguel throws the napkin down, stands up, and walks out.

After what seemed to take forever, Hector thinks, Miguel finishes the meal and gets up and leaves. As he watches Miguel go off to plant the tracker device, Hector turns to his phone to ring Rachel. The check arrives at the table. Hector figures he has to pay for Miguel's meal.

"Rachel, are you ready?"

"Don't you ever say hello first?"

"Hello. Are you ready?"

"Yes. I will be waiting in the lobby. Don't make me wait forever, darling."

"Sending the driver over now."

Hanging up, Hector tells the driver to go pick up Rachel at the Hilton Hotel. "Take your time, do you understand? Just say that it was busy traffic."

The driver acknowledges the order from Hector. *Of course I understand. You want to piss the woman off to no end. I've seen this played out time and time again.* "You're the boss. Am I to assume I am to pick you back up right away?"

"Yes, once you pick her up, get over here right away." *Clearly this driver only has a high school education,* Hector thinks.

"Yes, sir," the driver says, thinking, *What an ass. Stupid rich bastard. I hope the woman screams at you for making her wait.*

He departs the pub and gets in the limo in the driver's seat to go pick up Rachel.

Now I've got time to watch the soccer match without any more interruptions. Hector flags the waitress down to order another beer and stares at the TV playing the soccer game. The waitress just thinks about the fact that she has to readjust the check to add on another drink. *I hope he tips me well, as the heavy drinkers usually do.*

"Aaron, it's time for you to leave to go meet your friends."

"Yes, I know."

"You remember what to do now? I need to know you're still with me." Rachel checks Aaron again for any indications that he might double-cross her and switch sides.

"No, my love, we're in this together." Aaron affirms as he dreams of the island house they about to move into next week.

"OK, I gotta go meet with Hector, that slimy bastard, in a few minutes. He's sending the car around. You go off now. Go hang with my ex for a few hours and just make sure they both arrive safely at the meeting point."

"Anything else, my love?" Aaron stands in front of her and holds her hands in his tightly.

"Once Selma proves the device works, you must immediately shoot Jim. That's all you have to do, Aaron. I've changed my mind. I'll take care of Selma."

"Anything for you Rachel, you know that. It's all about us, and that's the way it will always be."

I think I'll have a host of beautiful women serving me night and day at our island house. What does it matter, anyway? We'll have plenty of money to spend and all the time in the world. Aaron smiles one more time at the woman standing in front of him as she replies in kind.

Chapter 26

Miguel walks the streets of New York City. He thinks about how relaxing it actually is to walk the streets, but this is the business sector and certainly not as exciting or action-packed as Forty-Second Street or Broadway. He takes it all in and pauses to realize he is free of boss man pestering him to do this and do that.

I should just shoot his ass and see how he would like that. Maybe he would stop barking orders all damn day. Roberto was always his favorite, but a lot good that did Roberto, as he's six feet under now. I need to be better than Roberto, or I'll be lying next to him.

Miguel shudders at the thought of being in a cold, dark box six feet in the earth. He decides to focus on something else. *Come to think of it, when I get back, I need to go to Roberto's apartment. I bet I can take a few things, like his guns and cash, that are probably just lying around the empty apartment. Hmm, must remember to do that when we get back. Roberto wouldn't mind, and it's not like he can do anything about it.*

He looks up to the sky and then realizes, as with Roberto, that killing is not going to have him heading upward; more likely downward. Miguel starts to chuckle until he realizes he should probably be looking straight ahead, at least for now.

Oh shit, here's the New York Stock Exchange building. Quick, bring out the camera and take photos to look like a tourist. Because what Mexican in New York City with a camera isn't a typical tourist? He laughs at his own joke. *OK, go up the stairs and try the doors just for the hell of it.*

He tries the door and, surprisingly, finds it unlocked. He continues to open the door and walk inside the building.

Immediately, he sees the guard standing up next to the metal detector. He greets the suspicious-looking guard only to realize that he is also of Mexican background.

"Hola, *hermano*," Miguel says.

"What do you want?" the guard enquires.

"Man, I just need to use the bathroom. Do ya mind?"

The guard looks him over and doesn't see a threat. "The bathroom is over to the left. Just hurry it up, will ya?"

"Gracias, amigo."

"De nada."

Miguel goes in the bathroom and plants the tracker device underneath the second sink. He actually then does use the urinal and washes his hands, confident boss man will be pleased about a job well done. *Finally, I'll get some respect*, he thinks as he waves to the guard on his way out the door, pausing to take a photo to reinforce the tourist façade he has been putting up so well.

Selma and I are enjoying every moment as though it will be our last, which may not be far from the truth. I take a couple of photos of her at various tourist scenes: out on the street on Broadway, in front of Rockefeller Center, and a classic photo with the Empire State Building in the background. We might as well have fun, and Selma certainly is playing the part of the fun girlfriend on a vacation. I wonder what she would have answered if I had asked a different question about us, but I decide to leave it be and relish the moments we are creating together. I still do not know what will happen in a few hours hence but remember that we need to go meet up with Aaron soon.

241

"Honey, I hate to say this, but it's time to meet up with Aaron."

"Oh, do we have to? I was really enjoying the day out with you. I wish it didn't have to end."

"Let's take the subway. We need to get off at…" I look at the map. "There's a stop near Trinity Church. That's where we need to be."

"Lead the way. You're the boss." We walk into the subway entrance.

"Maybe you can come up with a better nickname."

"Oh, I'll think of something really good for you, Jimbo!"

"Please call me something else." Of all things, she picks that one to call me?

"I gave you two names, and you don't like either," she sarcastically states.

"Our train is coming now. Come on." I smoothly take her hand and climb aboard the famed New York subway.

Fifteen minutes later in Lower Manhattan, we walk up to Trinity Church. We see Aaron leaning against a wall with a bag beside him. He has not recognized us yet, as he is distracted, playing with his phone. My phone begins to go off rather noisily, and I scramble to quiet it. Is Aaron playing around by calling me?

"Wait a sec, dear. I need to take this call." I answer the phone.

On the other end, Mad Dog says, "Jim, brother, I'm calling you to tell you something you ought to know." Then he pauses.

"Hey, Mad Dog, what's up?" I am surprised that it is not Aaron calling.

"Jim, I…I just need to tell you…"

"What? Tell me, man."

242

"Do not trust Aaron, no matter what. Do ya hear me, Jim?"

I find myself at a loss, as Mad Dog has never bullshitted me before, though his voice suggests something is amiss.

"I hear ya. Understood. Thanks."

"He's setting you up. Goodbye and good luck. Mad Dog out." And he hangs up the phone.

"Goodbye." Thanks, friend.

I hang up the phone and see that Aaron has finally spotted us. Selma rushes over to hug him, and they embrace. I walk up to Aaron, and we square off before resigning to hugging each other in a manly fashion.

"Aaron, it's so great to see you!" I play the excited card.

"Jimbo, how ya doing, bro?"

I am only thinking, as he is smiling, that Aaron is lying his ass off to me, and how and when am I going to inform Selma? How do I convince her that I do not trust him at all? This day just keeps getting better and better.

"Ok, guys, you're probably wondering what I've been up to," Aaron throws at us right off the bat.

Selma hugs him again and again. "It's so great to see you again. You look so alive!" She is so emotional right now that I think this is not the best time to tell her Aaron is double-crossing us.

"Aaron, buddy, we never properly thanked you for taking out what's-his-name."

"Roberto," Selma blurts out.

"Ah yes, thank you, Selma." I turn toward Aaron once more. "You had us pretty worried there, buddy." I have mastered the happy smile so well. Must have been from all the years of living with Rachel. Though Selma's reaction toward

Aaron seems pretty real to me. I hate to ruin it for her, but I must tell her ASAP.

"All right, guys," Aaron says, getting serious. "So what's the plan?"

Hector enters first, and then Miguel climbs in the limo with Rachel already inside. Hector sits next to his business partner while Miguel looks confused before sitting next to the bar, deciding it is probably the safest seat choice. Besides, Rachel is wearing this skirt that leaves her legs very exposed, especially when one is seated across from her. Hector doesn't seem to take notice of Rachel other than for business purposes. *Oh well, his loss and my gain.*

Hector speaks to the limo driver. "Take us to Wall Street Wine Merchants on the corner of Pearl Street and Pine Street."

"Yes, sir."

"Why are we going there, Hector?" Rachel seems confused.

"Well, I thought we'd get a nice bottle of scotch." Hector stops for a second and then continues. "No, actually, I'm leaving the instructions there for Selma on where to meet us at five p.m."

"Got it."

"We've arrived, sir." The limo driver shifts the vehicle into park and quickly runs to the other side in time to open the door for Hector. He steps out and enters the shop, proceeding straight to the proprietor.

"Greetings, kind sir. I have a favor to ask." Hector removes his gloves, opens his wallet to remove three $100 bills, and lays them on the counter. The proprietor looks around suspiciously but decides to hear this snobbish customer out first.

"I have some guests coming in shortly, and I want to surprise them."

The proprietor looks confused but gladly accepts all reasonable requests and takes the cash lying front of him.

"What do you need me to do? Is there something specific you're seeking? Perhaps something vintage for your discriminating taste, sir?"

"It's really quite easy. They'll be coming in shortly, and they don't know much about whiskey. I made suggestions on what to purchase, but they never listen to me, so I hope they ask you for a bottle of scotch, and I want you to direct them to a specific bottle. I want to have this note inside for them in the box when they open it up later on." Hector produces a piece of paper with some writing on it. "All I ask is for you to give them this bottle with the note I just prepaid for and, as you can see, I added a little extra for your troubles."

"I'm following you. Thank you for your patronage. Do you have a particular bottle in mind?"

Hector looks up to the shelf above the register and spies the perfect box. "Let's put the note in the box of Glenlivet up there." He points up and to the left.

"Fair enough. I don't sell a lot of those these days."

The proprietor moves over a ladder against the shelf and climbs up, removing one of the Glenlivet boxes, and brings it down for Hector to inspect. Hector looks at the bottle and box, nods his head in affirmation, and drops the note in the box.

"I trust your discretion in the matter. It's for my nephew and his new wife. Again, please keep the difference as a token of my gratitude." Hector smiles.

"Consider all the matter taken care of. Just make sure they ask specifically for the scotch, and I'll judge whether to give it to them. When did you say they will be coming in?" the proprietor enquires.

"They should be coming in within the next hour."

"Can you give me a description of who I should look for or at least their names so I can check their ID when I card them?"

Hector gives the details to the proprietor, including Jim's and Selma's names.

"It was a pleasure doing business with you, kind sir. Is there anything else that may interest you?" The proprietor figures if this guy has this much money to spend, he might as well milk this rich customer for all he's worth.

Hector thanks him and thinks about a nice tequila but declines the proprietor's request, turns, and walks out the door to the waiting limo.

Selma and I, along with Aaron, start walking down a random street in Lower Manhattan.

"Are you sure you know where you're going?" Aaron pesters Selma endlessly.

"Yes, yes. I have detailed instructions from Hector. He gave them to me earlier today."

I pipe up, "When did you get those?"

"Like I said, earlier today. Enough questions already." Selma pleads for us to shut up and trust her.

Aaron leans over to me and whispers, "I got what we need in case this goes bad. You never know." He shows his sidearm covered by his jacket.

Still playing the poker face, I say, "Good thinking. You never know what's going to happen at these things."

"You know it, bro!"

I only smile, thinking I really should tell Selma that I will probably have to shoot Aaron at some point today. But Aaron is my friend, and friends don't do this to one another, do they? What happened to bros before hos? What else is he not telling me? It is probably too late to glean any more information from Mad Dog. I can only hope he is not setting me up. I trust him, and he has never lied to me before. I guess I will have to play this out by gut feeling alone, with or without Selma.

We continue to walk down the street and follow Selma's guidance. When we turn the corner and walk to the end of the block, Selma stops suddenly in front of a liquor store, Wall Street Wine Merchants, on the corner of Pearl Street and Pine Street.

"Selma, don't you think it's a little early for a pick-me-up?" I quip.

Aaron adds, "I think we should play this one sober, don't you think?"

Selma turns to us. "OK, this is my show. You two wait outside, and I'll play this out per Hector's instructions."

We acquiesce and go meandering around the building.

Selma walks into the corner liquor store. It has a wall of various-priced liquor bottles and a very inattentive clerk. He takes no notice of her until she raises her voice to ask, "Excuse me, sir, I'm looking for a bottle of Glenlivet. At least, that's what I was told to get. What do you recommend?"

The proprietor lifts his head up and utters, "Yes, we sell Glenlivet. A beautiful scotch. Smooth and not too peaty in taste. Do you like scotch, kind lady?"

Selma replies, "Well, I might have tried it at some point, but I'm supposed to be looking for a packaged box of Glenlivet. Oh, like those up there on the shelf above you."

Now the proprietor is interested. "Are you sure this is what you want? Only those with the most discriminating taste prefer the boxed set. Are you sure that's what you were told to acquire?" He has to be sure this is the person that is supposed to receive the hidden message.

"I'm sure of it. I was told by my friend to ask for that specific packaged liquor box."

Feeling satisfied, the proprietor replies, "OK, OK, I'll get it for you. Coincidently, your uncle was in here earlier enquiring about this same bottle. He was so gracious as to prepay for it. I just need to verify your ID."

Selma goes along with the ruse. "Yeah, my uncle probably came in earlier to let you know what I should buy. He tends to make my decisions for me."

"Yes, he did comment on your poor decision-making choices." And with that, the proprietor steps down from the ladder and puts the package on the counter. He sees two males outside, waiting for the woman, obviously. He checks Selma's ID and comments on what a lovely name Selma is. "I don't hear that name too often, so I remember it when I hear it." He hands the ID back to her, as well as the packaged Glenlivet box in a plain brown bag. He adds, "You might want to check out the bottle sooner rather than later."

Selma stares at the proprietor but accepts the bag with the liquor bottle box.

"Have a great day, ma'am."

"You too," she replies and walks out to meet up with Jim and Aaron.

"OK, guys, that was strange. But let's move on to a park or someplace. I believe there's a message in this box." Selma shows them the packaged liquor box.

"There's a park up the street where we can check it out and chill before the showdown," Aaron suggests. "Because nothing says living like passing a liquor bottle around among friends in a public park."

Selma chimes in, "Seriously?"

I add, "Let's go then. Oh wait, don't we need a brown bag for the liquor bottle?"

Chapter 27

Miguel has been watching the three people the whole time. As they start walking up the street, he brings out his phone and calls Hector.

"OK, boss. The woman retrieved the liquor bottle from the store. The three of them are now walking up the street."

"Excellent. Keep me informed when she actually reads the note."

"Will do, boss."

Hector turns to Rachel, who is sitting by him on her phone reading the news or some website page.

"See, I told you everything is going exactly as planned."

"Yeah, yeah. You know it all." Rachel does not seem at all enthused.

Selma finds a small park up the street and sees an unoccupied bench, the perfect spot. She stops at the bench and opens the carrier bag. She pulls the Glenlivet box out and opens the box. Sure enough, there is a note within the box, which she reaches for and takes out.

She opens the paper and reads aloud, "Proceed to 45 Williams Street where a Charles Schwab branch office is located. There, you will enter the building. Look right and enter the second door that says, 'Authorized Personnel Only.' Punch in the code 0485 to open the locked door. Walk up three flights of stairs and enter the construction area. The floor is being remodeled."

"OK, guys, are you ready for this?" Selma questions us as we are chilling out on the grass next to her.

"Sure," I reply, though I am much more relaxed while lying on the grass staring at the sky.

"Yup," Aaron adds as he watches the traffic go by. "Hey, Jim."

"What is it, Aaron?"

He produces a gun from the brown bag he has been carrying. I look at the gun and thank him for supplying it. I stand up and put the gun in the top part of my pants in the back.

Aaron reminds himself that the gun he has given to Jim won't kill anyone. "Just don't point it at me, old buddy." *I've got a gun that will kill you, which I'll be doing in next hour.*

Rachel and Hector arrive in time before the others do. Hector scans the area and finds a table and chair for Selma to do her demonstration. Rachel just stands idly by, wondering why he is making such a fuss when he is going to kill them afterward anyway. Hector looks out the window and barely sees the New York Stock Exchange building off to the left of the city view.

"OK, Rachel. As soon as Selma proves it works, we take out Jim first and her next. Is that the plan?"

"Whatever you say. You're the boss."

"I'm starting to wonder—are you on my team or not?" Hector questions her.

Rachel responds quickly, "Of course. Why would you say such a silly thing?"

"OK, then. They should be here momentarily."

"Let's get this show on the road."

"I hear you."

Hector calls Miguel to find out the status of the party of three that should be arriving shortly.

251

Miguel is standing across the street and about five hundred feet from where Aaron, Jim, and Selma should soon be entering his field of view. As this is the first door they have to go through, following their every footstep and possibly getting spotted is not worth the risk. Besides, he had gotten his midday snack from Subway up the block. He had enjoyed a nice little sub before this shit starts to get real. It would really be bad to be in the middle of everything and have his stomach start growling.

Back at his old job, when he was a bouncer at Hector's club, he got to rough up people, throw people out who were too drunk or belligerent, and had knives and guns shoved in his face all the time. He only had to kill two people, and it did not bother him too much. They were scum like him, and he still sleeps at night not thinking about those two men whose lives he ended early.

It was actually a relief that boss man did not want him to shoot Selma dead. He sorta likes her and might have an issue wasting a bullet in her pretty head. But business is business, and Hector is paying him a lot of dinero to shoot people, not be friends them. Still, it would be a shame to shoot her.

The two other guys, Miguel ponders, he will have no issues with killing, and it will all be in a day's work. He will probably go to some bar afterward and do a couple of shots of whiskey in their honor. With the amount of money he is going to make from this job, he will be able to afford the good stuff, and a lot of it.

Oh, it's time, he thinks and becomes more attentive as he spots the three of them walking toward the first door.

Miguel grabs his phone and dials Hector. "They are through the first door on the street."

"Excellent. Now wait a few minutes to give yourself time to be out of sight. I do not want them—I repeat, Miguel—I do not want them to know that you are behind them. *Comprende?*"

"Yes, boss man," Miguel replies, trying his best not to add, "Asshole."

Selma punches the code into the locking mechanism. She then tries the door handle, and the door unlocks. Breathing out a sigh of relief, she walks through the unlocked door, holding it open for us. Aaron and I both share the same surprised face that the code works but proceed anyway without questioning or thinking about it too much.

Selma stares at the daunting flight of stairs in front of her. She turns to us as we stop short behind her. "OK, guys, this can go smoothly, or this can go really, really badly. I am this close to walking away." She shows us two fingers close together.

We both nod our heads in agreement.

She is trembling something fierce but manages to continue. "How do ya'll want to play this? Guns a-blazing, cool and smooth, or what? Tell me because I don't know, and, to be perfectly honest, I am scared shitless."

I speak up first. "OK, dear, relax and do what you need to do. Aaron and I have been through similar situations before." Well, that's partially true, thinking about the time we got into a fight at a German beer hall and were vastly outnumbered and then the German police arrived…

I pause before realizing Aaron and Selma are both staring at me, waiting for me to continue. "Yes. What we need to do first is have Aaron on point going up the stairs. Then he will stay to the left. You, Selma, are the center point, and I will take the right. Questions?"

"Sounds good to me, buddy."

"OK, Jim. Thanks. I feel better with you at my side." And she smiles at me in the way only I understand.

"Come on, you guys. Let's start moving up the stairs." Aaron wants the show to get on the road and not have to witness anymore more innuendos between us.

Miguel thinks that enough time has passed and crosses the street in typical New York fashion, bolting in front of cars blaring their horns and the drivers making obscene hand gestures directed toward him. He thinks about flashing his gun back at them and maybe that would make them drive off in a hurry. However, he thinks better of it and gets to the opposite side of the busy street in no time.

He opens the first door and walks down the corridor to the second door. He freezes for a second, as he can hear voices on the other side of the door marked Authorized Personnel Only. *Phew, I almost blew the surprise, and boss man would have been quite pissed off at me.*

The voices finally stop, but he decides to wait a few more minutes to make sure the coast is clear. At least he remembers the four-digit code to punch into the keypad.

"What is taking them so long? All they had to do is go through a couple of doors and walk up three flights of stairs. I mean, come on." Hector is quite impatient and rechecks his watch for the third time.

Rachel is listening to him but not really paying attention. "Maybe they got lost coming over here!" She snorts at her lame joke.

Hector is still pacing about.

"Why don't you phone Miguel to see what's up?" Rachel offers. "Isn't he supposed to be following them?"

"Naw, they might hear his phone ringing and figure out it's a trap."

"Then relax and sit down. You're making me nervous."

Hector glares at her for a second and turns around to look out the window and down onto the street.

"Suit yourself," Rachel mumbles and looks at her phone, wondering what she is going to say to Jim when she finally sees him again. *More importantly, how is he going to react when he sees me alive and well?* She giggles at the thought of the very surprised look he is going to have on his face. She really should take a photo of his shocked face. It would be priceless as the last photo of him alive with some stupid look on his face. *Surprise! Gotcha!*

"Here it is." Aaron pauses as he approaches the third floor. "Whatever happens, we three got to stick together, correct?" he adds for reassurance.

I look at Aaron, knowing it's all a lie, but Selma seems to relax a bit upon hearing him speak, as though he is preaching from the pulpit. I still need to find a way to let her know not to trust Aaron, no matter what. However, I doubt that she will believe me, especially as everything is about to kick off and she still thinks Hector is going to hand over $5 million and let us walk out the front door.

And what should I do about Aaron? Should I believe what Mad Dog just told me before this very moment, when I am supposed to be trusting my other best friend to help keep all of us alive? Why shouldn't I be trusting Aaron anyways? What has he done to me to make me think otherwise?

"Jim. *Jim!*"

Someone is calling my name. I turn to Aaron. "What?"

"Are you with us? You looked—well, you looked lost for a moment. Are you sure you're all right? That's the second time you've blanked out, man, in the last couple of minutes. We need you on your game right now. You're scaring me and Selma."

I glance over to Selma, and she has a blank expression on her face, but her eyes suggest a worried feeling. Are they both thinking that I am choking at the final moment of the big game? I look to Aaron and then back to Selma, who is now looking a little worried about the man she is deciding to be with for the rest of her life. Aaron is only expressing hope because he has known me a good part of his life but now is losing faith in me because of my recent actions.

I only reply, "Everything's perfect. Let's do this right now!" Though the thought of engaging in this situation and having to put our lives in Aaron's hands is a little off-putting.

Selma takes a deep breath.

Aaron opens the door to the third floor, and we all walk on through, ready to face what's on the other side.

Hector is standing next to the desk and still looking out the window. He turns toward Rachel's direction.

"Isn't it about time you disappear?" Hector looks toward the enclosed office over her shoulder. He wants to add "forever," but opts to keep silent.

"Yes, yes," she says as she checks her gun making sure it's loaded.

"I don't want your ex-husband to get any spoilers...yet," Hector chuckles. "I really can't wait to see the horrified look on his face when he sees his long-lost wife…right before we put a bullet in his brain."

He checks his six-shooter, making sure it is loaded and ready to go. He lifts his head, as he can hear sounds coming from the emergency stairwell. He tells Rachel it is her time to go, now. Rachel turns to remind him what the signal for reentrance is, and Hector confirms it. She blows him a kiss and walks to the first office on the left, closing the door behind her.

Hector stares patiently as the emergency door opens and Aaron, Selma, and Jim walk in and head toward him.

Miguel waits for approximately five minutes. He puts his ear to the door and verifies he doesn't hear any more voices, and it sounds like they went up the emergency stairs. He feels confident it is OK to proceed, punches in the code to disarm the emergency alarm, and opens the door. He closes the door behind him and slowly peers up the stairwell for any sign of them. It is dead silent. He walks softly up the stairs and stops behind the door to the third floor, following Hector's instructions to the letter. All he has to do is wait for Hector or Rachel to call out to him when needed. In the meantime, he can hear a lot of chatter on the other side of the door.

"Well, well. Selma, my dear, you're looking as radiant as ever. Especially when you have your bodyguards covering you on both sides!" Hector exclaims, greeting the three of us as we walk into the room.

Selma looks uncomfortable and hesitates, stopping short of Hector but gripping her backpack even tighter. Aaron slides to the left of her but leaves some notable distance. I am standing next to her but continue to scan the room before returning my eyes to Hector.

"Hola, Hector. Long time, no see. I've delivered Selma here as promised."

Hector seems taken by surprise by my serious tone but then laughs for a moment. "Well, it seems you have delivered the *goods*, old friend."

Selma blushes instantly. Hector and I are having a face-off, but neither of us is willing to back down. Finally, he breaks the silence and asks Selma, "So my dear, does it work or not?" He flips his suit jacket behind his hand to reveal the six-shooter holstered on his side.

She is not fazed by his display. She excitedly responds, "You're damn right it works! Do you want a demonstration? Did you bring the money as agreed?"

"Of course, my dear. I would never cheat you out of what's coming to you." Hector pauses to look over at me but then continues. "You impress me first, and then we'll talk about the money."

Selma conceals any emotion she has right now rather well and turns to me and asks me to help her set the device up. We unload the backpack. Meanwhile, Aaron finds a chair and takes a seat. Apparently, no one is bothered about what he is doing while the events unfold. He brings out his phone and starts playing with it.

Hector points to the table behind him and directs Selma to set up there with some electrical cords already in place underneath it. I am thinking the cords are probably what Hector is going to use to wrap around our necks as I start to reach for one to hand to Selma.

"Oh, I don't need that, Jim. This baby is self-powered."

I smile at her and gather up the rest of the extension cords to put in the corner near the private office. As I turn back toward the table, I am overcome by a strange feeling. This is not good. Something is not right.

Selma is unpacking the computer case and explaining the various components to Hector, who actually seems interested in what she is saying. She places the three different pieces on the table and turns the table to face the window.

"OK, Hector, listen up," she begins. "Years ago, you came to me asking how I could design a system that can be better and faster than any financial trading system currently on the open market. When I said that it was theoretically possible, you replied that you wanted to know specifically how I could build a system to target the stock markets. Or to manipulate the stock market; I think those were your exact words."

"Sure, it was something like that. Continue." Hector is getting very anxious.

"Anyway, I started to point out all the various people that have tried and failed and currently are sitting in federal prison. But you were insistent that there had to be a way that someone hasn't thought of and that didn't leave a trace that the police could find."

Selma plugs in the antenna to the device and powers it on. She adjusts the antenna so it points in the general direction of Wall Street.

"Weeks went by. I was at Caltech thinking about your proposal. Then a colleague came by one day and asked me to go out for drinks for a celebration that night. It turns out that he landed an engineer job at the New York Stock Exchange and had to share the excitement with someone. Well, what woman turns down free drinks and a chance to celebrate someone's good fortune?"

We all nod our heads in affirmation. Selma continues. "After a few drinks, he was little more relaxed and started telling me how easy a job this would be for him. He starts babbling about the schematics regarding the New York Stock Exchange system and how it was designed. He started to outpace me in drinks, and I started to slow up on the drinking as he babbled on faster. I took special note when he described in detail how there were six different main trunk lines carrying all the data that filters to all the brokers nationwide. There were two trunk lines for inbound traffic and two for outbound traffic. The other two lines were false lines, specifically in place to thwart would-be hackers from attempting what we are about to do."

I look at Selma in an odd way. She doesn't pick up on it, as she is in her technical mode and is enjoying being the emcee of the show. She proceeds. "So my friend drank way more than me and apparently more than I thought because he started revealing confidential information, the very information I needed to bridge the gap in my research. The two false lines have a very specific marker. Once you know what the marker is—and he actually told me how to identify it—it becomes rather easy to eliminate those two false lines from the original six. After that, it's obvious which two lines are the inbound and which two are the outbound.

"Once I knew how to differentiate between the real and false lines, I was able to build a system that can exploit this fact and get the end result: hack the inbound data lines in order to manipulate the stock market prices. The only problem was it had to be done remotely and had to be faster than computer chips easily obtained on the open market could handle."

Selma turns toward Hector with a dead stare. Everyone in the room is unnervingly silent, trying to comprehend the meaning of everything she has explained. She breaks the silence by asking, "Hector, did you have someone install the tracker device at the New York Stock Exchange building like I requested be done prior to the demonstration? I need it to isolate the targeted signals coming from the building."

"Consider it done, Selma dear," Hector replies.

"Good, let's move on." She pauses and turns back to the device but looks up immediately. "OK, I need everyone in the room to shut off their phones or put them in airplane mode," she blurts out in a commanding voice.

She speaks in a teacher-to-student way to Hector, "In order to start eliminating and filtering the lines, it is advisable to have everyone's cell phone in the general vicinity to stop streaming data. Hector, write this down because it's important to remember it prior to implementing the device."

Hector pulls out his cell phone and switches it to airplane mode, and Aaron stands up from his comfy chair to pull out his phone to do the same. I sense the opportunity, as Selma has not gone for her cell phone yet, and quickly send a text to her phone that reads *Aaron betrayed us* before I switch to airplane mode.

Selma finishes typing on the device and then remembers to switch off her cell phone. She reaches for her phone in her purse and quickly switches to airplane mode. I can't tell if she got the warning or not as she continues with the next part of her demonstration.

Selma is fixated on the computer screen, as she still sees two signals active that are within a twenty-foot radius from her position. One is in the direction of the stairwell that they just came up, and the other signal seems to be coming from one of the offices off to the right.

"And thanks to your Russian friends in the mob, Hector, we have the experimental yet powerful quark computer chips that are capable of processing faster than any computer chip that I know of currently in use. In addition, the antenna is a work of genius, if I do say so myself. I was working on this technology as a side project before you came into the picture, and it's funny how, in the end, I actually needed this component to make it all work."

I watch as Selma is now typing away at near blinding speeds, configuring and adjusting the antenna. Yet she can still talk about her work as though it was a "project." Amazing, my dear. You are so awesome, Selma.

"The antenna is capable of reaching distances of four thousand to five thousand feet, nearly a mile. That is more than enough of the distance required from this location to the stock exchange central computer, which, by best estimates, is about a little over two thousand feet. Hector, I see you have read my instructions to the letter as to what the requirements were needed in order for this to work. I find it amazing that you actually found a suitable location and secured this building with a cleaned-out section of the floor. What was this, an investment or banking company that used this floor?"

"It is no concern."

"Right. I'll continue momentarily," Selma says as she looks at me one last time and sends me a smile. I hope that means she has seen the text message. "Now everyone, gather around and watch what my pride and joy does."

Hector, Aaron, and I move in a little bit closer to watch it unfold up close and personal.

Selma still needs to signal to Jim that there are possibly two other people near them. She reaches for his hand as he moves closer, and she squeezes it tight twice. Jim is playing his poker face and squeezes her hand once before releasing it. She only hopes he gets the true message. *We'll find out soon enough.*

Selma reaches in the zipped inner pocket of her handbag and pulls out a flash drive. She holds it in her hand as Aaron walks up and stands behind her to the left, Hector moves to stand over her left shoulder, and I keep a little distance, standing behind her and off to her right. I am so tense that something is about to go down, but at least I get to watch how smart my girl really is, and now she is about to prove it.

Selma inserts the specially configured flash drive, and the light on it turns green. She returns to the computer screen on the device, and there is a program labeled Muerto Hombre. She clicks on it, and a box comes up. I let out a laugh as I remember a flashback to the restaurant when she handed me a piece a paper that read *Muerto hombre* and *Plaza 42* on the other side. An interesting yet odd coincidence to hear this expression again. Is she sending me a coded message?

Selma types the command *EXECUTE* in the box, and the program immediately comes to life. It takes a 3-D representation of a nearly one-mile radius of Lower Manhattan in basic transparent blue boxes to represent buildings. It reminds me of watching the movie *Tron*. Then with another click of a button, the screen is filled with green data streams coming every which way. Now I think of the movie *The Matrix* and wait for Morpheus to come smashing through the window in front of us.

However, it isn't Morpheus or Neo or any character from any movie that opens the office door to my right at this very next moment. Rather, this is not a fantasy, but real life, as my missing wife reappears from out of nowhere. She strolls from the open office door and walks up to me with a loaded gun pointing at my chest.

"Hello, Jim. It's been a long time."

It was almost instinct to lean in and kiss her husband, but Rachel catches herself from making an embarrassing mistake in front of everyone. Aaron is watching like a hawk as the events unfold in front of him.

I am in shock but muster in a hoarse voice, "Rachel…Rachel…*you're still alive?*"

"I thought you would be happier to see me, Jim!" This time she pushes the gun forcefully into my chest. *Legally speaking, I should say, "Ex-husband," but he doesn't know that yet.*

I watch my whole life crashing before my very eyes. Here, I have been living with the suppressed pain of my wife's mysterious disappearance many months ago, only to have her reappear right in front of me. Maybe I would be more excited about it if she wasn't pointing that gun at me the whole time.

I think out loud, "I guess it would be awkward to give you a hug, *wife*."

I am not really sure who to trust or what to believe anymore. I now believe whole-heartedly in Selma, but my chances of coming out of this alive have greatly diminished. The other odd thing about all of this, I think at this very moment, is that no one else in the room is reacting to Rachel's sudden appearance. Is everyone in on it, and was it all an elaborate plot against me, or, better yet, was everyone against me all along? Be it as it may, the paramount question for the moment is, why am I still alive? They could have easily shot me already. Why prolong the agony and draw it out for no other reason? So that means there must be a reason. What else is supposed to happen? I ponder all of this, hoping to discover the missing detail while the gun is still pointing at me.

Rachel barks at Selma, "Well, my dear, continue with your demonstration. You're doing a fine job thus far. I am impressed, my distant relative."

Selma stares at me, gauging my reaction to the relation revelation, but I am lost in thought, or I am still in shock, so Selma does only what she can do. The show must go on.

Selma says, "If everyone can analyze the screen closely, you will notice some interesting features. The green lines represent the data streams. The denser the line, the more likely it's a financial or encrypted line with a lot of data being transmitted. See, this is why I asked everyone to turn off the data streams on their cell phones, as it makes it easier to sort out all these data streams you see here. Now, I created some algorithms to help filter out some of it."

Selma types some more, and the screen appears to contain a lot less green data lines. She clicks the Zoom tool and focuses on where the New York Stock Exchange building is located. There are six lines that are solid green and thick.

"OK, here's what we want to find," she says, pointing to the six lines. "Do you remember what I told you, Hector? I assume you were also listening as well, Rachel? One can plainly see the representation of thousands of transactions happening simultaneously." She compares one of the six lines with one of the financial transaction data streams as she points to what appears to be an ATM transaction. Everyone nods their heads in agreement though they probably don't fully understand what they really see on the screen.

Selma clicks a few more times and enhances the stock exchange data lines so the computer screen display shows the six data lines that are parallel to one another. She clicks on each one and turns to the group. It is easy to ascertain which two are the false lines, as they have the markers. She clicks ones that are numbered 1 and 4, and a few more clicks, and those two lines fade to black, barely visible. Next, she clicks on Numbers 2 and 5 and enhances the lines and then speed clicks on the streaming speed bar and the lines are showing to go outward. She explains these two lines are the outbound lines. She clicks a few more times, and they nearly disappear. "That leaves lines three and six. Those are the ones we'll be targeting," she says, confidently displaying the two lines she wants to hack.

Selma directs the next question to Hector. "OK, Hector, which stocks do you want me to manipulate and increase their core price?"

Hector and Rachel look at each other and stare in disbelief, as if to say, "She really has done it. It really freakin' works." Rachel breaks the silence and lowers the gun as her interest moves to the device. "But how is it not detected by *anyone*?"

"Because the Russian chips are operating ten times faster than what the stock exchange has, and their silicon-based chips can't react in a normal way. This program I will be attaching will act asynchronous to their system, and it will not be able to differentiate between the two, as it will assume our input feed is part of the main system. Brilliant, I must say." Selma smiles as a smart scientist normally does when they prove their theories to the masses. "Watch now for the final demonstration."

"This is what we've been waiting for, Selma. Impress us," Hector demands.

Selma says first to him, "Give me the current price of the first stock."

Hector responds, giving the current price.

Then to Rachel, she says, "Look up this stock price's closing price as of Friday."

Rachel gives her the price from Friday.

Selma confidently says, "OK, I'm changing the price from $25.18 to $45.18. Watch before your eyes." She does a few clicks and hits the Enter key. "Rachel, check that price again."

Rachel hits the Refresh option, and the price of the stock changes instantaneously, up $20.00 from the previous close. She says, "OK, I'm impressed, but unless we own a million shares of the stock, how is this going to help us?"

"Because I rigged it so you can update ten stocks at a time. Imagine that you sent trades to initiate when the price hits a certain mark and you can manipulate hundreds of stocks in a matter of minutes. It will throw the whole system into flux. People will make tens of millions, and many will lose millions. But since we know which ones will be going up, we will be able to make millions, as you can initiate the sales of the stocks faster than you purchase them."

Chapter 28

I am watching all my plans unravel at once. It is often in these moments that the very thought of greed travels fastest in anyone's brain. When mentioning get-rich-quick schemes, pyramid schemes, or stock-manipulation devices, the very thought of making untold riches by doing little or nothing, well, supersedes logical process, and the pleasure process gets the utmost priority in the brain.

The moment after Selma said the last "millions," everyone except for her pulls out a gun and points it at someone. Even a thug of Hector's, I assume, who was hiding behind the door all this time, opens the door and runs across the room to approximately five feet behind me with a gun pointed in my direction.

Click. Click. Click. Click. Click.

Witnessing the very definition of a Mexican standoff, I go over in my head the sequence of events that happens after Selma says, "Millions."

Hector points a gun at Aaron.

Rachel points a gun at Hector.

Aaron points a gun at the thug.

The thug points a gun at me.

I point a gun at Rachel.

If it wasn't clear before, it most certainly is now. This is that moment of clarity, and everything now makes sense. The sides and alliances have now been drawn.

There are some facts that still hold true. One, Mad Dog was right about Aaron. Two, Selma successfully built the device but won't get her $5 million. Three, either Hector's side or Rachel's side is walking out of here victorious. It is not looking good for Selma and I, as we are as good as dead. It is time to change the odds in our favor.

"Rachel!" I scream out, "is now a bad time to talk?"

Every sound goes silent in the room, and everything moving stops, freezing in time.

"Jim, you really think this is a good time to talk? You know, your timing was never spot-on." Rachel exhales deeply.

"Sure, why not? We gotta clear up a few things anyways." It is my only witty reply at the moment.

"Well, what do you have to say? Say it now. Your time is running out."

"Shouldn't I be asking you that, dear?" I stall, knowing she hates being called *dear*.

"Fuck you, Jim." At least she has started to talk to me like she used to.

Hector says, "Rachel, *dear*, can you lower your gun on me?"

"Fuck you too, Hector."

Hector declares, "Hey, Jim, you know she left you for Aaron, don't you?" His gun is pointing squarely at Aaron's chest.

Aaron—my friend and comrade through thick and thin. After all we've been through in the army and afterward. Mad Dog was right. I don't know whom I want to shoot first: my wife or my best friend.

Unfortunately, Hector makes the decision for all of us first and announces, "Fuck you all."

Hector fires the first round and hits Aaron in the right thigh although he was aiming for his chest. Aaron starts to go down but not before getting in the perfect shot at the thug. Hector hits Aaron squarely in the head on the second shot, and Aaron is left in a messy, bloody pile. Thanks to Aaron's bullet, the thug's shot at me goes astray and grazes me in the right arm. That shit hurts like hell, and it causes my shot at Rachel to go wild and miss her by mere inches, or so I think. However, her shot at Hector is spot-on and nails him straight in the heart. It is either in retribution for killing her current lover or to end the business partnership to increase her share. Either way, Hector is now *el muerto hombre.*

Selma starts to reach for her gun, but Rachel already has her gun trained on her. Rachel looks up to me and starts to laugh when she sees I have my gun aimed at her forehead. "Go ahead, Jim, throw all those years of marriage down the drain," she says. She's really insane.

"Wait a minute—you *left me? For Aaron? You bitch!*"

I fire the gun, but she does not go down as expected. I realize why. The gun that Aaron gave me must be filled with blanks. I am an awesome shooter, and there is no way I can have missed her twice in one day.

Meanwhile, Rachel, assumed dead wife, is holding the gun on Selma, current girlfriend. Today is a strange day. What can possibly happen next?

Rachel turns toward me, and she lowers the gun. She starts to laugh in a very haunting manner. She always had a weird laugh, but one disregards their spouse's quirks. Or maybe I never noticed it before now.

"Jim, what are we gonna do?" Rachel lobs at me. That is a strange question coming from her at this moment, after everything that has transpired.

"Why, what do you mean, Rachel?" I am stalling, as I have no idea what to do, but something will come up. It always does.

I notice Selma rummaging around in her purse, obviously looking for something.

Rachel continues. "You're not going to let me walk out of here, just like I can't let you two walk out of here. You know, Jim, she is a pretty girl."

Rachel starts to point her gun in my direction. I look deep into her eyes and stare at the woman that I am married to, the woman that is about to kill me. It's a fair point. I have attempted to shoot her twice today, even though it was only blanks.

I look out of the corner of his eye and see Selma motioning to me with her head, face clenched. She is not looking at me with a look of terror because a gun is pointing at me but rather a look as if to say, *"Look out."* I am still staring at her when I see her jump in the opposite direction, leaving a grenade on the device's keyboard while flicking the grenade pin to Rachel as if to say, "Catch!"

Rachel is completely caught off guard and does what any human would do when something is thrown in one's general vicinity, and that is attempting to catch what is thrown at her. Selma rushes toward me as I turn away from the desk, and she grabs my arm just as the explosion goes off and the impact knocks us off our feet. I also see Rachel down for cover at the same time.

The piercing sound of a grenade explosion in one's vicinity often causes extreme pain and disorientation. I regain consciousness a few seconds later and spy the thug's gun a few feet away. I still have not regained my hearing, but everything is coming back into focus, and I see Rachel running for the door. I grab the gun and aim it at her. I fire off two shots in quick succession, though I probably missed. It is still worth the effort. I watch the emergency door close, and Rachel is gone.

I rotate around to find Selma face down and quickly dash to her rescue. She seems shaken up and has a few cuts and scratches but opens her eyes and, seeing me, smiles with joy. Over her shoulder, I see what's left of the device, in flames and obviously destroyed, which isn't a bad thing.

"What the hell were you thinking? Where in the hell did you get that?" I scream at her though she probably can't fully hear me.

"I...I just...have to tell you."

"Tell me what?" I hope she speeds this up, as the smoke from the burning device is starting to fill the room.

"The flash drive is missing!" she yells at me, but that could be from the ringing in her ears from the explosion. Nevertheless, it takes a moment for all of it to sink in.

"That flash drive contains all the programming. With it, she could build and operate another device eventually. It has to be destroyed."

Selma's last words finally click, but I have to know something first. "Hey. A while ago you wrote muerto hombre on a piece of paper and put in in my pocket. Yet, I'm still alive. Why did try to warn me?"

Selma stifles a cry. "Because I thought if you pursued this path, you would be the dead man. Like Hector, the thug, and Aaron." She looks around the room.

"Well, if we still want to stay alive, we best be leaving soon!" The sprinkler system detecting the smoke from the burning device will go off any second now. We will have to get up and make a break through the office doors rather than the emergency stairwell, lest Rachel is waiting for us in there. I look over to see Selma starting to shed a tear.

In a fit of desperation, she breathes, "Let's go get your wife."

I reply, "Before we do that, we have to do something unpleasant first."

"What possibly can that be?"

"We need to find some keys to a vehicle outside." Pointing to the dead bodies, I say, "And one of them has keys."

About the Author

R.J. Matthews began writing down his creative thoughts in 2015. Born and raised in Michigan, R.J. enlisted in the Army and became an intelligence analyst over his 10-year military career. He saw time in Hawaii, Texas, Bosnia-Herzegovina, and England. After leaving the Army he moved to Harrogate, England and joined the British Police staff. Returning to the United States in 2011, R.J. settled in Asheville, NC, met his beautiful wife, and started working for the Department of Veterans Affairs. He and his wife are on a quest to visit all 31 NHL arenas. They have visited 13 so far. R.J. just completed the screenplay for *Tequila Highway: Last Exit* and is currently writing a TV series.